Praise for STINGER

"A superbly crafted and highly recommended political thriller, *Stinger...* is a ripping good novel of page-turning suspense and plot-twisting intrigue."
— James A. Cox, *Midwest Book Review*

"Forget 'armchair adventure' – this is an edge-of-your-seat action thriller. If it isn't true, it sure as hell could be."
— Charles Benoit, *Relative Danger, You*

"The first book in the Nick Daley series is a captivating and thrilling excursion.... When I put the book down at the end, I had to say 'Wow'. Then I went in search of the next book."
— Randall Masteller, www.spyguysandgals.com

"This book moves fast, hitting one suspenseful peak after another until the final shocking revelation.... *Stinger* keeps readers on their toes trying to keep up with the plot twists. Highly recommended, but not as a bedtime book – not if you want untroubled dreams."
— Karen Treanor, *New Mystery Reader*

Also by Diana R. Chambers

The Company She Keeps

STINGER

Diana R. Chambers

Aventine Press

I wish to thank Michael LaRocca, Wayne Arnold and Leigh Walker for their thoughtful assistance along the way. I am grateful to Erin Boomer for her evocative cover photo and to Sofia Valko for sharing with me her great gifts as an artist. *Stinger* could not have been written without the constant support of my traveling companion in life, Everett.

http://www.dianarchambers.com

Stinger is a work of fiction. There was a secret U.S. operation to resupply the Afghan mujahideen in the early 1980s, but all names, characters, places and incidents depicted herein either are the product of the author's imagination or are used fictitiously. Any resemblance to actual persons, living or dead, events or locales is entirely coincidental.

ISBN-10: 1593303777
ISBN-13: 978-1593303778

Library of Congress Control Number: 2006923808
Library of Congress Cataloging-in-Publication Data
STINGER

To Everett

and

To Lili

We are content with discord, we are content with alarms, and we are content with blood... but we will never be content with a master.
— Afghan tribesman to British official Mountstuart Elphinstone, 1809

If leadership rests inside the lion's jaw,
So be it. Go, snatch it from his jaws.
Your lot shall be greatness, prestige, honor and glory.
If all fails, face death like a man.
— Hanzala of Badghis, 9C Afghan poet, translated by S. Shpoon

Prologue

Kandahar, Afghanistan
February 1986

Jamal knew what it was to be hunted. He also knew how to hunt. So he waited, perched high on a ridge, his rough shawl the color of the rocks.

Three silver SU-25 fighter jets swooped toward the valley. They released their bombs and soared upward, sun glinting off their wings. Two MI-24 Hind gunships wheeled in, rocket and cannon fire belching down on the village. The haze of smoke and dust blotted out the desert sky. Only piles of rubble remained.

One of the Soviet helicopters banked and headed north. The other touched down. Its cabin door opened and eight Spetsnaz commandos burst forth, rifle stocks unfolded. The Hind lifted off.

The special forces unit fanned out through the mud-brick ruins, assault rifles firing. Bold in their blue and white striped T-shirts, the operatives conducted their search with deadly efficiency. But they found nothing, no one.

A pimply-faced commando, scanning the rocky slopes, stumbled over a wounded donkey. He cursed and sprayed it with his AKS-74. After a final jab of the bayonet, he kicked the body and moved on.

Bandolier across his drab, long-tailed shirt, Jamal stepped out from behind a boulder and aimed at the blue stripe over the *Shuravi's* heart. With a crack, the pimply-faced soldier fell. The guerrilla leader ducked back out of sight.

More shots ricocheted from the surrounding hillsides. Blindly returning fire, the commandos dove to the ground. Their prey had found them.

Jamal reappeared around another rock, picking off two more Soviets. His fighters were few yet seemed to be everywhere.

The gunship roared back in support of the Spetsnaz forces, but it was too late: the enemy ambush had taken all but one.

Jamal leaped up, raised his fist to the skies and shouted, "*Afghanistan Zindabad.*" Then he was gone.

Moscow, USSR
March 1986
"Long live Afghanistan," KGB Chairman General Vitaly Petrov translated coldly over the hush in the darkened Kremlin conference room. Eyes fixed on the large television monitor, the austere man in the navy suit reached for his pack of Dunhills. The muscular visitor on his left—just in from Peshawar, Pakistan—leaned over with a flick of his gold lighter.

The other eleven members of the Soviet Defense Council watched the debacle from their regular places around the inlaid mahogany table. No one moved.

The surviving commando drags himself aboard the Hind. It lifts off, its Gatling guns raking the hillside. The soldier pisses out the cabin door, his stream joining the final rain of shells on the scorched fields below.

The sound of gunshots echoed through the former salon of the Great Kremlin Palace. The KGB colonel from Peshawar rose and walked to the bank of Japanese electronic equipment, hard-edged and in stark contrast with its ornate surroundings. He operated the controls to eject the tape and open the drapes. The light streaming through the tall windows revealed tight faces, averted eyes. Colonel Viktor Ivanov returned to his seat amid a silence broken only by the clicking of his heels on the parquet floor, the striking of a match, a cough.

It was no ordinary meeting. These generals and ministers were among the most powerful in the nation. But even the powerful could know fear. They were only too aware of what was at stake in that treacherous land on their southern border. Their failure to resolve the Afghan situation could mean the end of their privileges, internal exile—or worse. The Spetsnaz commandos were no ordinary recruits doing their "international duty," but crack army troops, the motherland's finest. Desert sands were turning into quicksand, and if the military could not extricate them—who could?

"That was China's new Type 81 series rifle." The chief of GRU military intelligence wiped his forehead with a handkerchief, vulnerable despite his chestful of medals. "The bandits do not suffer for equipment."

"That bandit doesn't seem to need the latest equipment. That bandit is making fools of us all. That bandit is Jamal… and he must be stopped!" Chairman Petrov's voice was quiet, but his message lethal. Non-negotiable. Drawing on his cigarette, he gazed out at the crocuses and snow, the River Moskva and across it the baroque panorama of old Moscow: the soul of the nation. As head of the Committee for State Security, he understood his duty. General Secretary Gorbachev had ordered the Afghanistan problem solved—by any means necessary.

"Once again, our so-called elite forces have failed in their 'special assignment.'" The KGB chairman crushed the cigarette into his ashtray. "Jamal and his band of ragheads are making a mockery of Soviet power. This counter-revolutionary bandit must be eliminated. Before the Americans have time to arm him."

The other men studied their papers or tea glasses or the intricately inlaid table. Vodka bottles glittered in its center, vodka that no one dared drink these days. At least not in the afternoon. The defense minister watched his smoke disappear in the high white ceiling. The GRU general wiped his forehead again. There in the center of the Center, they were all confronting the central question, posed by Lenin: *Who controls whom?*

As first among equals, Chairman General Petrov smelled their fear. The trembling of the smaller who faces the larger. He directed a tight smile at Colonel Ivanov. "Such a minor problem—this one man—but so irritating. It seems our army comrades require our assistance. The time has come to activate Operation Birdwatch." He surveyed his comrades through steel-rimmed glasses, his glance conveying a quiet but powerful threat. "I trust we all concur in this decision."

The stillness was broken only by a nervously cleared throat.

"Good." Petrov glanced at his operative from Peshawar, his specialist in "executive action."

Viktor Ivanov nodded.

Chapter 1

Peshawar, Pakistan

May 1986

The streak of silver became a Pakistani Air Force C-130 cutting through the pale sky. Pointing its nose toward the tawny earth, the cargo plane made a steep descent and landed with a roar. It taxied past anti-aircraft guns, F-16s and a water buffalo pulling a cart of mud-bricks.

With a flick of its tail, the animal plodded on toward a concrete foundation, one of many lining the tarmac, along with many piles of mud-bricks. The sleepy little airport thirty miles east of the Afghan border had been jolted awake by the war next door. The military was in expansion mode. New bungalows were needed. Yesterday!

The construction workers had been at it since dawn without a break. But the heat was relentless; there was not the breath of a breeze, only dust shimmering in the blinding light. They had finally taken refuge beneath a canopy of willows, drinking tea and lounging against the chainlink fence.

The access road on the other side of the fence was quiet. A bicyclist pedaled past a three-wheeled auto-rickshaw parked under a drooping eucalyptus. The passenger's jean-clad leg extended from its open carriage, his long fingers tapping its faded green canvas roof. The vehicle glimmered with tiny mirrors and ornate metalwork framing scenes of snowy mountains and valiant mujahideen. It had a motorcycle engine, like many in the region, which didn't do much for the air quality of Peshawar, once a pristine valley whose very name meant flowers.

But Nick Daley had no time to smell the flowers. What he could smell was opportunity. He had marked the young Afghan driver, Taj Akbar, as agent material from the first taxi ride, and over the past two years, their arrangement had worked well. So he put up with the "putt-putt's" lack of springs, air conditioning and space for his lanky frame. It was useful camouflage for getting around town. Or tailing a target.

Nick watched the C-130 roll down the runway, just as earlier that day he'd watched it land in Karachi and take on its valuable cargo. His flight had arrived here first... leaving him time to wonder if the plane had made some kind of side trip. Frowning, Nick stretched out his leg again, his made-to-order-in-Bangkok cowboy boot the same color as the dust. He traced the shape of a palm tree. A palm tree made of dust. Swatting a fly, he returned his gaze to the aircraft.

Taj sat up front, binoculars to his eyes, wearing white pajamas and a loose black vest. His back stiffened as the rear gate opened. A military-green jeep sped onto the tarmac trailed by a tarp-covered truck. Nick reached forward and grabbed the binoculars. The gate swung shut after a second jeep, which skidded up beside the first one.

A slim Pakistani officer in his late thirties hopped from the lead jeep. Five soldiers followed, waiting at attention as the C-130 lurched to a halt.

Nick recognized the officer as Captain Ali, General Farouk's man. Figures. The cargo bay opened and a younger officer in sunglasses walked down the ramp, a cigarette in hand. Enter Farouk's nephew. Lieutenant Rashid gave the captain a curt salute, then jerked his thumb toward the plane. Nick saw Ali's mouth tighten before he turned and ordered his soldiers to work.

They joined Rashid's troops in transferring several crates from the plane onto the army truck. There were nine crates in all, each about two-and-one-half meters long with the words DRILLING EQUIPMENT stenciled in red along their sides.

When the last one was loaded, Ali walked back to his jeep. Rashid wiped his forehead, lit another cigarette and followed.

Nick lowered the binoculars. "Rashid looks nervous."

Taj glanced back. "He is having good reason to be nervous. That is some cargo."

"Yeah, that's some cargo." Nick took a deep breath and then let it out slowly, thinking of the distance he had traveled that day... the distance still to go.

The purpose of his Karachi trip had been to monitor the weekly delivery of "captured" Soviet weapons for the Afghan resistance. The regular Saudi shipment was bound for Islamabad, the main mujahideen resupply center. But what really interested Nick were the nine crates of "drilling equipment" that arrived in an Egyptian container. Their actual contents were nine American-made Stinger missiles. The "mule-portable," shoulder-fired Stingers were viewed as a potent defense—possibly the rebels' last best hope—against the Soviet gunships that had devastated the country over the past five years. But their use shouted U.S. involvement at a time when policy dictated a whisper. As a result, these were among the first Stingers to report for action. Nick had plans for them. So, undoubtedly, did everyone else.

In the interest of deniability—for everyone—the Pakistani government limited foreign aid to two shipments per week, which were to be channeled through the "Afghan cell" of the Inter-Services Intelligence agency, the ISI. Nicholas Ross Daley knew all about deniability. An old hand at covert action, he was now playing an even more complex game. His only firm mandate was to get out alive, which he viewed as license to be creative.

Nick watched the men finish securing the tarp over the crates.

"All are arriving?" Taj asked.

Nick nodded. "All nine."

The military vehicles sped off the field and onto the peripheral road. The taxi followed, soon disappearing in the noisy flow of traffic. Taj managed to keep up with the convoy, trailing it northeast, then back along the Kabul River Canal.

Suddenly a line of camels lurched in front of them, the animals joined nose-to-tail by rope and piled high with timber, carpets and baskets. Taj slammed on the brakes. Seeing the convoy slip away, he hit the horn. But the *kafila* kept lumbering across the road. When the rear camel finally drew near, its young rider waved his embroidered hat, while his mount turned and leered through large yellow teeth.

Frustrated, Taj swerved behind the camel. "We must not be losing truck."

Nick shook his head. Local color had long since lost its charm. "One thing about Peshawar, the day-life is sure a lot more exciting than the nightlife."

"We are having no nightlife in Peshawar."

"You had to rub it in."

Taj grinned, relieved to be on the move again. "*Insh'Allah*, we are having other rewards."

"God willing." Nick nodded. "Now follow those rewards."

It took a few moments, but Taj cranked up the engine to what Nick called putt-putt speed, about fifty kilometers or thirty miles an hour. They regained sight of the convoy as it was winding its way toward the ancient Bala Hissar fort perched on a cliff overlooking Peshawar. Halfway up the hill, Taj parked under a clump of willows where they watched the vehicles approach the fortress. Sturdy iron gates opened, then slammed shut behind them.

Taj glanced at the CIA *malik*. "What is our program now, boss?"

Nick didn't take his eyes off the entrance. "We wait right here until the mujahideen—or whoever—pick 'em up. Then we'll have us a little 'hands-on' inspection." He shifted on his cracked leather seat, trying to get comfortable.

Nick had done plenty of waiting in his time. And watching. Other trucks, other planes, other cargo.

During the Vietnam war, Nick's special forces unit had been sent to Long Tieng, a Laotian mountain valley code-named Sky. Their secret mission was to train the Hmong guerrillas of General Vang Pao, a key ally in a neutral land. When operations were really swinging, the Air America landings were one a minute. Hmong children thought rice came from the skies. Their elders, who knew better, were freed to focus on a more lucrative crop—opium—which was used to finance Vang Pao's anti-communist offensives.

Nick learned about the opium one hot March day after hopping an Air America helicopter down from the highlands. Curious about the cargo, he tracked it to a hillside lab and eventually onto a waiting C-130. Only by then, the sticky black bricks had become some kind of white powder. That was when he realized America needed Vang Pao as much as the general needed America. After all, North Vietnam's supply line to the South—the Ho Chi Minh Trail—ran along the Laotian border. But with no official U.S. presence in Laos, the unofficial "Customer" had been brought in to support the war effort.

Later, the Customer tapped Nick on the shoulder, after he'd proved himself. So he shed his uniform and joined the CIA. He didn't question his role in any of this. One way or another, he was fighting communists, and had what he wanted—plenty of action and a ringside seat at the Purple Rose Bar.

In those days he'd been too young to care about getting rich. Too idealistic. He had learned a lot since then. About money, and what it could do.

About women, too. And what he'd taken for granted. In Bangkok, there'd been no shortage of women willing to scratch a man's itch. Little did he know he'd end up in Peshawar where even thinking about it could get you killed.

Nick sighed. Thinking about how he shouldn't think about it made him start to think about it. Then he thought about his ex-wife and the advantages of marriage. And the disadvantages. The time passed.

After an hour or so, as the light was fading, a battered blue truck drove into the fort. It reappeared a few minutes later, heading downhill. Taj followed it down the bumpy track, then along a pothole-ridden road that crossed a semi-industrial area of mechanics, furniture builders and tailors. On the outskirts of town, the vehicle merged with buses of workers going home, pickups full of mangoes or old tires and a few auto-rickshaws.

Soon the blue truck reached the low mud walls of an Afghan refugee camp. It turned onto a rutted dirt entranceway and stopped inside the wooden gate. Four armed mujahideen got out and stood guard.

Just then, Taj seemed to develop engine trouble. He parked and began poking around the engine while Nick hung back inside the cab. He stared at the camp, a chaotic jumble of mud-walled shacks, tents and dusty lanes. He had seen the results of war on civilian populations before, like the decimation of the Hmong in Laos. Here, too, the suffering was extreme. Women, children, old men and the wounded torn from their homes, accepting their lot without question, without complaint. In these congested conditions, the women kept strict purdah, living secluded lives inside a canvas tent or, if they were lucky, the mud walls that transformed a hut or tent into a family compound.

What struck Nick about the Afghans was their simple dignity, bravery and faith. He'd seen these qualities in Taj and so many others. Within the confines of this camp—as in camps all over Pakistan—refugees waited patiently for God's will to send them home. In the meantime, most of their young men risked their lives inside Afghanistan fighting to expedite God's will.

Dusk was falling and all was quiet. The air was filled with cooking smells—bread, rice, spices, frying oil. A few old men gossiped on a faded rug as they passed their *chilim*, an old waterpipe that had somehow managed to survive, just as they had. A goat scavenged near some drying bricks. Otherwise, the dusty paths were empty.

It was not long until the call for prayers resounded from the mosque. As the mujahideen guards moved to the front of the blue truck, Nick and Taj hopped the low wall into the compound. The compelling adhan continued—a sinuous, musical call of faith, *to* faith. The men placed their weapons before them, then unrolled their prayer rugs and kneeled west toward Mecca.

Taj stood lookout while Nick climbed inside the back of the truck, knowing he had just seconds before the muezzin's cry was over. There were five crates labeled DRILLING EQUIPMENT. He pried them open and pushed aside a layer of straw.

Three of the crates contained a complete "set" for the portable Stinger anti-aircraft missile system: a dull green launcher tube with computerized viewfinder, two missiles, a battery, reusable grip-stock and some spare parts, packed in Styrofoam. Their markings indicated they were made by General Dynamics, a California defense contractor, with serial numbers that matched Nick's records.

The remaining two crates were filled with straw, out-of-date Egyptian shells and used Chinese mortar parts. Useless junk.

Taj hissed for him to hurry.

Nick shut the crates. The two men slipped back over the wall and ducked into the taxi just as the guards returned to their post.

Taj wheeled the vehicle around and drove off. Once they were safely underway, he glanced back at his boss.

Nick shook his head. "Three Stingers and some junk."

"What are happening to other six crates?"

"Maybe we should ask General Farouk." There was grudging admiration in Nick's voice. "That enterprising bastard."

"Very smart man. He is bringing opium from Afghanistan, making heroin in mountain caves."

"While controlling the drug eradication money. The guy knows how to use the system, doesn't he? He gets rich from our military assistance program and plays the black market like Wall Street."

"Maybe saving for cattle ranch in America, like President-General Zia."

"Perks of power. The rich get richer. It's the old Third World shuffle." Nick shrugged. "Not my problem, though. Right now, my only problem is protecting my operation."

"What about Stingers in refugee camp?" Pronouncing it re-FU-gee.

"Forget 'em. As for the missing six—if we're right about the general, maybe we'll catch him in a generous mood. Get him to 'donate' them to us."

"General Farouk very big man."

Nick shrugged again.

"Everyone wanting Stingers nowadays."

"Very trendy," Nick agreed. "And hard to come by. Valuable to those who have them."

Taj stared into the darkness. "Everyone wanting Stingers nowadays."

Chapter 2

As the Pakistan International Airlines 737 descended through the clouds, Robin Reeves pressed her face against the window, trying to catch a glimpse of her future. To the north and west were the mysterious snowcapped peaks of Afghanistan, jagged peaks that meant danger—and opportunity—their vastness a reminder of the magnitude of her task. But her work would begin in the Peshawar valley, bounded to the south and east by mauve-gray slopes that became brown foothills ending in the dusty plains. Barren plains, broken only by scattered fields of cultivation.

As the aircraft began its approach, Robin was able to distinguish a few small villages, clusters of earthen houses surrounded by rectangular mud walls. Yet there were no other signs of life and she was struck by an eerie emptiness.

The pilot pointed out the Kabul River drifting through the arid Pakistani landscape, a river born in the highlands beyond the legendary Khyber Pass. A river could make the journey, but for a human the possibilities were few and they were arduous. Thirty miles to the east, the Khyber cut through the mighty Hindu Kush, a range whose name meant Killer of Hindus. Robin stared at those seemingly impenetrable mountains, the forbidding boundary with Afghanistan. Jamal was somewhere on the other side.

They had met at Berkeley in 1968. It was a popular Political Theory class, held in a large room, yet she'd noticed him immediately. Tall, dark and handsome had always been her type. Robin felt his glances and knew it was just a matter of time. When they finally spoke, on the outskirts of some protest rally, it was with a friendly inevitability. Besides the physical attraction, they were drawn together by a shared idealism, the highly charged intensity of the times.

Jamal Durrani was part of Afghanistan's ruling Pashtun clan. Raised in Kabul, he had been sent by his family to study at the University of California. It was expected that he would then return home to join the King's modernization program.

Robin was curious about his ancient and exotic homeland. Located in the hidden recesses of Central Asia, crisscrossed by the Silk Road, Afghanistan had a dramatic history that went back forever. She found some of its traditions equally archaic—especially the practice of purdah, which originally functioned to protect women, but now only imprisoned them. Jamal told her about the progressives fighting for change—including his own mother—but they were pitted against the mullahs who believed in tradition, and a woman's place.

Robin Reeves didn't know about her "place." Nor about tradition. She questioned every accepted value. Once she hit Berkeley, Robin embraced the excitement and turmoil, the intensity of the times. Jamal was gorgeous, intriguing and to the political left. Not only that, he wrote her poetry. She'd never known anyone like him.

They came at each other from exactly the right opposition to make for explosive sex, spending magical hours in bed. She taught him about a woman's pleasure. He taught her about passion.

Their friendship was equally fulfilling. They talked politics, smoked grass, danced at the Fillmore, marched against the war, and picketed CIA recruitment on campus. An art major, she barely found time to attend classes, but he never missed a one. He was more focused, more intellectual. He told her about the great seventeenth-century Pashtun writer, Rahman Baba, who had proclaimed, "An ignorant man is like a corpse." The Afghan ideal was the poet-warrior... not that he would ever want to go to war. He was a man of peace, a lover of beauty. A lover of her. Then he would look at her with those gorgeous eyes.

Robin almost envied Jamal. He had his people and a place where he was rooted. She didn't yet know what she wanted to do with her life, but injustice angered her. She believed in an ideal world order where people wouldn't go hungry and the military-industrial establishment wouldn't dictate foreign policy. Robin truly believed in banning the bomb and giving peace a chance.

Then it ended. He finished his studies and felt the pull of duty. He was a son of Afghanistan and Afghanistan needed him. He told her he must return to his mountain homeland and asked her to join him. But it was his world, a world to which Robin could never belong... and they both knew it. They said goodbye.

Robin considered switching to art history. Asian art history. However, she couldn't bear academia, nor—she realized—was she an artist. She also realized that the nearest thing to a paintbrush was a pen. And the pen was mightier than the sword. Or so they said.

Robin took out her notebook and contemplated the immense mountains. Barriers to change. She began jotting down notes for her newspaper article.

The pilot made his final announcement. "*Insh'Allah*, we will soon be landing in Peshawar, capital of Pakistan's North-West Frontier Province."

Robin opened her guidebook to the list of phrases. God willing. She frowned, then shrugged and looked back out the window as they continued their descent.

Right away, she noticed the F-16s facing the runway. The anti-aircraft guns. The army-green vehicles parked along the bungalows surrounding the field. Back home, the military didn't defend civilian airports. And what about Karachi? She had never been through security like that in her life! Robin didn't know if it all made her feel more protected—or more exposed.

She watched a cargo plane touch down at the far end of the field. Military vehicles drove up and soldiers scurried about carrying large crates. She wondered what kind of equipment was being offloaded. Weapons?

A wave of heavy air and blinding light hit Robin as she exited the plane amid a crowd of exotic passengers. They were mostly men in loose pajama-type outfits, sandals and a variety of headgear. Flat hats with rolled brims. Skullcaps. Turbans, tightly wound or loosely draped. In defiance of the weather, most wore vests or shawls. Or both.

The afternoon heat enveloped her. She felt weighted down. Every step took effort. Every breath tasted hot and dry. She trudged across the tarmac behind a black-shrouded woman following in the shadow of her swaggering husband. Robin looked around. There were few other females, and most were veiled in voluminous shawls or tent-like burqas with latticework slits at eye-level. The garments were varied in color but all appeared hot. Really hot. Robin couldn't imagine wearing one of those things. Yet these women had to. How could they see where they were going? She experienced a terrifying wave of claustrophobia, then new respect for those struggling to free them from the veil. That was something worth fighting for.

Several armed soldiers stood along the tarmac. Some of them stared openly at her. She felt the stares were hostile, but tried to tell herself they were merely curious.

Robin did not want to stand out. She had planned her wardrobe with care, intending to be nondescript, respectful and conservative. She was wearing a long-sleeved, beige shirt and trousers, typical journalist gear. Still, she felt uncomfortable. Robin closed her top button self-consciously and fiddled with her good luck pin, a small gold robin. She was the only Western woman, the only unaccompanied woman. And all the "basic beige" in the world was not going to change that. The place was starting to give her the creeps.

But then she noticed the cheerful potted plants lining the entrance to the modest one-story terminal. If you ignored the armed-camp aspect, it didn't seem so bad—at least not Third World dirty and poverty-stricken.

The arrival terminal was crowded with more men in floppy shalwar kameez. In contrast to Karachi, with its suits and jeans, Peshawar seemed a different world. Robin saw a big, bearded man with a red rose sticking from the barrel of his ancient rifle. She watched him greet and embrace an equally strapping friend. The two walked away, pinkies joined.

She passed a prayer area facing Mecca, then reached the baggage carousel—a jumble of burlap-wrapped parcels, rolled carpets, cartons of Japanese fans and VCRs. As she fought for her luggage, several taxi drivers accosted her, each trying to underbid the competition.

Finally, a tall, hearty man wearing a taupe, long-tailed shirt grabbed her bags. "Only twenty rupees."

The others looked at each other, shook their heads and moved away, amid grumbles. No one could match his price.

Robin exchanged glances with the tall taxi driver.

"You are news lady from San Francisco?"

Robin regarded him cautiously. "I am."

His leathery face relaxed in a smile. "I am Jhan. I am waiting for you. Welcome." He picked up her two canvas bags and headed for the exit.

Robin stared after him. She had been told someone would be meeting her, a driver who knew his way around Peshawar. She'd been there only a short time, but it was long enough to realize that she would need help. With a shrug, Robin followed the man outside. The brilliant light and heat again assailed her.

Jhan indicated his brown Toyota Corolla. He saw her glance at the feather duster in the rear window. "Very dusty, Peshawar."

She gazed around, then back at him. "Very."

He nodded. "I will be your eyes and your ears in Peshawar. When you are needing driver, tell hotel and I am coming with great speed." He tossed her bags in the trunk, then opened the passenger door.

Robin was unexpectedly grateful to have her own male protection. "A good man is hard to find."

The lines around his eyes crinkled as he regarded her.

She shook her head. "That just means, okay, let's go."

The moment she sat down, the jetlag hit her. Robin wondered what time it was in San Francisco. Then she took a deep breath and settled back, ready to ease into this new world. But as they plunged into Peshawar's chaotic traffic, she was soon on the edge of her seat. Jhan—and everyone else—appeared to view stop signs, pedestrians, animals and other vehicles as little more than irritating distractions. It seemed a matter of special pride to ignore red lights. Driving was evidently a question of manhood. At least there would be no jokes about women drivers: there were none.

The roadways were a jumble of lavishly decorated motor vehicles, bicycles, horse-driven tongas and bullock-drawn carts, as well as a sprinkling of older American and Japanese cars. "Petrol too dear for most people. I am having one of few automobile taxis," Jhan boasted.

"What other kind are there?"

"Most taxis are of the auto-rickshaw kind. Like that one." He pointed to a small, three-wheeled machine that seemed to be held together with spit and staples and sounded as if it had a lawnmower engine.

A sputtering lawnmower engine, on its way to the junkyard. Or maybe an art gallery? Robin studied the leaping tigers and Rambo-like warriors and was sure there was a story there. Folk art goes to war!

She knew she could make one hell of a travel article out of all this, if that were her intention. Talk about local color. Talk about an assault on the senses. Horns beeped, bells clanged, out-of-tune engines coughed, voices rose to compete with the din. The air smelled of smoke, spices, dung and exhaust fumes. The light and color were dazzling, the heat mind-boggling. All at once, she felt woozy. "Do you have air-conditioning, Jhan?"

Jhan turned a knob on his dashboard. "Oh, excellent air-conditioner."

Robin began rolling up her window. As a feeble puff of warm air came through the vent, she sighed and rolled it back down.

Jhan entered a residential district where the streets became wider and bordered in green. "Cantonment."

The air seemed cooler and the traffic less frenetic. Robin checked her guidebook. Once a British refuge from the congested Old City, it had remained a leafy neighborhood, with properties spread a civilized distance from each other and far back from the street.

"American consulate here," Jhan gestured vaguely.

"Where?"

Suddenly three army trucks rolled out of a guarded stone compound and blocked the street. Soldiers flagged down the oncoming vehicles, which all came to a respectful stop. A convoy of six jeeps full of armed men squealed out the gate.

"Who's that?"

"Maybe visiting general, maybe governor general. Maybe General Farouk." Jhan stared hard at the jeeps and shrugged. "Many military in Peshawar."

After the convoy was gone, the trucks drove back inside and the soldiers waved everybody on.

Robin shook her head, still wondering about the "many military." It gave her pause. She'd have to be careful in order to do her job, and still fly under the radar.

Soon the boulevards funneled into narrower streets. Buildings crowded upon each other. Garish signs announced their businesses. She hung on as Jhan continued to accelerate, brake and honk about every four seconds. Robin was tense and wondered about the local hospitals. "Jhan. I'm really not in that much of a hurry."

"It is my duty to do my best for you."

She nodded doubtfully, then gasped as Jhan hit his brakes to avoid piling into a truck. A large black animal lay dead in the road. Its furious owner had pulled a weapon on the truck driver.

Jhan made a quick U-turn and sped away.

Robin craned her neck to watch and then jumped at the loud crack. "Was that a gunshot I heard?"

Jhan shrugged. "Water buffalo is like family. Of course that man wants to kill lorry driver. But then, dead man's son must take vengeance. Or his son or *his* son. This is *badal*, Pashtun duty of revenge. Blood feud."

"When does the feud end?"

"We Pashtuns are most patient. We have a saying. 'The man who takes revenge after one hundred years, he takes it too quickly.'"

Robin thought of Jamal. He was Pashtun, too. She remembered the soldiers at the installation they'd just passed. The armed guards at the airports. There were macho armed men everywhere. Hijackings and bombings were a way of life. The weather was brutal. So, too, was the code of vengeance. This was a harsh, unforgiving land and she was about to take it on.

Robin experienced a rare moment of self-doubt. She wondered if she could really pull it off. Would she make it out of Pakistan a success? Or, would she make it out at all?

Then she scolded herself. She had never failed at anything she'd set her mind to. Well, except once. *Him*. And she wouldn't let that happen again.

Chapter 3

Everyone hung out at Lala's Grill. The simple, wood-paneled café was located off the lobby of a downtown hotel. Popular with locals, it had been discovered by Peshawar's foreign community—a mix of do-gooders and bad-doers all attracted to life in the war zone. Reporters and Afghan rebel leaders sat around its tables, along with aid workers, arms merchants, smugglers and diplomats.

Or those who called themselves diplomats. The small town had become a global listening post, a crossroads of spies, the point at which the Cold War got hot.

For Nick it had gotten even hotter with yesterday's Stinger delivery, followed by the juggling act that resulted in the disappearance of six of them. He needed to figure out who was behind it, and why. As he gazed around the table at his colleagues in the spy trade, he suspected one of them might know something—or provide a lead.

The restaurant was quiet. As usual, there was no Mr. Lala present, although he was said to exist. Perhaps in London. The balding manager sat in the rear tallying lunch receipts, while staff members gathered around mounds of rice, grilled mutton and curry. The Pakistani love songs wafting through the speakers were as sugary as the Coca-Cola and tea, both flavored to please the local sweet tooth, one that Nick had not yet acquired.

Nonetheless, over the past two years, Nick had developed an appreciation for the culture, a respect, even fondness. But now he didn't hear the music or taste the tea—or engage in idle conversation. He eyed a blue-eyed teenager in a loose turban seated by the front window. The youth was dipping French fries in ketchup, a vintage Lee-Enfield rifle leaning against the table.

"Ballsy kid, sitting next to the street." Nick turned to Syed Hussein, the Afghan trade representative. "These bombings have gotten out of hand, don't you think, Sid?" He smiled, knowing Hussein hated the nickname.

Even more, he hated being called the "Ox." Yet he was ox-like, a huge, barrel-chested man, a man of power in every sense. Hussein was a high-level operative for the Afghan intelligence agency, KHAD, whose agents were usually blamed for the frequent bombings in the Peshawar area. He stared darkly at Nick. "Many provocateurs and their patrons, yet all are blaming us."

Nick held his gaze, considering what the Stinger information would be worth to the Afghan spy.

"More *chai*." Ahmed Latif interjected, gesturing to the waiter. In the proud Pakistani tradition, the dashing security officer acted as host for these get-togethers of their foreign guests, whom he had also been assigned to oversee.

"I am already bringing." The waiter arrived, beaming behind his grand mustache. He filled their glasses from his porcelain teapot, then surveyed the table. "More sweets?"

Ahmed shot a quick glance toward the burly Afghan, then patted his stomach and waved the waiter away. He was a fastidious man, his uniform always crisply pressed. His reputation was equally rigorous. He was rumored to have arrested one of his brothers for tax fraud. He was also rumored to have started that rumor himself. He turned his eyes toward the blond Russian with the closely cropped hair. The Soviet "cultural attaché." "How is the weather these days in Moscow, Viktor? Much cooler, I am thinking?"

"Much." Viktor Ivanov replied shortly, unbuttoning the lightweight jacket he'd had made during his recent command performance at the Center. Thinking of the tailor—an old Kremlin favorite who had survived even Stalin—Viktor was reminded that his new mandate was a matter of his own survival. Or death, which in his mind included spending his career in Peshawar. He took out a silver flask and poured some clear liquid in his tea, then twisted the top back on.

"What am I, chopped liver?" Nick looked the KGB *Rezident*, a man whose high cheekbones protected narrow, watchful eyes, although his crooked nose was a testimony to less cautious times. He wondered about Viktor's trip home, what they were cooking up at headquarters. The two intelligence officers knew the value of an occasional swap of information, so Nick was working on the right bait. As to the Stinger operation, he was still debating how to play him. The Soviets would do anything to keep the Stingers out of the hands of the mujahideen—or bandits, as they called the rebels. Freedom fighters "'Chopped liver.'" Viktor poured some Stolichnaya in Nick's tea, then slipped the flask back in his pocket and pulled out a small notebook. He jotted down the phrase. "Excellent colloquial American humor."

"Maybe you'll be the next Vladimir Posner." Nick noted Viktor's blank look, but didn't buy it. The American-born Russian journalist was a popular media figure in both countries—KGB, for sure. Nick knew all about playing the fool—and the danger of underestimating your adversaries. Who's putting who on?

Ahmed stared at Viktor's glass. "Gentlemen, really I am shocked." An ironic smile belied his sharp words.

With a raised eyebrow, Viktor retrieved the flask and poured his Muslim colleague a shot. He turned to Mr. Yu. "Comrade?"

Bespectacled and thin, Mr. Yu accepted with a small, almost reluctant nod. He wore his usual dark suit and white shirt, a serious man with serious ambitions. No one knew his first name.

Nick couldn't resist. "I wouldn't think vodka is your 'cup of tea,' Mr. Yu."

"*Cha.*" Yu glanced around the table. "Or chai, as my colleagues here call it. You drink coffee. We all drink cha."

"*Chai,*" Viktor corrected him. "Russia, Afghanistan, Pakistan—we drink chai. You drink *cha.*"

Nick noted the Russian's irritation. These old comrades were headed for a divorce. "Thanks for the tutorial, Mr. Yu. After all, we Americans only speak English."

"A pity. All your wealth. So little education."

"Touché." Nick grinned wryly, studying the man. So far, he had been unable to get a handle on the elusive functionary. Yu represented the China South Industries Corporation, a weapons manufacturer licensed by the Shanghai government, for whom he collected intelligence as well. He was also rumored to handle off-the-books transactions, both military hardware and softer wares in powder form. Whether or not his government was aware of his sidelines, other governments—at least, their representatives—were.

As Mr. Yu returned to his tea, Viktor offered the flask to Syed Hussein.

The brawny Afghan placed a palm over his glass and stared at his Pakistani colleague. "No, thank you. We Muslims do not drink."

"Ahmed just doesn't want his guests to feel uncomfortable." Nick raised his glass. "To our impeccable host." He grinned. "And thanks for picking up the tab."

They all joined the toast, even the Afghan with his straight tea. Ahmed nodded graciously. "I thought it was your people paying the bills, my American friend."

Nick heard the dig. He was attuned to the different levels of banter, the politics and hostilities lurking just below the surface. "We wouldn't be in this backwater if it weren't for Vic's interest in the goings-on next door."

Viktor frowned. "The Soviet Fraternal Limited Contingent comes only at the invitation of our Afghan comrades for assistance in their struggle against the agents of international imperialism."

"Well, that's a mouthful." Nick smirked as he turned to the "Afghan comrade," noting his uncomfortable expression. "Your people are fortunate, Sid, to have such a generous neighbor."

The big man's eyes narrowed, swept past Nick and focused on Mr. Yu. "How you are finding the tea today, Mr. Yu?"

"Still too sweet, still rather weak." A running joke was whose national tea was better. Most thought the Chinese tea too bitter.

"Speaking of weak, when will you Chinese cease your feeble attempts to copy our weapons?" Viktor's tone was peeved. "Someday you may regret your assistance to the Afghan bandits."

"Someday, perhaps." Mr. Yu regarded him serenely. "In the meantime, we like how these 'bandits' keep you busy. So if you think our efforts feeble, we must try harder."

Nick bit back a grin. "We applaud your diligence, my friend. And the development of your manufacturing sector."

Mr. Yu nodded and checked his watch. "If you will excuse me, gentlemen."

"Anything we should know about?" Nick studied his face.

Mr. Yu rose, his eyes impenetrable behind the thick lenses. "We of the developing nations can never remain idle." He pushed his chair into place and walked to the door.

The brown Toyota braked hard outside a downtown establishment. Jhan turned and gestured triumphantly. "Green's Hotel."

White-faced and white-knuckled, Robin took a deep breath. She felt baptized, in a way. This half-hour drive had taught her she needed some toughening up. It would get worse before it got better. She watched a man unloading chickens from a dusty pickup onto the sidewalk in front of the restaurant. "These chickens seem to have reservations, too."

Jhan pointed to the sign over the entrance—LALA'S GRILL—then made a slicing motion, finger across throat. "A noble destiny, madam."

Robin winced as Jhan got out and opened her door. The dead chickens stunk, flies buzzing around their glazed, beady eyes. She thought of becoming a vegetarian. Then looking into Jhan's earnest face, she scolded herself for being a wimp when she had such challenges ahead.

As Robin sidestepped the chickens, she almost collided with a dark-suited Chinese man leaving the restaurant. "Oh, excuse me."

He gave her a blank look and hurried down the street.

Robin turned as Jhan clapped his hands twice.

A small porter scurried toward them. He saluted Robin. "Welcome to Green's Hotel, sir."

Robin blinked, looked at Jhan, then back at the porter. The man was addressing her. She nodded and smiled. "Thank you."

"Most welcome, sir." The porter beamed, collecting the bags from the trunk.

Robin followed Jhan, who opened the hotel door. She entered and looked around. "So this is Green's." She looked back out at the noisy street. "Great location."

The porter was trailing behind. "We are glad you are liking it, sir."

Robin studied the lobby with its columns, peeling paint and threadbare Persian carpets, the air of colonial British gone to seed. But the plants in the atrium were maintained and there was a little fountain. Men in the local wardrobe—and even a few suits—sat in cracked leather chairs, reading and chatting. "Plenty of personality."

"Excellent," the porter agreed.

Robin continued to the front desk. She presented her passport to the clerk and filled in the registration card. "I'd like an air-conditioned room in the new wing, please."

"No problem, madam. We are most pleased to offer you most beautiful, most refreshing, most modern room in hotel." With a dignified nod, he handed the guest an envelope with her name and the notation, "Hold for arrival."

She opened the envelope, skimmed the letter, then read it again. As Robin looked up, she saw Jhan standing there.

He regarded her seriously. "Remember. Anytime you are needing car, I am here. Besides, few taxis in town, only rickshaws."

"I'll remember that." Robin extended her hand.

He hesitated, staring, and then clasped it loosely.

Robin realized he was not used to shaking hands with a woman. "I appreciate your help, Jhan. Thank you."

He tilted his head sideways, then forward. "It is I who must thank you." With a final bob of his head, Jhan turned and left.

Robin watched him go, feeling oddly alone. She had entered a man's world where an unveiled female in slacks was deemed to belong to the male sex. When she became aware of the curious eyes fixed on her, she realized how hard it would be to keep a low profile. Then it struck her. She was the only woman in sight.

Robin had arrived in Peshawar.

Chapter 4

He did not care for Pakistan. At all.

Nor, Mr. Yu reflected as he left Lala's Grill, did he much care for these men. These "spies," with their games of power and petty advantage. He was a man of culture, or at least he had aspirations, while these men were rather common—especially the Afghan, this "Ox," forced to pull the cart of his colonial master.

Yet those were the exigencies of life. Survival had a bitter taste, and for all—except the American—the stomach ruled. In Yu's homeland, one did not ask, "How are you?" but "Have you eaten?" However, the days of the iron rice bowl were long gone, along with guaranteed employment from one's work unit. He was on his own, with no choice but to spend his time in activities as distasteful as they were necessary. Yu had a plan, a vision. It had to do with his name. His sons. Becoming an ancestor.

Mr. Yu hurried down the dusty street, shutting out the noises and confusion. He had to prepare. Soon it would be night.

Captain Ali drove west along Jamrud Road, proud of the responsibility entrusted in him by General Farouk. Yesterday, it had been the Stinger shipment. Tonight, the other business. A poor boy from the Karachi slums, he now enjoyed an important job, money and respect. His family was never hungry, and his wife no longer had to work the fields but could remain comfortably secluded at home, like the rich ladies. He owed it all to the general.

At the outskirts of town, Ali stopped the jeep in front of a rusty, wrought-iron gate set in a stone fence. He picked up a *Frontier Post*-wrapped bouquet, got out and looked around. It was a solitary place, dark, no moon. He switched on his flashlight and approached the gate, suddenly hesitant. You are a soldier, he told himself. The captain squared his shoulders, then entered Peshawar's old Christian cemetery.

Ali made his way cautiously through dense undergrowth, past shattered gravestones and neglected graves. Nonetheless, he almost tripped over a cracked piece of black marble jutting up through the weeds. Finally, he reached a lonely grave in a far corner. Ali unwrapped the newspaper and placed his red tulips in front of the sandstone slab, pausing to read its inscription:

> *Here lies Captain Ernest Bloomfield*
> *Accidentally shot by his orderly*
> *March 2nd, 1879*
> *Well done, good and faithful servant*

He wondered about Bloomfield, a man of his own rank, wondered if they would have been colleagues. Then he realized the Englishman would have never seen him as an equal—despite the distance his country had traveled since Independence. Lost in reflection, Ali jumped when a disembodied voice floated out to him.

"I am thinking he preferred poppies."

A tall, broad-chested man emerged from the darkness, his teeth and the whites of his eyes very bright. His turban was as dusty as the shawl he wore over his embroidered coat. "*Salaam Aleikum.*"

"*Manda nabashi.*" The classic Pashtu greeting, May you never be tired.

The Pashtun tribesman bowed. "*Zenda bashi.*" May you live forever.

"I am trusting your journey was safe." Ali continued the courtesies.

"The mountain passes are still snow covered, still full of *Shuravi* mines." At the mention of the Russian foe, Selim spit haughtily, then removed a burlap package from under his shawl.

Ali knew that merely handling this drug declared *haram*—sinful—was forbidden by the Qu'ran. But there was no alternative, for either of them. He had to obey orders and the Afghan had to fight the Shuravi. Both had to feed their families.

It was harvest season in Afghanistan. Springtime, the New Year. Terraced hillsides of white and gold, red and purple. Poppies swaying in the breeze. Petals falling... until the pods stood naked. The first cut released a milky sap, which dried into a black resin that smelled like new-mown grass. Selim's opium was of the third cut, finest quality, the creation of many poppies—two thousand for each kilo.

He had crossed the snow-covered peaks with fifty-five kilos of opium lashed to his camel, following secret trails to a laboratory hidden inside a mountain cave. This was tribal land that straddled both sides of the border—land that lay legally inside Pakistan, but was, in fact, beyond the reach of any government.

While Selim drank tea and rested, his fellow Pashtuns dissolved the opium in a vat of boiling water. They added some chemicals, then filtered the solution and dried it into brown morphine base, which was cooked again with more chemicals. By the next day, his fifty-five kilos of opium had been transformed into five-and-a-half kilos of the finest white heroin. Number four, crystal. After extracting a half-kilo in payment, the tribesmen-chemists packed up the crystalline product and wished him a safe journey.

Now Selim handed the five-kilo package to the Pakistani captain.

Ali gave him an envelope thick with American dollars. "This will buy more weapons for *jihad* against Russians."

"Many Russians will die." His eyes blazed, then he shrugged. *"Insh'Allah."*

There was a sharp but quiet pop. The bullet hit Ali between the eyes.

A second shot hit Selim in the back of his neck.

It was quick. A surprised cry. Blood. A grunt. More blood. The two men fell upon the grave, their lives flowing away in blood the color of tulips. Ali still clutching the burlap package. The envelope of money lying in the dust.

Mr. Yu emerged from the darkness, holding a silenced Beretta. Stuffing the pistol in his waistband, he grabbed the envelope and opened it, pleased to see that the contents were green. Dollars, not rupees. Thirty-five thousand US. With much more to come.

He placed the envelope tenderly in his breast pocket, then retrieved the package. Unwrapping the burlap, he peered through plastic at the fine white powder. In Peshawar, these five kilos of heroin had been worth thirty-five thousand dollars. Soon, each kilo would be worth that much. He was well along the path to becoming an ancestor.

Until then, he needed to proceed with caution. He checked each body for weapons or anything else of value. The Pakistani soldier was unarmed. In a fold of the Afghan's sash, Yu found a small toy, a plastic airplane. He stared at it, thinking of the toys he intended to buy his sons. With a sigh, he dropped the plane in his pocket, chastened again by the exigencies of life.

Then he unfolded a red, white and blue vinyl bag and placed the heroin inside. Mr. Yu had a moment's pause. This was a cemetery, after all. He frowned, then reassured himself that this place had been through worse... and would remain long after he was gone. It was an old land. Chinese pilgrims had been coming here for centuries to walk the path of the Buddha. He respected religion. There was time for that. Right now, he was on his own path.

He looked around, squinting into the darkness. No one. Mr. Yu pocketed the pistol and walked away, the striped tote bag swinging from his hand.

Chapter 5

Trying to look interested, Nick watched his boss, Ronald Hudson, making tracks on the Kashmiri carpet as he went on about the current spat between Congress and the Company. Nick was more concerned with the six missing Stingers—and the Farouk connection. He wondered if the general were running his own show. Or did he have the tacit approval of others? If so, which others? Which governments, or factions within governments? His train of thought led back to the home team. And his operation. And protecting it. Even from the boss.

His cool blue eyes arctic, Ronald Hudson regarded the latest communication from the latest congressional committee to investigate covert operations in the region. "These people are absolutely clueless. They simply do not get the strategic issues at stake here." He held the document between thumb and forefinger as if it were dirty Kleenex. "Now, they're inquiring about *diversions.*"

Holy shit! Nick shifted in his seat. That kind of talk set off alarm bells in his head. He did not want any investigating committee nosing around his territory. As for Farouk, he'd handle him privately. He stretched his legs toward Hudson's Victorian desk, a relic of the British Raj. "Oh, you mean the stuff that falls off the truck." Despite the grin, he felt wary.

"They're actually accusing us." Ronald looked at his papers. "Quote: 'Agency mismanagement of the covert aid program.' Unquote." His voice dripped scorn, which deepened as he focused on Nick and his dusty cowboy boots. "The Company used to have such fine standards."

Nick shrugged. "I guess I'm just a sign of the times. Declining standards and all." He believed in heading off an attack at the pass, which he figured came from all those summers in Texas, vacations spent with his Sunday School grandma who'd also taught him when to turn the other cheek.

Ronald returned his disdainful gaze to the document. "Armchair analysis from the gang who can't shoot straight."

Nick was sure there was a joke there somewhere, but… Diversions?

"To continue. Our supply pipeline to the rebels is leaky. Large amounts of aid are slipping through the cracks into the deep pockets of Pakistani intermediaries. Et cetera. Et cetera." He crumpled the report and tossed it in the trash.

Nick knew that Ronald didn't really care about the leaks—or the mujahideen's lack of equipment. The graying-blond, buttoned-down Yalie just didn't like being challenged on his own turf. It was ironic. The Afghan war had made Hudson's career, but its very heat attracted others. Others who also wanted control. Nick was less concerned with power than keeping a low profile. Not rocking the boat. "Way I look at it, the Paks deserve something for all the shit we've got 'em into. Refugees, drugs, guns, social unrest. Why not grab their piece of the billion-dollar American pie? I've noticed the guerrillas do their own skimming." He eyed the boss, but got no reaction.

"They're talking audits. *Nobody* audits the Agency."

Nick frowned. "Those Washington folks are all the same. They want to know, and they don't want to know. I'll tell you one thing. This resupply is running as well as most I've seen. The ragheads'd be down to their last slingshot if it weren't for us." He smirked, but his eyes took dead aim. "Speaking of leaks—the good stuff? Like the Stingers? Whose pockets are they landing in, d'ya think?"

Hudson shot him a look, then turned toward the window. "I don't know. I'm not interested, and neither are you. Distribution is a Pakistani matter. Policy dictates we keep it that way." He turned back and smiled. "Besides, Stingers are probably too complicated for the rebels."

"I've heard those things are just point and shoot."

"Nick. These are simple people. Rural folk. They have enough equipment to keep going. That's our goal: support the forces of freedom around the world."

"Right. Still, we know nothing works without grease in these parts. Only they call it *baksheesh* instead of diversions."

"Please. Spare me the lecture. I've been playing the game for too many years. And don't use that word 'raghead' around here—it's offensive."

Hudson stared at Nick's toe, grazing a finely carved desk leg. "Have I ever told you how valuable this piece is?"

"I have a dim remembrance of things past."

"Ah. The man has read Proust." He raised an eyebrow and nodded.

Go ahead. Patronize me, you sonuvabitch. Nick didn't really mind being looked down on. It was just another form of camouflage.

Hudson rose and headed toward the door. "Let's take a walk."

Nick was glad to escape the room—chilly in every way. Before leaving, he patted the belly of a smiling Gandharan Buddha. "Do you think he's mellow because he's stoned, or is he just happy to be here?" He didn't expect an answer because Ronald was already striding down the hall.

When Hudson had arrived from Angola in 1979, Peshawar was off the map, literally a nowhere assignment. By year's end, the Soviets invaded Afghanistan—poor, defenseless Afghanistan in the eyes of the world. A Christmas gift from Moscow, in Hudson's private view. His career soared as Peshawar developed from a backwater town into a global hotspot, while the Russian adventure went from bad to worse. The war was good for America—and certainly good for Ronald Hudson. He'd been in the right place at the right time. Now he was CIA chief of Peshawar base, with an official position as head of the U.S. Information Service.

They passed the research library full of Pakistani and Afghan youths, many of them students in Nick's experimental new Media Project. The idea was to teach them skills of photojournalism so they could report from the field. In Nick's "day job" as consular press attaché, he had spotted a need that these young men could fill.

It had been a difficult war for the Western media to cover. A few European and American reporters did manage to slip across the border from time to time. A very few. The Soviets had barred all foreign journalists. The U.S. government banned Americans, for their own safety. Still, if a journalist were hellbent on chasing a story, there was not much anyone realistically could do about it.

The two CIA officers walked down the front steps of the former suburban residence, now transformed into U.S. Government offices. In many ways, the war had been good for the local economy, bringing rising real estate values—as well as inflation. The men turned onto a path that led to the garden, well tended with leafy trees filtering the morning sun. The air was warm and sweet smelling, a respite from the frigid air-conditioning and the dense heat outside the gates.

Ronald finally got to his bottom line. "The media is stirring the pot. They're ecstatic over another diversion story."

"It's the CIA angle that turns them on. They think we're real sexy."

Ronald's smile was pained. "What we have here is a problem of media management—and that, of course, is your specialty."

"Ah luvs to sweet-talk our literary guests."

"I think it's your sleazy charm that goes over so well with them. What is it they say about 'birds of a feather'?"

"Maybe it's just my knowledge of Proust." Nick grinned. "But, yeah, I hear you. Our journalist friends have deadlines. They can't get into Afghanistan and yet they need to file—something. My job is to keep them out of mischief. *On* the beaten track. Too many Americans step on too many of the wrong Pakistani toes, they'll kick us clear the hell outta here." He eyed Hudson. "And we wouldn't want that to happen, would we?"

Ronald was studying his roses. "I've put a lot into this garden." He reached down and yanked out a weed. "I've put a lot into this war, too." A pair of fighter jets streaked across the sky and he paused to observe their trajectory. Then he took out a small pruning shears and snipped a white bud. "This is a good clean war—not one American life has been lost... well, except that Arizona journalist. We're winning major propaganda victories against the Soviets every day. If I do say so myself, we've shaped things well."

"Enough weapons to wound the Russian Bear, just not defeat him." Nick stared at the twin plumes of jet exhaust. "With luck, we can keep this thing going on for years."

"That's a rather frivolous remark, crude even. Our objective here is to achieve military balance with the other side. Which may or may not include victory. Military, that is."

In other words, stalemate rather than checkmate. Nick knew what the Afghanis thought of "military balance." In the previous century, they had managed to dash British hopes of expansion in Central Asia. Now they were battling Russia. It was all part of the ongoing "Great Game" that the world powers persisted in playing. But there were games, and there were games. Games within games. Which was where he operated.

The American Congress didn't care about the Great Game, its subtle rules or intricate moves. They just loved the black-and-white, David-and-Goliath nature of the war. They were gung-ho Afghanistan, and CIA allocations were as large as Vietnam. Too large. With too little control over where the money went—to whom. But it was a war even the liberals could love, the chance to prove they weren't soft on communism. Everyone admired the heroic freedom fighters. Congressmen had their pictures taken with visiting mujahideen, some even traveled with them inside Afghanistan. It was a macho thing, an emotional thing. A noble thing. They were simply not interested in "military balance." The real romantics were even thinking the Afghans might win!

Ronald eyed a snail and slowly ground it underfoot. "Our Congressional friends don't understand the work we're doing. They seem to prefer clean hands to success."

"Depends how you define success. Or maybe they just don't grasp the concept of military balance." Nick shrugged. "Of course what do they know? Those guys can barely make their way off the Beltway. They couldn't find the real world if you gave 'em a map."

"I certainly can't argue with you on that, but so what? We simply have to be smarter than they are, outthink them. That shouldn't be too hard." Ronald sniffed his rose thoughtfully. "Their interference is hurting us all." He gazed at Nick. "I want you on top of the press situation. I need you to downplay this diversion and black market talk."

"How about putting them onto the cemetery murders? I'm sure there's plenty to 'dig up' out there."

Ronald gave him a murderous stare.

"Seriously, don't you wonder what that is all about?"

"No, I do not. And neither do you."

"It was a thought. Don't worry, though, I've got more."

"Why does that scare me?"

With a grin, Nick walked to the gate and then glanced back at Hudson, still contemplating his rose. He knew his boss considered him a loser, but didn't give a shit. The goal of intelligence work was to lull the opposition into overconfidence, by any means. You couldn't afford ego trips in this business. Not if you wanted the real payoff.

Chapter 6

Robin awoke in a dazed sweat. Almost a panic. It felt as if a dentist had been drilling in her head. Where was she? She heard the mosquito dive-bomb her ear again. Flailing wildly, she kicked off the damp sheets—and remembered. This godawful hotel room. Peshawar. Not a drop of air, and no escape.

Still jetlagged, she managed to raise herself on an elbow and look around. The room had been bad enough last night and was even worse in the unforgiving light of day. Fortunately, she hadn't unpacked. Mentally she surveyed her supplies of cotton clothing, books, clipping files, binoculars, camera and film, granola bars and water-purifying kit. It seemed she was prepared for everything.

Everything but stepping on that moldy carpet, undoubtedly home to all manner of wildlife. She pulled on her socks, aware she was reacting like a spoiled American tourist. At the moment, though, Robin didn't care. She grabbed her watch. A little after ten—and already almost a hundred. She flopped back on the bed, her T-shirt dripping.

San Francisco seemed very far away.

Robin had always known she took things too personally, too seriously. But better that than being a superficial, hipper-than-thou Beautiful Person, like most of the other guests busy seeing and being seen at the hot-ticket opening. The "art" left her cold: she would have rather written about the fashion parade, although the kissing-cheeks game was beyond her. It was the nature of her profession to be an observer, and she cultivated the skill of being at once inside and outside. Yet sometimes the disconnect was extreme.

Stuffing her notepad into her bag, she stalked out of the gallery, relieved to have finally escaped. Free at last. The falling dusk seemed an apt metaphor for the lack of clarity inside the packed storefront. In her opinion the work was pretentious and empty, the product of a con artist who styled herself as a Zen-master but whose actual genius lay in self-promotion. Yet even the local journalists bought into the hype. Her colleagues. It all seemed so cynical and pointless. Robin believed there was something wrong with a system that worshipped novelty, fame and money above all else. Art was supposed to be uplifting. She only felt downtrodden.

Thinking of the review she was to write, Robin set off toward the *Gazette* office a few blocks away. This was SoMa—South of Market—San Francisco's answer to SoHo. She remembered Huxley's *Brave New World*, and the miracle drug soma, which acted to smooth out life's rough edges, its dosage determined by just how rough things were. Like the character, "hers had been more than a one-gramme affliction." Robin sighed.

As the light faded around her, she was hit on by a line of strung-out dealers. Too far gone to know the neighborhood was now trendy, they offered bargain rates on reefer, crack and new, improved stuff to fry your brain. Or freeze it. Robin had never been afraid of winos or dopers. She remembered the smiles of the Flower Children. But these people had a desperation that made her shiver. In a way, though, she understood their desperation. How did you make life matter?

That was the question that drove Robin. In her passion to make life matter—to achieve the grand gesture—she had always scorned the easy way. Avoiding the conventional, she sought challenges, even danger. What attracted her was life on the edge—the edge of society, the edge of safety. But at that moment, she felt as false as the Zen-master artist. As much a *poseur*.

Suddenly a woman with matted hair and raging eyes emerged from the darkness and put out her hand. Robin slapped a five in it, then hurried on. Depressed and angry, she trudged up the granite steps and inside the large building that housed the *Gazette*.

On her way to the newsroom, Robin passed the conference area where several colleagues were watching the evening news. Normally she would have joined them, but she was in no mood to socialize. She did pause, though, as anchor Dan Rather switched to Afghanistan. Then stopped dead in her tracks when she heard Jamal's name.

Robin turned. She had read about him, of course, but this was the first time she'd seen him on TV. The image was different from the one she carried in memory, different even from the grainy photographs that accompanied news reports. She realized the significance of a network crew shooting the tape. He was obviously making his mark in the Afghan conflict—and everyone was taking notice.

She stared at the tall, bearded man with thick, tousled hair and powerful eyes that commanded attention. She noted the brass glimmering from ammunition belts crossing his long-tailed shirt, the dusty pants and leather hiking boots. It was more than a pose, she knew. There was an energy about him. He almost leaped out at her from the monitor. For an instant, she had the strange feeling he could actually see her, and know the truth in her heart.

Robin regarded him closely. Time had merely tiptoed across his face. He was more handsome than ever. His features were fine but emphatic—high cheekbones, long aristocratic nose, wide brow, firm mouth. A sensitive face, but strong. Determined.

From a great distance, she heard Rather's voice. "Jamal, the controversial Afghan mujahideen leader, is seen by some as the only man charismatic enough to unite the various resistance factions."

The memories washed over her. Jamal was charismatic, all right. Dangerously so.

Jamal draws a battle plan in the dust with a sharpened stick. He is surrounded by a group of about twenty armed mujahideen, all in similar loose, drab clothing, all watching him with expressions ranging from respect to devotion.

"Others, however," the voice-over continued, "view him as a dangerous egomaniac spitting in the face of both the Soviet Union and the United States."

Then the anchor's face reappeared. "There are widespread, though unsubstantiated, rumors that he is banking U.S. aid money as a cushion against his uncertain future—"

"Give me a break!" Robin crossed her arms, radiating scorn, as two copy editors turned to stare.

"What?" asked the brainy one who had asked her out, more than once.

She shrugged and swept past them. Robin was used to men being intrigued by her and understood the value of mystery. If the guys had a thing for her, let them. But she kept it strictly professional, businesslike. She wasn't interested in a relationship—or an affair. At least, not with them. What she cared about were ideas and ideals, and somehow making a difference. So she fixed her eyes on the horizon and refused to be sidetracked.

Robin reached the newsroom, then sat down at her desk behind the barricade of newspapers, magazines and books. Determined to get it over with, she popped a piece of paper into her IBM Selectric and rolled it into place, clean and white and waiting to be filled. It was not really a bad job.

Assigned to the city beat in "The City," Robin covered the spectrum: crime and corruption, the environment, fashion and, of course, food. She was currently following the extradition case against a right-wing Argentine general who had hoped to end his days as a North Beach restaurateur. Just thinking about the slimy rat got her going all over again. Still, the practical side of her recognized the value of the case to her career, as a segue into international. Afghanistan was on her radar.

Robin soon knocked out a review dealing with the art of business and the business of art. Done. She set off to pay a visit to her editor. Let him send someone else next time.

Robin poked her head into the windowed office of her prematurely balding editor, Paul Terry. She marched over to his desk, slapped her review down and crossed her arms defiantly. "You wanted it, you got it! Read it and weep."

"From joy?" Paul gazed at her through his horn rims, thrusting his thumbs behind striped suspenders.

"More like sorrow. Or pity."

"What's the headline?"

"Fashion Victims Worship at the Shrine of Art."

Paul smiled. "I'm pleased to see you're so happy in your work."

"Even happier now, since after this…" She jabbed a finger at her review. "You'll have to get another sucker for the art scene. I'll be persona non grata everywhere south of Market."

Paul released his suspenders with an abrupt snap. "That settles it. I was going to promote you to art critic. But now that you've burned all your bridges, you're useless to me."

Robin froze, staring at him in dismay. Being fired wasn't in the game plan. She needed this job.

He paused, then reached in a drawer and handed her an envelope.

Her mouth opened in protest, then widened into an amazed smile when she realized the envelope held an airplane ticket—not her final paycheck.

"How long you been bugging me about this Afghan trip? Your big career break. A move from local to international... well, go for it!" He feigned impatience.

Robin looked at the destination, shaking her head with delight. For a moment, her heart danced in her eyes. "You're a rare bird, Paul. You make this B.S. media game worth playing."

"A left-handed compliment that I accept with grace."

"If only there were more like you. I just saw Dan Rather do a number on Jamal. Sounded like speculation-in-search-of-a-story to me." She scowled.

Paul regarded her fondly. "My last angry woman. It's your turn now. You can tell the story your way." He leaned back in his chair. "How do you know he'll see you?"

"He'll see me." She held his look. "We were at Berkeley together."

He studied her face, its calm certainty. "Pretty close were you?"

"We were friends."

He nodded. "I sure as hell wouldn't forget you."

"Thanks."

He kept staring. "Berkeley was why they started calling us the Left Coast."

She frowned. "Now they're all studying Business Administration. Our college ideals may seem dated today, but Jamal and I really believed. Only he is fighting to achieve those ideals, while I'm hanging out in San Francisco with the BPs—and yes, that is related to B.S." Robin shook her head. "It all seems so unimportant, so frivolous—life here in Yuppieville." She smiled ruefully. "No offense, Paul."

"None taken. I was there too, you know, back at the barricades. It's just, ideals don't pay the mortgage, so you have to grow up." Paul shrugged. "Most of us, at least. Go get 'em, tiger!"

Robin nodded, eyes ablaze. Then her look softened and she grinned. "Uh, Paul? One last favor?"

"Have I ever denied you anything?"

"Not lately. I just realized I don't have anything to wear over there. Okay if I come in late tomorrow?"

Paul waved his hand. "Take the day off. Now get outta here."

She didn't need to be asked twice. This day had been a long time coming. "I won't forget you when I get that Pulitzer." What she was really seeking, though, wasn't fame, but rather something exciting and important. Something real.

The heat brought her back. Robin wiped her forehead, realizing it was only going to get hotter. She sat up and stared, taking a good hard look at her current reality. Her "modern, air-conditioned" Peshawar hotel room. The paint was peeling, the plumbing leaked rusty water and the mattress sagged.

She rubbed her back, then picked up the phone and called the front desk. "This is Robin Reeves, Room 207. There must be some mistake. I requested the new wing."

"But, madam, that is new wing."

"And air-conditioned."

"But, madam, you will simply go to wall and activate switch and the fan will commence operation."

Robin looked at the sluggish ceiling fan. "Of course. Thanks." She hung up. Oh well. She hadn't expected a four-star hotel and did not intend to stick around any longer than necessary. She rummaged around until she found the list of possible contacts. Starting at the top, she dialed a number. "Hello, my name is Robin Reeves. I'm a reporter from—"

CLICK.

She looked at the receiver, wondering if they'd been cut off. She tried again. "Hello? I'm a reporter from the *San Francisco*—"

"Maybe you will be going back soon?"

The line went dead. Robin blinked, then dialed another number. "I'd like to speak with Gul Omar, please."

After a short pause, a man replied, "Sorry?"

Robin checked her list and repeated the name carefully. "Gul Omar." Looking down, she noticed a cockroach scurry around her feet.

"He is not available at the present time, sir. May I be of assistance?"

"I need help arranging a trip to Afghanistan to interview the mujahideen leader, Jamal."

Silence, then, "It is very difficult. There is no one to speak with you at present. Everyone is very busy."

"When?"

There was a long pause. Finally came the grudging reply, "Maybe in one day's time."

"Good. I will come tomorrow morning at ten." She crushed the cockroach with the ball of her left foot, then removed her sock and tossed it in the corner.

Jhan's brown Toyota turned onto a tree-lined street. The sycamores were slender and young. Robin thought it looked like any neighborhood in California—low-slung stucco houses fronted by broad, well-tended lawns. But in California, there were few walled and gated houses. Even fewer guard shacks.

She got out of Jhan's car and entered the guarded post outside the U.S. Information Service compound, feeling the intense gaze of two armed Pakistani soldiers. "My name is Robin Reeves. I have an appointment with Ronald Hudson."

One of the men ran a metal detector along her body. The other guard checked her bag, then picked up the phone and dialed. "Miss Robin Reeves is having appointment with Mr. Hudson." He hung up. "You may pass."

They didn't mess around here. Robin crossed a broad expanse of lawn toward the front door of what had probably once been a private estate. Inside, a receptionist in a green silk tunic was seated behind a desk, a sheer green scarf covering her head and shoulders.

The woman nodded at Robin and pointed down the corridor to the right. "Mr. Hudson is expecting you."

Robin walked along a white hallway decorated with colorful Pakistani textiles, then entered a waiting room where she sat in a carved wooden chair. She studied the Persian and Indian miniatures on the walls, and was impressed by their quality.

After a few moments, Ronald Hudson appeared at the door, extending his hand and a professional smile. He welcomed her, and said it was a pleasure.

Right. The handshake was weak and his smile plastic.

"San Francisco, my favorite city."

"I guess it's everyone's favorite city, isn't it? Seems pretty tame compared with this place, though." She grinned. "Peshawar is what we used to call far-out."

A slightly raised eyebrow noted her mispronunciation of the town's name. Then Hudson nodded affably. "Far-out. Haven't heard that one in a long time, but yes indeed, an apt description." Gesturing toward his office, he ushered Robin to the sofa, then sat facing her. "The first thing you must learn is—it's pronounced puh-SHOWER. Not PESH-awar."

Robin took pains not to show it, but she was embarrassed. Dumb. She shrugged. "Puh-SHOWER."

"Don't worry, ninety percent of first-time visitors make the same mistake," he said, eyeing her bush vest. "This is your first visit, I take it?"

"Why, yes. Although I've done extensive research." She felt he was trying to throw her off balance, and didn't like it. "And I've got a different slant." Robin was determined to take control of the meeting. She looked him dead in those icy eyes. "I intend to interview the guerrilla leader Jamal at his base outside Kandahar."

Hudson laughed. "Base? That guy sleeps in a different place every night. Doesn't trust anyone. He's almost a myth the way he appears and disappears." He regarded her pointedly. "And have you heard about the new Russian shoot-to-kill policy? Any foreign reporter found wandering around is history. They got one from the *Arizona Republic* recently. Fifty-year-old family man."

Robin blinked. "I wasn't aware of that, but I'm not worried." She paused. "I know Jamal."

"You've got to be kidding!"

Now she had his interest. "Of course he was 'Jim' in those days. We studied Political Science together at Berkeley."

Hudson nodded, probing. "So you two go back a long ways."

"Very long."

"He expecting you?"

Her expression was modest, yet mysterious. Let him read it however he wanted. "Not exactly."

"Then he should be pleasantly surprised."

Smiling guilelessly. "I certainly hope so."

"It's very enterprising of you, I'm sure, but the trip is simply impossible. Don't worry, though. There's plenty to cover right here in Peshawar— refugee camps, Red Cross and Red Crescent hospitals, schools, women's issues. Marvelous human interest material."

Robin tossed her head. "Don't patronize me! I'm not here for the girl stuff."

Hudson's manner was placating. "Now, Robin… may I call you Robin?" She gave him a short nod.

"I certainly didn't mean to offend you. I'll introduce you to my press officer, Nick Daley. He'll get you oriented, help in any way he can." He paused, looked straight at her. "But Afghanistan is strictly off-limits."

Robin met his eyes. "Officially."

"And unofficially." His look didn't waver.

"Right." Her manner was tough now—no nonsense. She needed to establish her credibility. "One last question. What about diversions of U.S. covert aid away from the resistance?"

Hudson didn't bat an eyelash. "You're a smart woman, Robin. Whatever you hear, just remember there are many stories floating around. Hidden agendas that could make your head swim. My advice is stay away from rumors. It's not worth it." He smiled, raised his palms in a shrug. "The Paks are sensitive. After all, this is their country and their business. If you snoop, you'll be on the first plane out."

Robin searched his face but couldn't get beneath the surface. She smiled back and nodded, noncommittal. "I see."

"Now, Robin, I've got some useful info for you, background material on the conflict, as well as a list of names and organizations based here. Consulates and NGOs, media contacts. And a good local doc in case, God forbid, you get a dose of Delhi belly." He picked up a stapled packet from his desk, stood and handed it to her.

Robin rose to her feet, without looking at the papers. It was beyond her who would want to rely on a government press kit. She preferred her own research. Glancing at the door, she noticed the carved stone Buddha along the wall. The figure appeared to be smiling right at her. A wise, all-knowing smile that briefly gave her pause.

"I'm hosting a party here tonight. I'd love you to join us. You'll meet Nick and everyone else worth knowing." He looked at his watch.

She got the hint. "Wouldn't miss it. Thanks for your time." Robin turned, opened the door and walked out.

Chapter 7

A hot breeze circulated through the garden, carrying the scents of night-blooming jasmine and exotic cooking spices, along with the singsong rhythms of a dozen languages accompanied by sitar and tabla. The U.S. Information Service reception was a mix of worlds. To some guests, Pakistan was a faraway, romantic place. To others, it was home.

Or at least a place to hang your hat. That was how Nick saw it. You went where the action was. Peshawar was the international hot-spot-of-the-day, with the Soviets and American proxies engaged just across the border. Some would represent the conflict as a civil war—Afghan vs. Afghan, reformers vs. traditionalists. There were elements of truth in that view, but it was not the whole truth. And no one here was so simple as to think so.

The Soviets had possibly anticipated a quiet little invasion, but suddenly the Cold War had found a new playing field. And Peshawar was as much a battleground as the rocky terrain of Afghanistan. The party itself was an engagement in the war, and the guests were a savvy, often cynical bunch. By now Nick knew them all—the diplomats, aid workers and arms merchants, the Pakistani powers-that-be and would-be, although their wives and daughters remained safely at home. The media was out in force, including a movie producer scouting a low-budget feature. And of course, there were journalists.

One of them, looking quite smashing in a turquoise Indian gauze number, was the new reporter in town. Nick had already checked her out, having been ordered to get "on top of the press situation." But there was more: his boss had just slipped him an interesting tidbit. The woman knew Jamal—well. Nick started easing in her direction.

Robin was already at work, pumping Eddie Girard for information. Girard was a wiry, ex-street kid turned journalist who boasted he'd never met a war he didn't like.

They were hanging around the bar, which served soft drinks, fresh fruit juice and bowls of spicy nuts. An action junkie and old Asia hand, Eddie was also trying to arrange a trip "inside." His seventh. "So this time, I've been waiting at Dean's Hotel over five weeks for them to get it together."

"Five weeks! I don't have that kind of time."

"You may have no choice."

"Who's the 'them'?"

"One of the seven 'official' resistance groups headquartered in Peshawar—all controlled by President-General Zia's purse strings, all on big power trips. Their rules are one of 'em has to agree to escort you inside."

"Why not just hire a guide to take you in?"

"It should only be so simple. Truth is, it's too damn dangerous to travel there without some kind of clout—protection, insurance, whatever you call it. Besides the Russians, you gotta worry about running afoul of one of the rival mujahideen groups."

"Rival? I thought they're all supposed to be on the same side."

"In a pig's eye! Although I guess they don't have any of those around here. Maybe a sacred cow's eye?" Eddie glanced at Robin, who nodded at the joke. "These Afghan 'leaders' are so friggin' busy jockeying for power, it's amazing they have time to fight the Russians! In fact, they don't. They leave that to their foot soldiers, who happen to be the bravest, most selfless men I've ever seen. Unfortunately, it's the leaders who control the weapons distribution and make the rules. Bottom line? They control access, and no one gets in without their approval."

"That sounds like an invitation for a payoff."

"Grease can help, but it's not enough on its own. It's more a matter of bureaucracy meets the battlefield. Things happen in their own time, according to their own rules. Like I said, I've been waiting five weeks—and I'm a man."

"What the hell does that have to do with the price of an E-ticket to the war zone?"

"Yeah, weren't those the days? When an E-ticket would get you on Disneyland's wildest rides." Eddie gazed at her. "I bet those were the only ones you rode." Seeing her mysterious smile, he shrugged. "But here? They're not real big on independent women in these parts."

A frown took over her face. Robin knew about the woman's place in this society. Jamal had taught her that. The chapter on women came near the end of the Qu'ran. Right after "The Cow." But she had resolved to ignore the entire issue through sheer force of will. "That kind of stuff doesn't bother me."

"Nothing like an undaunted American female to ruffle a few feathers."

Robin gave him a saucy grin. "You mean, as in tail feathers?"

Eddie shook his head. "I'd like to help you, Robin. Unfortunately, my contacts are now on the fundamentalist end of the spectrum. 'Nuff said?" Then he nodded toward a tall, lean man in jeans and a linen jacket who was ambling across the lawn. "Maybe you should talk to Nick Daley—the government press officer. Among other things."

"What other things?"

"Who knows? No one here is what they seem, no one says what they think. Part of the mysterious local charm." Eddie saw Nick swap greetings with a man in a tie, then continue heading their way. "The guy can be helpful, but his personality has a few raw edges, to say the least."

"Sometimes raw can be preferable to slick." As in Ronald Hudson. Curious, Robin watched Nick close the gap between them, cowboy boots and all. Marlboro Man.

Nick grabbed Eddie's hand and pumped it. "Eddie, old pal." Smiling all the while at Robin. Trying to pick up her vibes.

"At your service, Nick. Robin? Meet our faithful government servant, Nick Daley. Nick, this is Robin Reeves, ace reporter for the *San Francisco Gazette.*"

He released his grip on Eddie and extended his palm to the newcomer, noting her nice mouth with the little dimple next to it.

Robin took his hand and met his gaze coolly. The handshake continued a bit longer than necessary.

"Ahh, Lois Lane. Girl reporter for a great metropolitan newspaper. This old town has been hard up for some beautiful new talent." Nick liked her thick auburn hair. The legs were nice, too. And smooth, unlike those of most of the aid workers, bless their Good Samaritan hearts. But her gray eyes were standing guard, eyes that didn't let you in.

Robin was glad it had been Ronald Hudson who'd corrected her pronunciation, not this guy. She let go of his hand. "And how is life in Peshawar, Nick?"

"A little lacking, if you know what I mean."

That was an invitation to a two-step. "No, what do you mean?"

Nick held her look. "What I mean is my grandma used to cook up a mean stew. Plenty of veggies—the good-for-you stuff—but what made it were the spices. Can't live without the spice." He flashed a big, good-old-boy grin.

Robin stared. "I've heard so much about you... but nothing about your culinary expertise."

Eddie placed an arm around Robin's shoulder. "Robin needs to get connected with some of the Afghan political groups in town. I'm sure you can help her out."

Nick enjoyed the way Robin neatly sidestepped Eddie's arm. "I'd love to show you around—refugee camps, historical sites—introduce you to quotable locals, anything." He wagged a finger. "But if dear Eddie has given you any ideas about any Afghanistan excursions, you can forget it. It's too bloody dangerous. And believe me, the pun is intended. Besides, there's no toilet paper over there—not to mention toilets, clean water or food." His eyes twinkled. "Other than that, it's a great country. Ain't it, pal?"

Eddie nodded. "Scenic, too."

Robin shook her head in disbelief. The government was in worse shape than she'd thought. "Excuse me, but are you for real?"

"Maybe you'll be lucky and find out."

"An irresistible offer. But I'll get my own tour guide, thanks."

He shrugged. "I'll be around when you change your mind, hon. See y'all."

That was the last thing she needed. Robin watched him walk away. Marlboro men had always been her downfall. But this was definitely not the time or the place.

Probably more trouble than she was worth. His smile fading, Nick crossed the lawn toward the house. The smile reappeared as he rounded a corner and almost collided with the imposing, broad-shouldered figure of Major General Babar Farouk. "We've got to stop meeting like this, General."

"The pleasure is all mine, Nick."

"Thanks for coming tonight. You tried any of the fresh mango juice yet?"

The general nodded. "Superb. It promises to be quite a season. You know, when I was away at Sandhurst, that was the one thing I really missed. The mangoes."

"I know exactly what you mean." Nick bit back a smile. Farouk never missed a chance to remind you of his illustrious background, which included his British schooling.

Farouk wore his lineage with pride. Scion of a powerful North-West Frontier Province family, named after the first great Mogul emperor, he had attended the Royal Military Academy, where he'd received the "Silver Stick" award as best overseas cadet. He still had his clothing tailored in London and was at home in many worlds. "And your chicken tikka is commendable. It is evident your staff grinds their own spices."

"But of course. The local cuisine sets a high standard." Nick appreciated Farouk's style and flair, just as he understood it to be an effective means of camouflage. For despite his worldliness and charm, the general never questioned his right to use his might.

Farouk gave him a mock tip of the hat. "As do we. Your American aid money is of great help to the people."

"The question is, which people?"

"It is a pity, but there are fortunes to be made during times of war."

"Sad but true." Nick fixed him with a look. "We're very disturbed about the increasing flow of drugs through Peshawar."

"That is one thing we simply can not tolerate."

"There was another drug-related murder just last night."

General Farouk nodded gravely, but remained silent.

"One of the victims was an army captain."

"Greed is most dangerous."

Nick watched Ronald Hudson introduce a Swiss Red Cross nurse to a man from Boston public television, then returned his attention to Farouk. "Yes, General, most dangerous. Perhaps you'll want to keep a closer eye on things. I understand the Islamabad brass are keeping their sights on you. They've got long memories."

General Farouk stiffened at the reference to his failed coup attempt, then squared his shoulders and tossed his head. "Ancient history. I only seek to do my duty to the nation." Then he stood taller still as Robin approached. His eyes gleamed.

Nick could see she didn't waste a moment getting next to a source. "Say, Robin, I'm sure you'd like to meet the famous General Babar Farouk. General, may I present Ms. Robin Reeves, just in from San Francisco."

Farouk placed his left hand over their two clasped right ones and beamed.

Nick grinned. "The general may agree to an interview. If you play your cards right."

Robin extricated herself from the handshake, while turning her eighteen-carat smile on Farouk, and shifted into her no-nonsense reporter mode. "General, we keep hearing rumors of massive leaks—up to seventy percent—in the flow of CIA-purchased arms to the mujahideen." She pinned him with her eyes, continuing to smile. "They say most of them make it only as far as the black market."

"Aw, it's probably no more than thirty percent."

Robin ignored Nick, maintaining her laser-like focus on the general.

Farouk smiled back at Robin. "You Americans seem obsessed with this ridiculous story. My dear, the mujahideen are our Islamic brethren fighting our communist enemy. Why would anyone want to deprive them of needed supplies?"

"My question exactly."

He regarded her intently. "If you uncover anything—absolutely anything—you must come to me. Immediately. And I will do everything in my power to put a stop to it." Farouk glanced at Nick. "Our host is serving some marvelous mango juice this evening. Have you tasted it yet, my dear?"

"Not yet."

"I should be honored to serve you your first glass."

Robin nodded. "South Asian mangoes are world famous."

"At least the Pakistani ones."

Nick was impressed by how smoothly they both operated. "Remember, hon, anything I can do. Anytime."

She shot him an enigmatic look. "I'll remember." Robin turned back to the Pakistani general.

Farouk bent his head toward hers. "I do so admire the spirit of you American women—your *joie de vivre*."

Nick watched them go. She was just what this old town needed. But there was something going on. Why did he have the feeling she wasn't really interested in aid diversions, that her inquiry was merely a smokescreen for something else? But why? Maybe she just wanted a little adventure or to rekindle the affair with her macho mujahideen hero. He smiled to himself. His boredom was obviously breeding paranoia and weird fantasies. Whatever her game, he welcomed the opportunity to play.

Chapter 8

Jhan drove north through town until the streets narrowed into dusty lanes. He turned into a bumpy alleyway that led to a high-walled, yellow stucco compound with watchtowers at each corner. Robin saw several armed guards hanging around the gate—burly, bearded men wearing crocheted skullcaps, flat Chitrali caps with rolled edges or oversized turbans. They made a move on the car as it was rolling to a stop. Suddenly all Robin could see were massive torsos and Kalashnikovs.

Jhan poked out his head. "She is expected."

The guards didn't move. They stared fiercely.

Robin felt nervous, then steeled herself and opened her door, forcing one of the guards to give way. She got out and saw them fall back a bit further. "I'm a journalist from California, here to see Gul Omar." Robin felt their hostility—and discomfort. Odd. She was making them uncomfortable. Well, good. She held her ground and stared back.

The standoff continued until a tall youth with peach fuzz emerged through the gate. "Commander Omar is very busy."

"I'm sure he is. However, we do have an appointment, and I know he is a man of his word." Robin smiled sweetly, then moved past them, feeling a bit like Moses as the waters parted. As she continued through the gate and into the courtyard, the back of her neck felt prickly. She thought of their rifles. Hearing footsteps behind her, she whirled around to face her attackers.

Jhan!

His eyes were anxious but he stood tall. "It is my duty to help you, Miss Robin. These kinds of men..." He shrugged.

Robin nodded. Obviously no one was willing to disturb the great leader for a mere woman. There were rules in this society, rules that grew out of a hierarchy dedicated to marginalizing women—including her. Only a male escort could make her real.

The teenager rushed ahead and led them inside the faded, two-story house. They entered a living room sparsely furnished with carpets and cushions. He gestured to the only chair. "Some tea?"

Robin sat down and shook her head. "Thank you, no."

Jhan, standing behind her, watched the boy turn and leave. "Having tea a good thing. How can a man be good host without chai?"

Robin glanced at him, pondering his point. "Next time." She looked around the dim room and noticed a picture of Ayatollah Khomeini. Beside it was an idealized portrait of a younger man, a warrior with sharp, austere features. She removed a notebook from her vest and began fanning herself.

A heavyset man entered, his tan, long-tailed shirt taut over a massive belly. His eyes swept over her and then settled on Jhan. "Commander Omar agrees to see her—"

"Oh, great," Robin said, rising to her feet.

"After he finishes his phone call." The man ignored her interruption. He turned and left.

He didn't even look at her. Robin stared after him. She had known this would be a feudal, chauvinistic place, but nothing could have prepared her for the reality of crash- landing in the Middle Ages—or what seemed like it. The situation made her feel powerless, small, even invisible. She felt grateful for Jhan's help, despite a certain embarrassment at such a feeling. It was a shock to her sense of herself to realize that being independent and resourceful wasn't always enough. Robin sank back down, filled with a new, visceral understanding of Jamal's world, and why she had to find him. She began fanning herself again.

One day Jamal had taken her up to Mount Shasta in Northern California. Against the stern mountain backdrop, he'd told her about his ancient people and their unbending code of honor, hospitality and revenge. Their powerful faith. "Our faith makes us invincible. We have a saying, 'Every Afghan has God and a gun.'"

Robin stared at him, as if he were a stranger, aware suddenly just how different his background and values were. "What would it be like for me in Afghanistan?" She was curious, yet wistful, already knowing the answer.

He touched her cheek with great gentleness. "'The times they are a-changing...'"

"Slowly." She searched for something in his eyes and then let out her hopes in a deep sigh. Robin knew she could never belong to his world, except as a jarring intrusion. She looked away, shaken by the sense of loss... then turned back to him and nodded.

They smoked some Afghani hash and made love in the alpine spring meadow. He wrapped himself around her, fiercely. She fantasized that she was his wife and he had just slipped off her veil. She belonged solely to him. Only he could behold her.

Their lovemaking had a passion and power as never before. He was no longer a sensitive sixties male, but an Afghan chieftain who never questioned his right to own his woman, to use her as he wished. She had never been taken that way and was astounded at the part of her that enjoyed his force and wished only to submit.

But she would never submit. She would never belong to anyone. They began to drift apart after that day.

A drop of sweat stung her eye, causing it to tear. She blinked and all of a sudden wanted to cry, then scolded herself for being unprofessional. Robin looked at Jhan and saw he was watching her. She opened the notebook, pulled out a pen and started to write.

After a few more moments, a small, white-haired man appeared. "He will see you."

Robin peeled herself off the chair, shirt sticking to her back, and nodded at Jhan. They followed the old man down a long hallway to a large room with closed shutters and a ceiling fan.

Gul Omar sat behind a pine desk, hands folded before him. He was thin and ascetic, with narrow, dark eyes peering from a long, angular face—the man in the portrait next to Khomeini. His beard was full but neatly clipped, his nails clean, as was his crisp, white shalwar kameez.

Three armed men stood behind him, while several other guards were lounging around, yet not really at rest.

Robin extended her hand. "My name is Robin Reeves. I'm a journalist from San Francisco."

Gul Omar stared at her hand, but did not touch it. He looked at Jhan and frowned, then gestured to two wooden chairs.

Ignoring the slight, Robin took her seat and pushed on. "I wish to go into Afghanistan to interview my old friend Jamal in Kandahar." The blank stares were disconcerting. She fought the instinct to turn to Jhan and have him explain. "I want to tell the American public the truth about the Afghan struggle."

Gul Omar adjusted the papers on his desk with great precision. Finally, he raised his head, his chilly eyes staring somewhere beyond Robin's left shoulder. "We have no connection with your 'old friend.' Commander Jamal is foolishly refusing to accept our political leadership. Moreover, we are finding dangerous his... Western orientation." He shuffled his papers diligently. "I am sorry we cannot be of assistance, but perhaps we can be arranging a tour of refugee camps and hospitals."

"Thank you, but I have no shortage of such offers." Robin straightened her spine. "What I must and will do is go to Afghanistan and interview Commander Jamal."

"We are wishing you good luck in your quest. Now, if you are not taking tea, you will excuse me. I have much work." He returned to his papers without waiting for a reply.

Jhan rose from his seat. He cast a quick look at Robin.

She got up and followed him out of the room. Again, as when she arrived, Robin felt dark eyes watching her. The hallway was dim, and all she could see was Jhan's back.

As they left the house, Robin almost recoiled from the blast of sunlight. She blinked once, then again and took a deep breath, filled with relief. It was as if she had flung open a prison door and stepped back into the twentieth century. Afghanistan was trying to open that door. But those guys planned to slam it shut. She thought about it as they continued through the courtyard. Whatever she could do to ensure the defeat of Gul Omar and his ilk, she would do. In a way, she was glad for even this small experience of their tyranny. Despite the heat, she shivered at the thought of being enslaved to a zealot like him. Being some helpless ten-year-old bride! She walked out the gate, ignoring the teenaged boy and the other guards.

Jhan opened the car door for her, then got in and started the engine. "Taking tea can be good thing..."

"You already told me that," she retorted, staring out the window.

"Even with our enemies." He glanced back at her. "A host must be serving chai. It is a matter of honor."

"Sorry, Jhan. I didn't mean to snap at you." Robin sighed. The honor thing. Their sacred code of behavior. Jamal had told her about that, too. "So we must drink tea with our enemies?"

"There are things you must learn, Miss Robin. I am only wanting to be of service."

She nodded. "I need to try some of the other groups."

"Of course. We will go tomorrow, but if you are not succeeding with any of them... maybe we can try something else."

Guardedly. "What?"

"Other ways."

Robin ran a hand through her hair, pushing it off her damp forehead. Private guides. "Thank you, Jhan. I know you're here to help, but it would be better if I can go in with one of the 'official' groups. Like the other journalists."

"Of course, official channels are better. But please to remember, success is best."

Robin frowned as they sped off through the dust.

It was morning and an intimate party had just wrapped up in the Pearl Continental hotel suite. The air-conditioning remained on high and the green velvet drapes were still drawn, creating a cool, oasis-like darkness.

The gold velour bedspread lay in a heap on the floor. Pillows were tossed about, sheets torn loose. A pink bra hung from a brass lamp. Lieutenant Rashid sat on the edge of the bed, wearing only his open uniform top over leopard-print silk briefs. His face was relaxed, his hair disheveled and eyes glazed.

The two blond German nurses had left, yet their perfume remained. Rashid inhaled with pleasure. His encounter with Taj Akbar the previous day had been a fortunate one. Taj had mentioned the two women, newly arrived—and lonely. Rashid, a hospitable sort, had volunteered to show them around town. Although in the end, they had preferred the entertainment right here in the room. The timing was right—after the stress of handling his uncle's Stinger shipment.

Rashid would have preferred business to a military career but had not been given the choice. His father, Farouk's younger brother, had made his fortune from military patronage—armor-plating on cars and tanks, bulletproof clothing, etc. The family's foreign bank accounts were due solely to General Farouk's good will, good will also extended to Rashid, in the attempt to "shape him up." His uncle was a stern taskmaster, demanding and difficult to please. So difficult that sometimes Rashid got loose bowels from the pressure—and fear. Nothing like some highly sexed foreign women to release the tension.

There was a tap on the front door. "It's me. Taj."

Rashid smiled. "My friend. One moment, please." Rising, he grabbed the pink bra from the lamp and stuffed it in a drawer, then pulled on his trousers. He moved to the mirror on the opposite wall, smoothing his hair and buttoning his shirt.

Still smiling, he opened the door. "You are welcome."

Taj entered. He was followed by two large friends, Amin and Kamal.

Rashid raised an eyebrow, surprised to see the other men, but nodded when Amin offered the package of Johnny Walker Black Label.

"A gift," was all Taj said.

Rashid shrugged, aware of the benefits of family connections.

Kamal brought a glass and some ice from the bar. He handed it to the young lieutenant, while Amin unwrapped the bottle and then poured.

"Another small gift..." Taj opened a cabinet containing a TV and video recorder, then gestured to the bed. "Please take a seat."

Rashid sat down, a bit dazed by it all. As Kamal and Amin took their places on either side of him, he tossed back the drink.

Taj pressed rewind and then removed the cassette.

Rashid stared. A videotape. He shook his head in bewilderment. "What?"

Suddenly Nick entered the room and plucked the tape from Taj's fingers. "Good morning."

Rashid looked from Taj to Nick. American? His eyes darted back to the tape. Then to the unmade bed. The girls. A cloud spread over his face. "How did you do this?" Frightened, he shot up and tried to grab it away.

Nick flashed a grin, sidestepping him. He turned and pushed the mirror aside to reveal a tiny hole in the wall. "The technology is really coming along these days. I thought I might pick up some pointers."

Rashid blanched. He reached for his .38 on the side table, but was restrained by Kamal's persuasively strong arm. He sank back onto the edge of the bed.

"And not only me, but I think your wife's father would also be interested," Nick continued blithely. "Isn't he that nasty Afridi chief, Najib, who takes his sense of family honor to the max?" He gave Rashid a look of mock horror.

Rashid became intent on the carpet's complex geometric pattern.

"It's said he cut the balls off the doctor who dared to examine his wife—your mother-in-law—after her miscarriage. The doctor was his own cousin." Nick shook his head, shocked. "But that story's ten years old. Surely you've heard it before?"

Indeed, he had. Still staring at the carpet, Rashid could feel his bowels start to loosen. Beads of sweat danced on his forehead as he frantically gripped his sphincter muscles.

"Or maybe he's more liberal these days?"

"What do you want?"

"Merely a little information. Then the tape will be yours to enjoy. But me? I'd destroy it. That way, save both family honor and family jewels. If you get my drift."

Rashid lifted his gaze to the brown flocking on the wall. "Go ahead. Ask."

"That Stinger cargo you rode in from Karachi the other day? Nine made it to the base. An Afghan rebel group picked up three of them. What about the other six? Where are they?"

"How would I be knowing that? My orders were bring them to the fort. Beyond was not my concern."

"What is your concern is another family member." Nick smiled. "No pun intended. Somehow I don't think General Farouk would be pleased to discover his nephew sullying the illustrious family name. Although his enemies might. I can't imagine what will become of your career."

Rashid stared at Nick with pure hatred. "Typical American bully. Pushing us around in our own country."

Nick shrugged, looking at the tape in his hand.

Rashid again reached toward the bed table, as Amin and Kamal moved to block him. Trapped, he pointed at the pack of cigarettes next to his pistol. "What? Must I give up smoking? Along with my pride!"

The others shared a smile, not without sympathy at the man's predicament.

The ritual of opening the pack of K-2s, removing the cigarette and lighting it gave Rashid time to get a grip on his whirling brain. He took a deep drag, then another. "My uncle must never know I am telling you this." He stared at Nick.

Nick met his eyes. "My lips are sealed."

Rashid frowned. "All right. My uncle does some business with a Chinaman. I do not know his name."

"Based in Peshawar? Always wears a dark suit, thick eyeglasses?"

Rashid nodded.

Nick nodded back. "What kind of business?"

"The Chinaman has many customers. My uncle has many weapons. Sometimes 'surplus' ones are being transported under bales of rice to the Peepul Mundi grain bazaar. Sometimes the Chinaman makes a rice purchase. Other times he makes introduction and someone else is making purchase. Somewhere more quiet." Rashid shrugged. "Black market, gray market. Many people are wanting weapons these days. Many governments, even."

"Good system." Nick paused, thinking of Taj—and his fluency in the other Afghan dialect, Dari, the language from the days of the Persian empire. "I wouldn't be surprised if the 'Chinaman' has a buyer for the six Stingers—probably Iranian. Might take a couple of days, though. Make sure Farouk doesn't unload them first." He smiled at Rashid and glanced at the tape. "I appreciate your cooperation. Once the client takes delivery of the Stingers, this 'souvenir' will be yours."

Rashid took a long breath, but there was nothing more to say.

Nick checked his watch. "Oh, and Rashid? It's almost checkout time. You'd better hurry, or they'll charge you for another day." As Taj and his two friends moved toward the door, he turned back to Rashid. "Sorry, I've got to run. I have an important appointment." He smiled again. "With your uncle."

But not just yet. In order to put a little space between himself and the Afghans, Nick had a mango juice in the dim, air-conditioned lobby bar before walking out into the harsh midday sun. Blinded for a moment, he blinked and then found himself face-to-face with an elaborately-carved wooden sign:

> *HOTEL POLICY*
> *Arms cannot be brought inside the hotel premises.*
> *Personal Guards or Gunmen are required to*
> *deposit their weapons with the Hotel Security.*
> *We seek your cooperation.*
> *— Management*

Nick stared. He must not have seen it walking in, too focused on the operation. The sign told you everything you needed to know about Peshawar. In any case, it was new. What you might call, a sign of the times.

Chapter 9

It was the regular mid-afternoon meeting of minds at Lala's Grill, a welcome respite from the heat. Although the temperature inside was rising.

Syed Hussein of the Afghan secret police continued his tirade. A man of imposing height and bulk, the "Ox" was usually impassive—except when reciting poetry—but now he was angry. "Our revolutionary people will purge our land of mercenary terrorists. We will annihilate the enemy, especially the marauding banditory leader Jamal. That fool—"

"That fool is smarter than us all." Mr. Yu regarded Syed Hussein closely. "I would like that fool's business. Soon he may be ruler of Afghanistan."

After the morning's fishing expedition, Nick stared at Yu with special interest. He needed to reel him in. Quickly. "I'm sure he'd like to do business with you. So?"

Mr. Yu was rueful. "I have my bottom line to consider. I am unable to extend credit. However worthy the customer. Jamal is a poor man, his weapons are primitive..." He cast a triumphant glance at Viktor. "But most effective."

Yu's people were content with the Afghan war. The Russian Bear's clumsy misadventure had led to a boom in the arms business, drawing America's *Soldier of Fortune* magazine to their factories. Yu had leveraged his official connections into some lucrative side deals. He was becoming rich and bringing honor to his name. As to the other, less savory deals, they would be soon behind him. Merely the unfortunate means to an end.

"Imagine if Jamal didn't have a cash flow problem." Nick ignored the Afghan, smiling at his Russian boss. "Then he'd really cause you guys some mischief! Or is that what your Moscow meeting was about?"

Syed Hussein scowled, angry at both the American enemy and the Russian friend. The Soviet "advisers" treated the Afghans like dimwitted country cousins and had long ago usurped all power and taken control of all operations, with only their interests in mind. They were bleeding his country of its natural resources and charging his people the cost of their own occupation. Hussein felt his Afghan comrades had made a bad bargain, but were trapped: They were dead men if the Russians withdrew in defeat. As a Pashtun, he knew only too well of their ancient code of *Pashtunwali*, with its emphasis on retribution.

Viktor stared at Hussein, then turned to Nick. "I am sorry to disappoint you, Nicholas, but I doubt anyone in Moscow has ever heard of the man."

Nick just nodded. Then he saw Robin enter, looking frazzled, definitely the worse for wear. She sat down at a window table and gestured to him. Excusing himself, he got up. His companions looked at Robin, then leered at Nick. He grinned. "What can I say? Business."

Ahmed nodded. "Then business is good."

"Not bad, fellas, not bad at all. And Viktor, I'm still interested in your thoughts on Jamal."

"And I am interested in yours."

"Let's take a raincheck on that."

"Of course, I accept your raincheck. But please bear in mind that when it rains it pours." He gave Nick a look.

"Good point," he replied. "I'll keep that in mind."

With a glance at Nick, Ahmed also rose to his feet. "I'll be pushing off now, gentlemen. Carry on." He slipped on his gold Cartier sunglasses and left.

Nick joined Robin, taking the seat opposite her. "For you, I don't mind braving the window seat."

"What does that mean?"

"This is the war zone, my dear. In case you haven't noticed." He saw something in her face. "Everything okay?"

"Just great," she snapped.

"Sounds like it. Some tea?"

"Tea? Truthfully, I'd give anything for an ice cold beer."

"Anything?" Lasciviously, he fondled an imaginary mustache.

Robin groaned, clutching her stomach. "Don't you ever give up?"

Nick grinned. "Nothing ventured, nothing gained."

"I guess you never met a cliché you didn't like." She gave him a stern look, but he merely shrugged. "Anyway, how about it?"

"In this town? You gotta be kidding! You think the desert is dry, try Pakistan. Still, it's not impossible. You just have to know the right people." He winked. "In the meantime, why don't you have something cold—and legal—to drink, and tell me all about it."

Robin realized she needed to consider some alternatives. And there was something about talking with another American in a remote part of the world, a connection. Even one you'd never give the time of day to back home.

Nick gestured to the waiter Issa. "Two Cokes, no ice."

"But, Nick," he replied, "you know we are making our ice cubes with purified water."

"Humor me, Issa, we've got a guest with a virgin stomach."

With a blush, the man tilted his head sideways in assent before hurrying off.

Robin glanced at Nick's companions, who were still eyeballing her. "Who are those guys?"

Nick replied flippantly, "Spies."

"Oh, right. Just like in the movies, I suppose."

"Just like in the movies."

Robin studied him. "And you're CIA, of course."

"Of course."

"My, my, fascinating. Tea with the CIA. What would my sorority sisters say?"

"You? In a sorority? I don't think so."

She regarded him narrowly and then shrugged. "Well, they weren't exactly the happening thing in Berkeley back then."

He nodded. "Now how did I know that?"

She half-smiled. "How did you know that?"

"Just a good guess."

"Or good research."

"Nah." He grinned. "You're not the type."

"What type am I?"

"I'll take the Fifth on that one." Nick's grin widened. "However, if you did happen to have any sorority sisters lurking around Peshawar, I'm sure they'd be green with envy."

"That's debatable." Her smiling eyes belied her words, though. A pragmatist, Robin knew that you use what you have to use. Yet now, it was more than that—and less. It could have been the heat making her lightheaded, but she found herself giving him a certain look. "Let's put that debate on hold."

There was something in the air and both could feel it. They were surveying the territory. Curious.

But Robin had far too much at stake to let up on the brakes.

As did Nick. Although he was still admiring her mouth, and the dimple right below.

Issa returned, carrying two frosty green bottles with Coca-Cola spelled out in English and the swirling Urdu script. He bowed to Robin. "Two Cokes, no ice, madam."

"Thank you very much."

"Welcome, madam." The waiter left with a proud smile.

She took a long sip and grimaced. "You think I could have a little Coke with my sugar?"

Nick shrugged. "The local formula. They do love their sweets. "

Robin rolled the cool glass across her cheek and forehead, then set it down. She pushed back her limp hair and looked at him. "Okay, Nick, some answers. Please. Like how the hell do you crack this town?" She was frustrated and willing to admit she needed help. It had been a bad day.

Nick felt her irritation and had some idea what she'd been through. Sure, she was too impatient. On the other hand, he knew the crowd she was trying to deal with. He nodded sympathetically.

"And what's with these men?" She gestured around the restaurant. The only female present, she felt all eyes on her. "Have they never seen a woman before? They stare at me as if I'm from another planet!"

"ET with curves." He couldn't resist.

"More like cooties. Like I'm exotic, but dangerous."

"I think that about says it. You'll get used to it."

"Will I?" She frowned. "I read in the *Frontier Post* this morning, some guy killed his wife because she couldn't prepare meals on time! This is more than another country. It's another world."

"Yeah, you could say that. It's a traditional Islamic society and an unattached Western woman is unusual, makes 'em uncomfortable. Shakes 'em up, threatens their way of looking at things."

Robin stared at him, absorbing his message. "It's one thing to hear or read about it, another to feel it. So some roll out the red carpet, others blush…" Nodding toward Issa. "And still others look at you like a whore?"

"Something like that. Makes me seem real liberated, don't it?"

She kept looking at him. Okay, it was more than a case of heat stroke. There was definitely something about him. But no way, José. "You are cute"Ma thought so—"

"—but not that cute."

He played crestfallen and then broke into a boyish grin.

Robin grinned back, but felt the frustration return. She shook her head. "So I wasted half a day with a bunch of fundamentalists who seemed to hate Jamal as much as me *and* the Soviets. I've gathered the resistance is not exactly united around here. They seem to have forgotten they're supposed to be on the same side."

"In Peshawar, the only side anyone is on is his own. Many factions, all jockeying for religious and political power and limited aid money. They're united about one thing, though—they don't like aggressive females knocking on their doors. For your information: the guys you met used to throw acid on the faces of unveiled women back in Kabul. I've seen a few of the survivors…" His eyes grew soft and she saw it.

Robin swallowed hard and gazed out at the street. Remembering Jamal tell her that every Afghan had God and a gun. They played hardball around here.

He searched her expression for clues, but there were none. It was as if she wore her own veil, only not one of fabric. Nick wondered if she were naïve or just playing dumb. The boss was interested and so was he. On many levels. "I hear you know Jamal?"

"That's right. And that's why I'm sure he'll grant me an exclusive interview. It'd be a big break for my career. The only problem is getting there."

"Getting there is everything. You forget: There's a war going on—as in dead bodies."

"Of course, there's a war. But plenty of journalists have covered it from the inside. And I will, too."

"Now, Robin, let's be realistic. I don't suppose you want to get in the way of some napalm, or step on a butterfly mine, do you?"

"My choice. My risk."

Nick shook his head. She was a ballsy broad and he liked her spirit. Maybe not exactly his type, but she was starting to grow on him. He wanted to learn more about her and Jamal and whatever or whoever else there was. "Stubborn little thing, aren't you?"

"Are you for real?" Robin glared, despite the warmth she heard in his voice. Didn't he know that Neanderthal stuff went out with the cavemen, or hadn't he gotten the news? "Talk about another planet! Do you try to irritate me, Nick, or does it just come natural?" She didn't wait for a reply, didn't want any more jive song-and-dance excuses. "It's your job to help me."

"But it's not my freaking job to help you break official U.S. policy and get yourself killed. You can do a helluva story right here in Peshawar—local color, unforgettable characters, human tragedy. Just let me show you a couple of refugee camps—"

"If I hear that one more time, I'll scream!"

"I wouldn't want an hysterical woman on my hands." His smile was placating. "Sure, I'll help you. But first, you still want that beer?"

She regarded him warily.

"Ya got two choices—my place or the Bamboo Bar."

She kept eyeing him. "Where is this Bamboo Bar?"

Nick's look was mysterious. "Someplace different every week, once a week. But you're in luck—tonight's the night. I'll pick you up at seven-thirty."

Robin had few options and knew it. "Why not?"

"My thinking exactly, hon." He patted her hand on the table, then pulled quickly away before she could get pissed off or call the PC police or anything.

"See ya." He got up, nodded to the guys in the back and left.

The sun hit him full in the face as he walked out the door. Through the glare, he saw Taj's putt-putt parked down the street. When he reached the vehicle, he poked his head inside... Ahmed. Still wearing his gold sunglasses, smoking peacefully. The Pakistani intelligence officer smiled in greeting.

Nick looked at Taj, who shrugged helplessly, ashamed to have let him down.

"What a coincidence." Nick climbed in.

"Somehow I knew I'd run into you here. Of course, I am aware that our Afghan friend is your agent." Ahmed tipped his head toward Taj.

Taj stared straight ahead, stony-faced. Nick felt his wounded pride at being found out. And fear—a justified reaction, given his undocumented status in this country. "It's okay, Taj. Let's go for a ride."

Taj hit the accelerator and pulled sharply into traffic. Horns blared around them. He honked back.

"I asked him what you have on him, Nick, but he refused to tell me. Loyal. Or is he afraid? Or is greed the motivation? In any case, it bothers me terribly to be underestimated. It is true that we of the Special Branch have our hands quite full. All our 'guests' so busy spying on each other. We do, however, manage to keep informed." Ahmed's smile showed his pleasure at one-upping Nick. "But don't worry, I won't blow his cover or double-check his rickshaw license. After all, we are on the same side."

Nick nodded, waiting for whatever would come next.

"Which reminds me—if you are free, we have some business to discuss."

"I'm never free, but I am available. After all, we're on the same side."

Ahmed tipped his head. "Let's go someplace quiet."

"You call this quiet?" Nick grinned, appreciating the man's sense of humor.

"At least, we will not be overheard," the Pakistani spymaster replied.

Streaking, shrieking through the skies above the Peshawar airport, several of Pakistan's prized F-16s were performing sophisticated maneuvers. Nick and Ahmed strolled along the field, admiring the show.

It was a beautiful sight. Inspiring. Ahmed gazed toward the heavens, proud of the fleet. At the same time, though, the planes were an uncomfortable reminder of his nation's subservience to America. The forty F-16s had been purchased at twenty million each from General Dynamics, a neat way for the Americans to recycle some of their three-point-two-billion dollars in aid. "So much American generosity."

"What else ya got?"

"What else indeed?" Ahmed paused to wait out the roar of another takeoff. "She seems like a nice girl."

"Who?"

"The journalist. You American men are so lucky. Your women."

"You want her? You're welcome to take a shot. You heard of woman's liberation?"

Ahmed shrugged. "I fear Pakistan may never become liberated like America. The path to development is rocky. We must be cautious, even unscrupulous."

Nick looked up at the air show, waiting for the other shoe to drop.

"Seven years ago, our annual U..S aid was a few hundred thousand—peanuts, as Zia called it. Then the Soviets invaded Afghanistan." Ahmed shook his head. "A terrible thing. But now, as a 'frontline state' and America's new best friend, billions are flowing here." He opened his arms and glanced around. "From a trickle to a torrent. Imagine this blessing—like water in the desert."

"I realize there are those who never want to go thirsty again."

Ahmed nodded, his eyes hidden behind dark glasses. "You understand."

Blankly, Nick cupped his ear, pointing at the roaring jets.

"War is never silent." Ahmed returned his gaze to the metallic ballet in the sky. "There is an American saying: Make love not war."

"Innovative concept, huh?"

"The Afghans would not understand. They have a passion for war, feel alive only in battle. Do you know that in Pashtu, the word for cousin and enemy are one and the same? In early days, the name for their country meant 'Land of the Unruly' or 'Land of Insolence.'"

"How about 'Land of Rebels'?" Nick joked.

"That, too," Ahmed replied seriously. "Armed resistance is their favorite sport. You might say the Soviets have given them a reason for living." He flashed an ironic smile at Nick.

"An interesting perspective."

"Their ideal is the great warrior. Commander Jamal is such a man. He may even succeed in uniting the resistance and booting out the Russians. This would be good, but premature for us. Pakistan cannot afford U.S. blessings to cease flowing through this thirsty land."

"Okay, Ahmed, cut to the chase." Nick had grown impatient with the exposition.

"With pleasure. We would like to find someone to eliminate Jamal."

Nick burst into laughter. "All that leading to this? And why the hell me?"

"Your vast and varied experience in Southeast Asia is well known. We have heard about the Phoenix Program, for example—organizing

assassination on such a broad scale is surely a skill of which to be proud."
Ahmed fastidiously pushed back a cuticle.

Nick remained silent. Faulty intelligence could lead to half-truths, or
worse. In this case, it had led only to an inflated reputation. He hadn't
"organized" anything. He'd been there, though. Just not in Phoenix. An
earlier program, Operation Counter-Terror had used the CIA's Vietnamese
assets to combat Viet Cong terrorism, setting off a spree of retribution
and killing that Nick would never forget. Wanted to, though.

Ahmed was watching Nick's face. "Also well known are the propaganda
advantages of this war to your people: Soviet bully invades defenseless
Third World nation. Superb."

"So what else is new?" Nick shrugged impassively, as his mind raced
to catch up with the unexpected development. "Besides, if nothing else,
it's too risky a proposition. Jamal is a shadow, appears and disappears like
a phantom."

Ahmed removed his sunglasses, wiping off some dust. "I think two
hundred thousand U.S. might provide sufficient inspiration. Nothing like
a good challenge."

Nick could appreciate Ahmed's position. It made sense—on many
levels. "Some people do like challenges. Particularly for a cool, say…
quarter mil." He smiled. "U.S." Nick cast a sideways glance at Ahmed, who
gave him a hard look and then slowly nodded. "It would surely be a shame
to deprive the Afghans of their favorite sport."

"My sentiments exactly." Ahmed slipped on his dark glasses, gazing at
the sky.

Nick clapped Ahmed across the shoulders, struck by the reflection of
a F-16 streaking before the man's eyes. "It goes without saying that U.S./
Pakistan friendship is important to us all. So if I do hear of 'someone,'
you'll be the first to know."

Chapter 10

Taj pressed past the Old City's moneychangers squatting on handknotted rugs, heads bowed over calculators and currency, their safes behind them. Filled with urgency, he hurried across Chowk Yadgar, the central square, and then turned into the murky Street of Storytellers, lined with tall, narrow buildings that crowded out the light. Feeling the shadows weighing on him, Taj elbowed his way through twisting lanes as old as time.

These days there were modern vehicles, but still the rickshaws and horse-drawn *tongas*. There were modern uniforms, but soldiers had always been here. The people, too, had been here forever: old tribesmen, young mujahideen, a holy man from the plains of India, veiled women with little girls clinging to their burqas, boys chasing mangy dogs, butchers swatting away flies.

Taj took in the smells of grilled kebabs, rice, tea, sweat, cow-dung, smoky fires. This was the perfume of life... and it took him to another place, with a similar perfume. The sweet scent of childhood. The sweet lime tree in his courtyard. His dear Afghan village. His home. The air was cleaner there. Quieter.

This was a noisy world. The sounds of parrots and nightingales echoed through the bird bazaar. Vendors called out in Pashtu, Farsi, Urdu, Punjabi and English, hawking shawls, baskets, fruit and nuts. And then it struck him: Here, there was life. But in his homeland, death reigned; the *Shuravi* was killing his land. He redoubled his pace, finally nearing his destination.

In the Bazaar of Coppersmiths, the light seemed to return—shop after shop piled high with gleaming trays, bowls and urns. Each stall looking the same. But there was one that Taj sometimes visited on similar missions, and soon he found it. "Poor Honest Ali" was seated on an embroidered cushion in his raised doorway. Beside him lay a leather album with photographs of P. H. Ali himself and his celebrated customers. In addition to a flair for public relations, Ali knew how to accumulate favors. Even a meager service could be money in the bank. Seeing Taj arrive, he beamed, aware of the young Afghan's secret employer. American goodwill was a valuable currency. "*Salaam Aleikum.* Some tea?"

"*Aleikum Salaam.* You are too kind." Taj had an intent look on his face, no time for tea. What he needed was a scarce commodity in the bazaar: a secure telephone.

Ali read his expression. "I am having some special new items to show you."

"With great pleasure." Taj climbed the rough wooden steps into the shop and followed the proprietor to his back room.

Ali removed a hand-beaten copper bowl from the center of a low brass table, revealing a black telephone. He gestured. "Please to make yourself at home and please to excuse me. My customers await."

Taj nodded, trying to mask his impatience. After Ali left, he sat on a pillow and dialed.

Nick answered. "Yes?"

"Our friend is on the move."

Nick tapped an index finger on his desk. "Where?"

"He has just entered Mahabat Khan Mosque. Praying perhaps?"

"Or perhaps should be." Nick didn't do much of his own praying these days, not since his grandma died, but right now he did ask for something. And sent it Out There. He needed to nail Mr. Yu, at something. "Stick with him."

"I am returning to wait."

Nick hung up, shut down his computer and prepared to leave. As he grabbed his jacket, the doorknob turned and Hudson entered.

Nick grinned. "Why, Ronnie, you didn't have to—"

"I believe you received my memo about the budget meeting tonight?" Hudson's eyes were hard.

"I sure did. But, hey, I got a live one out there. You wouldn't begrudge me that, would you?" He opened his hands. "Seriously, though, it's business. Remember? You gave me my marching orders. To ride herd on those pesky reporters. I take that to include the new one from San Francisco."

Hudson stared. "You are aware that staff meetings are obligatory."

"And you know what you can do with your obligatory staff." On his way out the door, Nick turned. "Take good notes."

He hurried from the compound and across the street to his white Mazda, dusty from lack of use. The engine kicked right over, though, and Nick was soon turning onto Jamrud Road. Peshawar's main drag, it headed west through the Khyber Agency to the Khyber Pass, then into Afghanistan. Eastward it became the Grand Trunk Road, which eventually reached India.

As Nick drove east across town, he knew that changes were in the air, that he'd be on the road again. That twisty, turny road that had been his life. He remembered the day he'd set out, the seventeen-year old he used to be.

At the time, it was all Nick had been able to do: split before the folks split. Not deal with it anymore, the black moods and alcohol—and now the final disintegration. He needed to escape. Get out of Dodge.

And so Nicholas Ross Daley had stuck out his thumb and hit the road. It was but a short hop down Highway 35 from El Dorado to Wichita. He'd kept going, on to Oklahoma City and Dallas. At San Antonio, the first truck that stopped was traveling east to Houston. In Houston he got some fake papers and enlisted in the Army. Simple.

Nick didn't write home until he reached Fort Bragg, where someone tapped him on the shoulder and he was shipped to Hawaii for war games with the Special Forces.

He was upcountry in Nam when he got the "sorry" letter from his mom. Sorry that she'd had to sell his collection of old cars and guns, but the divorce was final, and she was off to California. Sorry that his girl Nancy had gotten engaged to a longhair. And—worst of all—that his beloved Sunday School-teacher grandma had died, the woman who'd taught him honesty and goodness. For Nick, surviving was difficult enough. He had no time to mourn the death of his past, just as he had no time to figure out where he was going. He was on the move, that was enough.

Then for a while, it all started to make sense, and the faith in what he was doing supplanted all that he had lost. He was fighting for the apple pie and motherhood and back home that was no more. Soon he was tapped on the shoulder again for a top-secret assignment in Laos, counterinsurgency training of some mountain tribesmen—the Hmong, traditional enemy of the Vietnamese dog-eaters.

But later, it stopped making sense. He realized he didn't know what he was fighting for—but also that this life was all he had. His father had remarried and landed back on his feet with a new wife down in Texas. His mother was slipping into a rootless alcoholic abyss, the freedom offered by California only a taunting reminder that "freedom was just another word for nothing left to lose." His sister had been busted following a 7-Eleven robbery, too loaded to see her drugged-out boyfriend's gun, until too late. Both brothers were also headed for the joint, one way or the other.

By then he had hooked up with the Company. They sent him back to Virginia for a course in Media Communications at George Mason University. Then for advanced intelligence training at the "Farm." Along the way, he also did advanced research on American women, even married one until she figured out he wasn't her kind of guy.

Over the years he spent time—did time?—at headquarters, but preferred those years out in East Asia Division. It was a good gig, plenty of money, freedom, the space in which to think and read; he liked the weather and the women and didn't know what he'd do back home anyway. Besides, where the hell was back home? El Dorado, Kansas? Texas, California, DC? No. His life was where it was... wherever. As the Thais said, usually with a fatalistic shrug, *mai pen rai*—it doesn't matter, what will be will be.

Mai pen rai. Que será. Whatever. At least, he'd never knocked anyone up; he had none of those poor Amerasian orphans on his conscience. Nick liked to stay loose. His possessions amounted to a couple of suitcases, some books, a few grand in the bank.

Others he knew had done better, others who believed that making money was the American Way. Who thought it better to be a rich patriot than a poor one. And maybe there was something to that. He sure as shit didn't want to end up a broke and broken bartender in Pattaya Beach, nor did he want to be bumped upstairs with the other Rear Echelon bureaucrat assholes like Ronald Hudson.

In the meantime, he had things to do. Like protecting his op, nailing the target... and checking out the new girl in town. All at the same time.

Wearing his linen jacket and a smile, Nick opened the lobby door for Robin. He was in a hurry to get to the mosque, but took time to check out her legs as she preceded him to the street. He liked seeing her in a dress. "You're a sight for sore eyes, my dear."

She gave him a narrow look. "I shaved my legs just for you."

"I'm not kidding, you look great."

"I'll take that for what it is. Thanks."

Nick opened the passenger door and waited for her to sit before moving around to the driver's side. He got in and grinned. "Together at last."

"Well, from you, I guess this is good behavior."

"Someday you'll appreciate my finer qualities."

"Someday I may. Someday."

With a honk, Nick slipped the Mazda into the flow of traffic, passing a pickup full of bleating sheep. It was dusk, men and animals going home. He drove quickly, expertly along Shahrah-e-Pehlavi and then turned into the Khyber Bazaar en route to the mosque. It was unfortunate that Mr. Yu had intruded into their first date, but... He swerved around a buffalo tonga blocking the road.

Robin gripped her seat and gave him a look.

"Exciting, huh? Makes you forget you're in the twentieth century sometimes."

"Boy. Isn't that the truth!"

Nick shot her a glance. "Lot of history here." He pointed out the remains of the Kabuli Gate, one of the sixteen gates to the ancient walled city, and then began to maneuver through the maze of cobbled lanes. Normally overflowing in noisy profusion, the Old City was now emptying. Shops were being shuttered, while street vendors were busy covering their goods.

The scene had a certain charm and Robin watched intently. Still, she sensed that Nick's mind was elsewhere, and began to wonder what was up. And where were they going, anyway? "I guess this is the scenic route?"

"Sure is." That was it. He let it go. Later. He'd have time later.

Robin's mouth tightened at his dismissive attitude. She suddenly didn't like being stuck in the car with him. At all.

Nick drove through Chowk Yadgar, turning left onto a narrow, steeply rising road lined with tall old buildings that almost met overhead. The Andarshahr Bazaar was home to the gold and silversmiths, the jewelers and coin-dealers. Many shops were closed, but some windows still had their wares out—masses of amber, coral and turquoise beads; piles of silver, bronze and ivory bangles—all displayed in a careless but stunning jumble.

Nick took a sharp right into an alley, which was also lined with tiny shops and workshops and barely wide enough for them to pass. Then he came to a sudden stop in front of a tiled archway. Behind it rose the dazzling white minarets and triple domes of the seventeenth-century Mahabat Khan Mosque.

"What?" Robin looked at him as he got out of the car.

"Hang tight, Robin. Sorry, but something came up. I'll be right back."

She was forgotten as his eyes traveled across the road. Next to a dangling light bulb in an old storefront, Taj gave the usual sideways nod and then disappeared in darkness.

Robin did not notice. By this time, she was fuming.

Nick hurried up the steps and under the elongated arch, entering an airy courtyard that ended in a domed prayer hall. Evening prayers were over and the mosque complex was deserted. He kept to his left, hugging a low, arcaded wall of locked rooms. Passing the central fountain, he heard a cough and froze into the shadows.

"*Nyet!*" The voice came from the prayer hall.

Nick slipped through another archway and stood behind a frescoed column, peering into a large space covered with carpets. Beside another column, Mr. Yu was talking to a broad-cheeked, narrow-eyed man in a brown leisure suit, whom Nick recognized as Nikolai Krigori, a Soviet trade representative. He was interested in the black leather attaché case next to the man's pointy-toed left shoe... as was Yu, whose eyes kept darting in its direction.

Then Yu reached into his red, white and blue striped tote, pulling out a small plastic bag stapled across the top. He opened it with caution and passed it to Krigori. Under Yu's unblinking gaze, the Russian fingered the white powder, as fine as talcum.

"Best number-four-quality white. Crystal. Five full kilos," Yu informed him.

Krigori unwrapped a piece of silver foil from a pack of Marlboros and placed it in his left palm, then tipped a small amount of the powder onto it.

Yu held out his hand for the bag and rewrapped it with care, never taking his eyes off Krigori. He tensed as the Russian reached in his pocket... and relaxed when only a Bic lighter emerged.

Seeing Yu's reaction, Krigori shot him a dour smile. Then all business, he lit the tissue clinging to the silver paper. Instantly the powdered heroin dissolved into a black liquid: proof of purity. A glint of blue showed through his pale lashes and he nodded, crumpling the foil. "*Da.* Yes. Good."

Mr. Yu nodded back, picking up the black briefcase. He opened it and began counting the stacks of greenbacks, awestruck in the presence of one hundred seventy-five thousand dollars. He thought of his growing bank account in Singapore, soon to be home.

Nick stepped forward, pointing his Colt Commander toward Mr. Yu and the money. He grinned. "I'm delighted to see the dollar is still the international currency."

Yu made a move to his pocket.

Suddenly cold sharp teeth were all that remained of Nick's crocodile smile, as both index fingers met on the trigger of his .45. "That wouldn't be too prudent, Mr. Yu. In fact, it would be the dumbest mistake you ever made. Now, gentlemen, I'd advise you to unburden yourselves of all weapons."

Yu scowled at him for several seconds before removing the Beretta from his pocket and dropping it to the ground. Krigori didn't budge until he found himself staring down the gunmetal barrel. Surly, he reached in his boot and pulled out the Tokarev.

"A 'Toke,' huh? The old Soviet faithful. I'll have a look at that, if you don't mind," Nick said politely.

Eyes lost in the anger distorting his face, Krigori handed him the butt end.

Nick held the Tokarev in his palm, recalling its widespread use by the VC—and later by the good guys, who considered it a "sterile" weapon due to its Russian origin. Then he shoved the pistol into his jeans, shaking his head in disgust. "You guys amaze me. I've heard about religion being the opiate of the masses. I guess that was before profit became the religion of the elite."

"Fool!" Krigori sneered.

"Now, now, Mr. Krigori, you'll get an ulcer that way."

The Russian blinked, realizing the American knew his identity. As a trade official, Krigori was the front man for his Georgian syndicate. The *bizinesmenki* had organized the heroin's transport in a consignment of Afghan raisins by rail from Kabul to Leningrad. Some would be shipped to London's Tilbury docks, the rest distributed in the Soviet Union. While the Georgian gangsters stood to make almost two million dollars, his own commission would be barely enough to buy a Japanese car or two to take home. It was a dangerous time for the scheme to be discovered, given Gorbachev's new anti-corruption campaign. Rumors about the fate of Brezhnev's family were surfacing. Krigori was frightened. He had visited Siberia. Once.

"Why don't you guys have a seat, relax a bit." Nick pointed a toe at the column. The two businessmen sat on the floor, facing opposite directions, backs against the stone. Nick pulled out a piece of rope and bound them tightly. Then he grinned. "Don't worry. Muslims pray five times a day. Someone will rescue you, sooner than later."

"You will regret this," Mr. Yu warned grimly, but it was all bluff. China was a firm advocate of the death penalty. Administered neatly: a bullet to the back of the head. There were thousands of executions a year for everything from murder to robbery to swindling. About the only capital crime Yu wasn't guilty of was pimping. He had to keep this quiet.

"I regret it already. I am shocked to see citizens of two such crime-free societies engaged in this nasty drug business." Nick regarded them sadly. "Although I do admire your capitalist initiative. So in the name of international friendship, I'll try to forget it. I only hope you'll use your time in this holy place to reflect on the error of your ways." He reached over and plucked the bag of heroin from Yu's pocket. "So sorry, my friend."

As the men glared at him, Nick tossed the dope into the red, white and blue bag along with the Beretta and Tokarev, then grabbed the black briefcase. "No, don't get up." He grinned. "The pleasure has been all mine, gentlemen." A double pleasure: He had Yu in hand *and* an unexpected windfall. A cushion for the future. He turned and left.

Satisfied, Nick hurried through the courtyard, slipping his mind into another gear. He was looking forward to the evening with Robin, and decided to cool it, tone down his routine. Nick knew people considered him a smartass. It was as good a cover as any and he didn't give a shit what most people thought. But Robin was too serious and too smart to buy his act; already he felt her digging, trying to see beneath his skin.

Returning to the dark street, he looked eagerly at the car. The front seat was empty—Robin was gone! This was not the place for a lone woman. Worried, he looked up and down the deserted road. He called her name. No answer. Not even an echo.

Chapter 11

Nick locked the briefcase and totebag in the trunk, then began his search. He crossed the road to the dingy old jewelry shop from which Taj had signaled him. Empty. He had no idea where she could have gone. The girl was so damn cocky and self-reliant. Clueless, yet arrogant: a dangerous mix. He became irritated. Hadn't she yet figured out that a woman's place was not in the dim back alleys of Peshawar? But no, Robin thought nothing could happen to her. And now, it probably had. Although what exactly, he could only imagine. Kidnapped for ransom or revenge or into some damn harem. They had kidnappings everyday here—even entire busloads of people—even government officials.

He pushed open a cracked wooden door next to the shop and entered a small courtyard. Normally humming with activity, the workshops and businesses were all closed. In the distance, he heard a forlorn hammer pounding against metal, probably a young boy working long into the night to support his mother and sisters in one of the refugee camps.

Then the scope of his concern changed. What if someone were trying to get to him—through her? What if her disappearance had something to do with the events in the mosque? That could be embarrassing. Whatever it was, he begrudged the favors he'd have to use up trying to find her. Favors he'd saved for more important business.

"Nick?"

Nick rushed back out to the street. In the dim light, he saw her walking toward him, seemingly safe, as casual as could be. She was smiling, and his stomach untwisted in relief. As she moved closer, he noticed her changed appearance—arms laden with ivory bangles, turquoise necklaces, an air of accomplishment on her face.

"Do you realize how pricey this stuff is on Union Street?"

He wanted to throttle her, like a frantic parent whose kid has finally turned up safe. Taking a deep breath, Nick grabbed her arm and steered her toward the car. "How much you pay?" he demanded, not wanting to reveal the extent of his panic.

"About two hundred dollars." She smiled proudly.

Nick rolled his eyes. "How much did the seller ask?"

Her smile faded. "About two hundred." Then she added, "Discount for dollars."

"You paid the first price asked?" He laughed at her with pity.

Robin stared at him. She didn't understand why he was mocking her.

"My dear, this is Asia, not Bloomingdale's. You never pay the first price, or even the second or third. Maybe half, and that's if you're a foreigner!"

Now she definitely felt deflated, even foolish.

"And you want to go to Afghanistan." He laughed, wishing to give her a hard time. "Well, maybe I'll teach you a few facts of life around here, if you behave yourself."

Robin ignored him, busy calculating the cost of her ignorance. She tossed her head. "I don't care. It's still cheaper than San Francisco. Besides, where's your social consciousness? Maybe I wanted to give the guy a break. He was a hard worker—so late at night. Better than handouts to a beggar."

"I admire your charitable instincts, hon."

"And better than sitting by myself in a dark alley—Mr. Sir Galahad!"

They exchanged glares, then Nick let her into the car. As he walked around to the other side, his eyes swept in all directions. The street was quiet, but he did not want to be there when it hit the fan and the two guys were found.

With a final glance out the rear view mirror, Nick drove off. Satisfied that he was in the clear, he relaxed. His sense of humor restored, he reached over and patted her thigh. "Nothing more feminine than a woman shopping."

She shifted her leg. "It's obvious male chauvinism is alive and flourishing here."

"It's definitely a man's world in these parts, hon. You don't have a clue yet just how much."

The Bamboo Bar was "open" every Thursday night with rotating hosts. Everyone would bring a smuggled bottle from his local black market contact and everyone would show up with a hangover at work the next day, which being the Islamic Sabbath was usually pretty slow. The regulars represented a cross-section of Peshawar's foreign community, a few hundred odd souls—if not odd, at least eclectic, as Nick joked to Robin— ranging from UN officials to adventurers and rug dealers.

Tonight's gathering was being held at the Dean's Hotel bungalow of a well-known professor of Afghan history, whose Princeton home was gathering dust these days. The host had laid out a spread that included chicken tikka, sliced cucumber, humus and chips. People nibbled, but it was really too hot to eat. This was drinking weather. Those residents who had acclimatized their digestive systems to the local bacteria enjoyed long cool drinks with ice. Others drank straight scotch or chilled vodka, thank you very much.

The general eclecticism was also reflected in the music, from Willie Nelson to Indian disco. Just now there was a string trio of sorts—guitar, sarod, and the long-necked tambur. Nick pointed to the musician playing it. "That guy's an Afghan star."

"What's he doing here?"

"What do you think? Driving a cab. Waiting for better times."

Robin sighed and nodded. They were sunk into two cushiony bamboo chairs on the veranda. The air was warm and the sweet breeze seemed to have blown away the remnants of their anger. Nick turned to her, and liked what he saw. He touched one of her bangles. "You know that looks kind of old. You may have got a good deal, after all. And you do look great in that stuff."

Robin presented him with a half-smile. "Thank you, Nick." She recognized the apology and would be gracious about it.

He continued looking at her, then pointed to the little gold robin she always wore. "You seem to like that pin."

"My good luck," she said simply.

Nick noticed her empty glass. "Refill?"

She nodded and he poured two more generous shots of Stoli—known locally as "Gorbachev," one of the main supplies flown in from the motherland for her "advisers" to the Democratic Republic of Afghanistan.

"But how does it get here?"

"This is the smuggling capital of the world. There's nothing can't be bought here." He raised his glass. "To ingenuity and free enterprise."

Robin lifted hers, slowly, thoughtfully. "To this small dot on the map, a unique corner of the world."

"And you haven't even scratched the surface." He looked in his glass. "You ever seen *Casablanca?*"

"You mean how many times?" She smiled and their eyes connected.

"Well, Peshawar is like Casablanca—full of intrigue and spies. All that fun stuff."

She scrutinized him. "So it's not boring being media babysitter here?"

"Depends on the baby."

She let it pass, determined to keep it light. "Are you really a spy?"

"Are you really a simple girl reporter?"

"Good question," she parried. "Anyway, I think it's awful how the Russians have rolled over that poor little country."

"Typical liberal naïveté."

"What the hell does that mean?"

"The Afghans love a good brawl, keeps 'em from fighting each other. Resistance is their national sport. So it's not all that bad."

"That's pretty cynical, don't you think?"

"Cynical? Maybe, if you're from the Left Coast. On the other hand, I've spent most of my time in what is commonly known as the Real World."

"I've heard of that place. Isn't that where the U.S. buys right-wing dictators and calls them friends, uses other people to fight their enemies?" Robin caught herself and shook her head. "Look, I don't want an argument. I'm just a journalist here to do a story."

Nick wouldn't be sidetracked. "The Afghan rebels fighting our war?"

"Well, sure, it's their war. But ours, too. Our enemy. As in, the enemy of my enemy is my ally. In this case, the ally is doing the heavy lifting, wouldn't you say?"

"Funny, the professor told me about an Afghan friend, lives in Oakland, who views the mujahideen as private armies for America. Only that guy's a Marxist. Maybe you ran into him at Berkeley?" He eyed her curiously. "But never mind, tell me about this story you want to do."

"I want to tell Americans about Jamal. He's an idealist, a great leader. And I know he'll help educate the women, try to bring them out of the dark ages."

"So I gather helping Jamal and some of the other mujahideen is okay in your book? That here at least, Uncle Sam is on the right track?"

She shrugged and took a sip of her drink.

He was clocking her, trying to read between her lines. Nick was used to everyone having an angle, a price. What was hers? Was it a trip across the border or something else? Or was she simply a naïve idealist? "You as straight as you seem?"

"I'm just an old-fashioned girl. I believe in truth, justice and the American way." Her smile was open and innocent.

Nick studied her face. "Of course."

"Just like you. Only you're a boy."

She was flirting now. And he liked it. "Indeed." Nick glanced toward the garden and spotted General Farouk. Catching the man's eye, he nodded. They got up and walked down the steps.

"Good evening, General. You remember Robin Reeves?"

Hand over heart, Farouk made a small, courtly bow. "How could I forget?"

Robin gave him a professional smile. After all, he was a source. And Nick was… well, she wasn't sure yet. She looked from one to the other. "I'm not sure which of you is worse, or which one I need more."

"You are a woman of wit, with a practical mind as well." Farouk regarded her approvingly.

Nick noted the general's glass, half-filled with a clear golden liquid. "What brings a good Muslim to this illicit gathering?"

"Maybe fate," replied Farouk, still gazing at Robin.

"You certainly have a way with words," she observed.

"I am a Pashtun tribesman and we Pashtuns are all poets at heart. And my heart sings at the poetry before my eyes."

Nick shared an amused look with Robin. "Aw shucks, General. How can I compete with that?"

"You have other advantages, my friend." Farouk smiled, changing gear. "I understand you viewed some F-16 training maneuvers this afternoon."

Blandly. "I was very impressed."

Farouk's smile remained in place, but his eyes held a warning. "You will be careful, won't you, Nick? Airports can be dangerous places these days. You are our guest, and we wouldn't want you to come to any harm." He included Robin with a warm glance. "Especially considering your importance to our other guests. And Robin, remember, anything I can do for you… anytime. Now if you'll excuse me. I'm off for a refill on my uh—apple juice."

Nick watched him walk away, wondering what kind of threat that was? Did he know of Ahmed's proposition, was he in on it? Were the two of them setting him up? Or was Farouk playing his own game?

Robin didn't understand the exchange, but she, too, was wondering. "What a character."

He looked at her from a distance, then returned. "Peshawar abounds in them, better than Saigon, Vientiane and Bangkok put together."

Suddenly Robin was able to see through Nick as through transparent layers. At the core was a little boy, awed at the strange world he'd found himself in. Having caught this unexpected glimpse, she wanted to see more. "Where you from?"

"From?" He shook his head. "Much less interesting than where I'm going. I'm starved. How about some of the best tandoori chicken in town?"

"I don't much care for spicy food."

Nick grabbed her wrist. "Trust me, you'll like it. C'mon."

She didn't say no.

The jacarandas were in bloom, lavender blossoms glowing in the faint moonlight. Forming an extravagant canopy, they lined the driveway to the Peshawar Club, a faded-yellow, colonial-era oasis of gentility.

Robin gazed around in surprise. "So peaceful. It's hard to imagine this is the same town."

"The same, but not the same."

The neatly sprawling compound had been home to Nick ever since he'd arrived kicking and screaming from Bangkok two years earlier. He had missed the grace and charm, the easy Thai manner that didn't intrude, but finding this place helped smooth the transition. He liked its calm ambience as well as the privacy offered by his secluded garden bungalow. It was a congenial atmosphere for a bachelor; they cooked and cleaned for him, took messages. There was companionship when he so desired, a few other foreign guests—including a handful of elderly Brits who had "stayed on"—some Pakistani professionals and their families. The "Club" had its traditions, including one of British reserve. No one tried to get too close. It worked for Nick, his perfect compromise with an imperfect world.

He pulled into a stone garage. While he was poking around the trunk, Robin got out and took a deep breath. Gardenias. They set off on a pebbly path lined with the white-flowered shrubs. The night had turned still and heavy, and Nick was carrying his jacket, as well as a totebag, briefcase and newspaper-wrapped package. Robin was glad his hands were occupied, so he wouldn't think of trying to take her arm. They reached the front lawn, an inviting expanse with a low-slung main building behind it.

The grass was a communal area with scattered seating areas, each grouped around an electric fan. Nick and Robin settled into a pair of comfortable rattan chairs, the parcels at his feet.

Across the lawn, two Pakistanis were relaxing in front of a large television. The evening news had just wrapped up and they were watching the commercials—lots of enticing consumer goods—followed by an episode of *Bonanza*.

A turbaned waiter approached, tall and dignified. "Good evening, Mr. Daley."

Nick smiled and handed him the newspaper-wrapped package. "Mangoes to knock your socks off, Mohammed. The season has begun. Half for you, half for me."

"Thank you, sir." The waiter sniffed the fruit and smiled.

"I notice mangoes have gone up lately. They say it's because of all the Afghan refugees."

The smile faded. "What can we do? This is our sacred Pashtun duty, hospitality to the guest. *Melmastia*."

Nick nodded. "'The bigger the man's tablecloth, the bigger the man.'"

"You know us well, sir." Mohammed bowed in respect. "I will bring dinner."

Robin ended up eating her words about not liking spicy food—along with every morsel of chicken on her plate. And piece after piece of hot-from-the-tandoor naan, with which she learned to scoop up the rice. She washed it all down with mango juice, and had no desire for dessert.

She wiped her hands. Again. "I love all these smells."

"A reminder you're not in Kansas anymore. In case you ever were. Which I was."

She gave him a look. "You've come a long way."

"Yeah. I've lost my taste for Kentucky Fried."

Robin grinned. "It was wonderful, Nick."

"As good as home cooking."

"That it is." She gazed around the 'living room' lawn. "It is like a home, isn't it?"

"About as close as I've got."

She turned back to him, but couldn't read his expression.

Then he smiled. "How about a nightcap?"

A hint of wariness returned. "I suppose it can't be served out here on the lawn?"

Nick became aware of her catlike eyes. He stared in their cool grayness, so at odds with the heat and anger he felt beneath her professional exterior. He was curious to know her better. "My ice cubes are made with bottled water."

She met his glance and held it. "Well, in the name of intestinal health..."

He took her hand, she left it there. Something about time and place and out-of-context, because the big city writer and the CIA cowboy were drawn to each other, despite themselves and certainly despite their better judgment. But they both kept telling themselves it was just part of the job.

Picking up the briefcase, Nick led her through the garden along a narrow path overgrown with roses. The air was heavy with their scent, mingling with the jacaranda and jasmine. The effect was sensual, silky, almost overpowering. They both felt it.

"*Luxe, calme et volupté.*" His voice was quiet.

Robin stared at him. How did he know Baudelaire? A cricket chirped, a long rubbing together of wings. She nodded. "My sentiments exactly."

The path stopped at his bungalow, covered with purple bougainvillea and more jasmine. They walked up two steps to his door. There was a brief pause; he could feel her holding back. Then he turned the knob and they entered.

The small foyer opened into the living room, but Robin stood there a moment. Uncomfortable, suddenly not sure.

Nick had his own discomfort. He gestured. "This is it. Make yourself at home. I've got to put some things away. Be right back."

Robin looked around, trying to get a feel for the man. It was cozy and casual, mostly leftover Victorian. Definitely lived-in. Sun-bleached, floral chintz curtains. A once-dark-green armchair, paisley quilt tossed on its matching but less faded ottoman. An old Royal typewriter on a small teak desk. A crowded bookcase, stacks of the *Frontier Post* and *International Herald Tribune*. A man who moved with typewriter and books and didn't pay much attention to where he landed.

She put her bag on the desk and noticed the map of Pakistan behind it. There were others, tacked around the wall. His own history, perhaps?

Southeast Asia, India and Iran. Afghanistan. A topographical map of the North-West Frontier Province. At least, no girlie calendars. Reassured, Robin sat down on the overstuffed brown sofa, avoiding the spring poking up from the middle seat cushion. She noticed a little carved ivory elephant on the wrought-iron coffee table. It was all quirky and non-threatening.

"You like Armagnac?" he asked, from a small alcove off the living room.

Robin was again surprised and impressed. "Guess we won't need ice after all."

"Tell me if you've heard this one. " He popped in a cassette. "Ravi Shankar and Yehudi Menuhin. My kicking-back music."

The music was both floaty and energetic. "I like it." He was still puttering around and Robin appreciated him giving her some space. "It's cozy here. Like a California bungalow."

"Comes from the Hindi."

"What?"

"The word bungalow." Nick reappeared with the brandy snifters and bottle and joined her on the sofa. "A legacy of the British Raj. Another kind of import. Like 'pajama' and 'chintz.'"

She glanced at his curtains. "I thought chintz was Victorian."

"It is. By way of India."

"I take it men walk around in pajamas there, too."

He nodded. "Just like here. Ever been to India?"

"No."

"You'd be hard-pressed to know when you crossed the border. India and Pakistan had a bitter divorce almost forty years ago."

"Partition."

"You've done your homework. So you know that before, they were 'married' for centuries."

"And their culture is community property."

"All the way from muslin to Muslim." He couldn't resist.

She smiled. "Including pajamas in the street."

"You think maybe they know something we don't?"

"You mean how to dress in hot weather?"

"Yeah." He poured two small shots, then lifted his glass in a toast. "To—Jamal."

Pleased with the oblique reference to her trip, she raised her glass to his.

There was a musical clink. Then a sweet warmth trickled down their throats. The scent of jasmine drifted through an open window.

Nick placed his glass down and moved toward her.

Robin tensed. But seeing that he was merely trying to push the spring back inside the cushion, she smiled, relaxed and reached with her left hand to help. Their fingers touched. She stared down: their skin was the same golden color, they blended together. But her hand was chilled, while his was hot.

Nick plucked her glass away and placed it next to his on the table. He looked at her face and realized it had been dancing through his brain since they'd met, her intensity drilling into him. He felt a mystery, whose answer he needed to know.

Their fingers were still touching, in fragile connection. His other hand was drawn to her thick hair, moving across her head as if he wanted to get inside. Robin froze. Gently his fingers crossed her cheek, circled her dimple, then took her stubborn jaw and turned it to him. The hands that had met on the sofa were now entwined.

They looked at each other and then kissed. A tentative kiss. Shy but firm. Delicious. Their lips drew apart, but only slightly. His mouth moved to the dimple on her chin; his tongue explored it first, then teeth and tongue and lips. She shivered; he had discovered a new erogenous zone. She touched his cheek with her right hand...

Suddenly Mr. Yu burst through the door, waving a pistol. Still in his business suit, yet resonating with frantic menace.

Robin tensed with fright, her fingers digging into Nick's arm.

He reassured her with a pat, while simultaneously shifting gears. Nick sensed that Yu was an explosion waiting to happen. "Why, Mr. Yu, a new Beretta. Already?"

"Quick trip to Darra, no problem."

"You found a shop open this time of night?"

"Good customers in Darra. They do me a small favor this evening. Now, finish talking. You will be pleased to return my property." Despite his ingrained civility, Yu had a ruthless determination. He would not allow the American to thwart his dreams.

Bewildered, Robin glanced from one to the other. He knew this man. Nick didn't seem worried. Should she be?

"I'm sure we can work something out, my friend. But please, stop waving that gun around. There's a lady present."

Mr. Yu didn't budge, nor did the .22. "Nothing to work out."

"I wonder how your government would feel about a trusted official sidelining in drugs while the guest of an important ally, who also happens to be an important customer? And not for just the small stuff. Right?"

Mr. Yu's mouth tightened.

"I understand that long-range missile technology is quite lucrative." Nick paused, then shook his head. "International relations are at stake, not to mention foreign exchange. The Pakistanis pay with dollars, as I'm sure you're aware." He stared hard at Yu. "Just as you are aware of China's stringent anti-drug laws. They're not too big on murder, either."

Mr. Yu slowly lowered the pistol.

Robin followed the unfolding events with a complex range of emotions. Fear had turned to confusion... to fury. Guns, drugs. Turned-on, turned-off. Just what was Nick up to and who was he, really? More important, how would this situation impact her plans?

Nick continued to stare at the Chinese businessman. Having finally succeeded in smoking Yu out, he needed to enlist his services for the next step of his operation. But first, he had to make sure he didn't get shot. "Of course, I do understand your desire for dollars. The Chinese yuan is not exactly the gold standard, is it?"

Yu directed a murderous look Nick's way.

"I'll tell you what." Nick paused. "I promise to keep my mouth shut and return those nasty drugs. But I do need a small favor."

"What about my money?"

"You mean the Russian dope dealer's money? There's an old American proverb: Finders keepers, losers weepers.

"Old Chinese proverb: Fuck you!" He sputtered in anger.

Nick laughed—and mad as she was, Robin fought back a smile. It was all too incongruous.

"I like to think we're old friends, Mr. Yu. Am I right?" Silence.

"And I know all you do for us, your help keeping the rebels in—the necessities, shall we say? So I'd like our relationship to remain friendly. I could use you as a 'consultant' on a little deal I'm working on. Very simple, nothing to it. The day after the transaction, you get the dope back, in a convenient manner. In the alley behind Lala's, for example? Say, the first garbage can from the right."

The last thing Robin needed was to get involved in some crazy dope deal. She'd seen *Midnight Express*; she knew about the prisons in this part of the world. Her first instinct had been right after all: the guy was a loser. Wrong, she corrected herself. He was trouble—even dangerous—a threat to everything she hoped to accomplish. She felt disgusted and angry at being suckered in. Angry at herself. Angry at him. Robin leapt to her feet. "It's been really swell, Nick, but I want to forget I ever saw the inside of this room. I'll leave you two boys to continue your discussion in private."

"Sorry, Robin, business."

"Get it while you can, Nick." She turned sharply to go, but kept her ears open. The bastard didn't say a word to stop her. Well, good riddance! So what was that little grain of disappointment she felt? She slammed the door behind her.

Chapter 12

Nick punched his pillow and turned over. Again.

He was wired, as usual at the start of an operation. Then, too, there was the situation with Robin. He knew she had a right to be pissed off about what had gone down earlier, but it was a matter of priorities. Now he remembered his problem with women. Every time he got close to one—or close to being close—something more important came up. Like duty. Or what they called duty. Women didn't like being second.

Nor did Ronald Hudson.

Nick knew he infuriated his boss by his refusal to kowtow. He viewed Hudson as a kiss-up, kick-down sort of guy, although maybe being a pretentious wimp was what it took to succeed vertically in an organization. Or maybe he'd spent his career so far from home that no one had caught on to him. Still, Nick saw opportunity in Hudson's weakness. He also had a grudging admiration for the guy's creativity in the realm of dirty tricks. Especially that secret counterfeiting program.

However, he doubted Hudson would be too happy about his plans for the bogus bills. Not that it mattered. Nick needed working capital to kick things off. The one hundred seventy-five grand he he'd confiscated from Yu and the Russian would serve other purposes. The Pakistani offer was like money in the bank. He didn't have to touch it. But it was there.

When the birds started chirping, he decided to forget trying to sleep. He lay there awhile longer, studying the map of Afghanistan etched in his brain. The bed tea arrived at five-thirty, and he was at the Consulate by six. As he passed the guardhouse, Nick noticed its occupant wrapped in a blanket, dozing. He walked inside, knowing he'd have the place to himself. At least for a short time.

He entered Hudson's office, opened the safe and began transferring piles of U.S. "dollars" to his brown briefcase, a woven Bottega-style number knocked off by an expert craftsman in the leather bazaar.

Suddenly the door swung open. Ronald stared at Nick. "Somehow I missed the FPO you filed." He was not at all surprised that the man had "forgotten" to submit a Field Project Outline, required of any officer who got anywhere near the counterfeit money.

Nick added one last stack of bills and then clicked the lock shut. "Maybe you should check again. I'm sure it's in there somewhere. In any case, can't just let this money sit idly in the safe. Time to get it into circulation." He gave the briefcase a breezy pat.

"Oh, really, under what authority?"

"Just my own rogue resupply operation," he replied affably.

Ronald studied the man. There was something going on, some groundwork being laid. He could see who was doing the digging—and smell the manure. It was time to get out his own shovel. "Don't give me that cowboy shit. Where's the money going?"

"I believe that's on a need-to-know basis."

A slow burn had ignited behind Ronald's eyes. "Damnit, I need to know! ULTRA is one of our most delicate programs. You can not run with this on your own. It gets back to the wrong people in Washington or Islamabad—we're out of business." Besides the creation of fake afghanis, which the mujahideen "spent" inside Afghanistan, Hudson was behind a yet more secret program. ULTRA involved a similar use of counterfeit American currency, intended to subvert Russian soldiers and ultimately continue its mischief in the Soviet Union's underground economy.

"Just cable them a backdated FPO. Or how about an OPR?" Frequent Operational Progress Reports were supposed to follow the initial FPO, an alphabet soup of BS Nick did his best to avoid. "They'll never know the difference." With a grin, he picked up the briefcase and moved to leave.

"You arrogant fool, don't you realize we walk on eggs here? Break too many, we're history! Whatever your game is, it could jeopardize our entire covert aid program!"

"I don't think so, Ron. I've got my own marching orders on this one. But if you're still concerned, I suggest you check it out with the Director."

"Of that you may be very sure."

"If that's all, I'll be off now. Got a busy day ahead. Oh, and don't worry, I'll help you dig up that report. Later."

Ronald reined in his anger. He looked forward to nailing the SOB. After all, this was his town. He was paying most of the bills around there and nearly everyone owed him, whether grateful or not. His smile was cool and tight. "I understand the days of the rogue elephant are numbered: he's now on the endangered list."

Nick was already at the door. He paused, with a wink. "Not to worry. I made a large contribution to the World Wildlife Fund. Ciao for now." He strode down the hall, looking forward to a productive day.

A black Mercedes with darkened windows drove through the flat, dusty scrub country north of Peshawar. It was followed by an old green Bedford truck painted with flowers, mosques, snowy mountains and a soaring F-16. Periodically, the two vehicles passed mud-walled, turreted compounds with gunholes and tall iron gates. They were now inside tribal territory, where each man's home was a fort and only the main roads were controlled by the central government: the land to either side was ruled by local *maliks*, the traditional chiefs.

The road was lightly traveled, but the vehicles did not travel light. Buses, trucks and "taxis" spilled over with men and boys hanging from windows, sharing roofs, trunks and hoods with supplies, animals and a range of equipment—including weapons. Some of the passengers were tribesmen and some were refugees; most were armed.

The green truck was strangely empty in comparison, just two men in the front and a tarp over the back. The Mercedes drove slowly and more than once the two vehicles were overtaken—usually on curves—by overloaded pickups and jeeps, honking, careening wildly.

The road meandered uphill and they passed several deeply etched gullies that became raging rivers during the rainy season. But the rains were long past. Now all was dry. Few spring wildflowers remained; fewer still would remain after today. The sun had just begun its rise, but it was already white-hot.

A helicopter circled overhead. An army jeep appeared from behind a crumbling wall and sped forward. The drivers of the Mercedes and the green truck accelerated, following the jeep into a narrow ravine. There, they slowed, bouncing cautiously over the rocks. Then after rounding a bend, the three vehicles parked, hidden from the road.

To their left, a group of men stood under a rocky outcropping. A half-dozen armed soldiers were covering General Farouk, who was sitting atop a stack of five crates labeled DRILLING EQUIPMENT. A sixth crate lay on the dirt in front of him. The helicopter buzzed overhead.

Mr. Yu emerged from the Mercedes with a dark, slim man dressed in an easy but well-cut Italian suit. He was tieless and unshaven, in the Iranian fashion.

Lieutenant Rashid had led the Mercedes to this meeting place—as his uncle had ordered—and was still in the jeep, just lighting a cigarette as the two men got out. He was not surprised to see the Chinaman, but there was something about the Iranian... Then, Rashid recognized Taj beneath his disguise. And was stunned. He glanced at the truck. Amin and Kamal were inside. Noticing his look, Amin smiled knowingly.

Rashid swallowed hard and stared straight ahead. There was nothing he could do or say without revealing his connection to them. They had locked him into their scheme to entrap his uncle.

Mr. Yu and the new customer walked toward General Farouk under the soldiers' watchful gaze. "Good morning, General." Mr. Yu tried to cover his nervousness. "I would like to present our client, Mr. Hassan. Mr. Hassan, General Farouk."

General Farouk rose to his feet and smiled graciously. "Good morning to you both. It is a great pleasure, Mr. Hassan."

Hassan/Taj placed a fist to his chest in the traditional greeting and inclined his head. "And a blessing. Thanks be to Allah from whom all blessings flow."

General Farouk cast a glance at Yu. "Mr. Yu speaks highly of you."

Mr. Yu's eyes darted between the two men. "We have been doing business for some time. Yes, Mr. Hassan?"

Hassan/Taj nodded gravely. "From small arms to Silkworms, China is always there with best price, quickest delivery—a true friend of our revolution." He looked at the crate in front of the general.

"We hope to join you in friendship." General Farouk scrutinized the Iranian businessman, noting his Bottega briefcase.

"That is our wish as well." Hassan/Taj stood proud, despite the anxiety of these negotiations on which so much rested.

"Perhaps you would be more comfortable if we proceed in Dari, a language related to your own Farsi?"

"Comfort is good between friends." With a nod at Mr. Yu, Hassan/Taj switched into Dari, an Afghan dialect in which he was fluent. "We are quite interested in your merchandise, General. However, our funds are limited. The fluctuation in oil prices, you know."

"I understand completely. We have much to offer, including a most generous bargain rate in honor of our special new relationship."

Hassan/Taj rubbed the stubble on his chin. "And what is this bargain rate, if I may inquire?"Only fifty thousand dollars each."

"Do you take me for an idiot? Or a Libyan? We have not that kind of money to spend. Forty thousand each."

General Farouk regarded him with an ambiguous expression, indicating perhaps approval or amusement, but clearly not anger. He shrugged. "And where else could you obtain such valuable weapons if not through me? Are you planning to hijack some mujahideen in Afghanistan?"

"Not a bad idea. If forced to, of course we will. We must continue our holy war against the Iraqi devil, Hussein."

Farouk sensed the Iranian was holding the line. He squinted his eyes, now less amused. "Forty-five. Or I will find a less tightfisted customer."

Mr. Yu was squirming in discomfort. But not from these hard-line negotiations—transparent in any language. He, too, understood the necessity of bargaining as a matter of face. And he, too, understood they would eventually reach a deal.

Hassan/Taj stared hard at the general. "First, I will inspect the merchandise. If all is in order, I will agree to the forty-five thousand."

Farouk nodded at one of his men, a captain. The officer pried open the crate and removed the straw packing material.

Hassan/Taj moved closer and peered at the dark-green launcher tube and missiles, the grip-stock and battery. He began his inspection.

Mr. Yu patted his pockets, then turned to General Farouk, clearing his throat apologetically. "Excuse me, General. I seem to be out of cigarettes."

"I have never seen you smoke," Farouk replied absently. He gestured to his new aide, the replacement for Captain Ali, who, it was said, had been moonlighting in drugs and paid the price.

Mr. Yu stared at the aide and suddenly saw Ali himself. But that was impossible, for he himself had dispatched the man at the cemetery. It must be a ghost! He blinked. The ghost was gone. What remained was a heightened sense of his own vulnerability. He was playing a dangerous game. Dangerous games with multiple roles—and multiple possibilities of detection. From the new aide, he accepted one of the general's Silk Cut cigarettes and a light. He coughed, then covered his mouth fastidiously.

Oblivious to Yu's agitation, Farouk watched the Iranian inspect the Stinger's battery. He respected the man's expertise, for only a serious buyer would know that sometimes their batteries were defective.

Hassan/Taj brushed off his hands and nodded. "My people are pleased with your friendship and cooperation." He passed General Farouk his woven Bottega briefcase.

Farouk opened it and glanced at the neat piles of green. "The exact amount, no doubt. I trust you and do not count it." His smile was both pleased and ironic. "Persians are known to be clever businessmen—"

"Iranians, please!" Hassan/Taj interjected. "Our name in our language."

"In any case, you do your people honor. You were quite sure we would agree upon forty-five thousand each?" He shut the briefcase and placed it next to him.

Hassan/Taj opened his palms, eyes gleaming in a blend of spirituality and pride. "Of what matter is a few dollars more or less? There is no price among brothers."

Yu, watching the exchange, coughed again and dropped the cigarette, grinding it in the dust. Farouk cast him a curious glance. Rashid, however, still watching from his jeep, was not at all surprised by his discomfort.

Holding General Farouk in his glance, Hassan/Taj gestured to his men, who jumped from the truck and moved toward him. "Besides, I am trusting you, also. I do not inspect the other five crates." As he spoke, Amin and Kamal began carrying the crates to the truck and loading them under the tarp.

General Farouk nodded at the captain who pointed his right index finger toward the sky and made a circling motion. Churning up great clouds of dust, the Sikorsky S-76 landed, rotors still spinning, ready for immediate departure.

Farouk gazed at his new customer. "Until next time, Mr. Hassan."

"I look forward to it."

The general turned, strode briskly to the copter and stepped aboard. His men continued to cover him as the machine lifted off.

With a quiet look at Mr. Yu, Hassan/Taj walked to the truck and climbed in. Kamal spun the wheel hard and sped back toward the road.

Lieutenant Rashid got out of the jeep and strolled to Yu. "Another cigarette?"

Mr. Yu shook his head, no thanks.

"I can see you are under so much stress," Rashid said with a meaningful look, handing him an envelope. "General Farouk asked me to give you your commission." He pierced Yu with his eyes. "My uncle never forgets loyalty—or anything."

Expressionless, Mr. Yu glanced inside the envelope and placed it in his breast pocket. "General Farouk is a most wise man."

Rashid hawked and spit in the dust near Yu, who turned and hurried to his car. Lighting a cigarette, Rashid watched the black Mercedes drive away.

Out of nowhere, a watchtower appeared to the southwest, baked red clay jutting into deep blue... skies that rolled toward the distant mountains of their homeland. Taj sank back in his seat and took a deep breath. It would not be much longer.

A brave man could still know fear. Of course he would walk through burning sand for his family, his people, for Nick. And yet the danger had made him sweat. It seemed not possible that General Farouk would know him, and yet Taj had felt the fury of Rashid's glance. Surely the lieutenant would not jeopardize his career by informing on Taj, and yet....

It had been necessary to concentrate very hard back there with the Pakistanis. Images of his sweet, shy wife and two lively sons kept dancing through his mind. They would starve without him. The fifty-rupee monthly allotment per refugee was a myth. Everyone got a cut until there was little left for the Afghans. The rations, a myth also. Every day you saw UN food and supplies in their original boxes for sale on the black market.

Taj did not care about Pakistani corruption. His people were strong and independent and had never relied on official generosity. Hospitality was one thing, being weak and dependent entirely another. Taj would not be dependent. He had been studying English at the American Center when he met Nick. His work for Nick supported his family as well as fellow villagers Amin and Kamal—and their families. One day he would return to his mountain valley outside Kabul. Until then, *Insh'Allah*, he would be loyal to Nick.

The watchtower loomed closer as the stone and mud fortress separated from the tawny landscape, its blank walls broken only by firing slits. Turrets rose on either side of the ten-foot wooden gateway. Faded red doors opened and then closed behind the truck. The three Afghans jumped out, laughing and poking each other in boyish relief.

Nick was sitting on the veranda of the long brick shed that formed one side of the courtyard. He swung his legs down from the rickety table in front of him, got up and joined them. Smiling, he watched Taj rip off his suit jacket and pull out his shirt-tails. "You look almost normal now, Taj."

Taj gestured at the truck, a proud grin crossing his face. "Mission accomplished."

Nick nodded. "Well done."

"What is the program now, boss?"

"I have a little plan that should work out very well for us—and kill many birds with the same Stinger." His look merry yet mysterious, he placed a hand on Taj's shoulder. "Things have been a bit quiet lately. But we'll fix that, won't we? I want you to get a truck—a plain one this time— and arrange for supplies, men, animals. We'll store the crates here for now." He indicated the locked doors in the brick shed.

Taj felt a sense of anticipation. He didn't exactly understand Nick's words about "killing many birds," but he knew the American would tell him more when the time was right. Nick had promised he'd go home a rich man. It sounded as if they were on the road.

Taj hopped behind the wheel and drove to the shed, where the men began unloading the truck. Nick stared at the painting on its rear, a victorious mujahid astride the body of a dead Russian soldier.

Chapter 13

Nick and Viktor Ivanov walked down the unpaved main street of Darra, a small dusty village southwest of Peshawar. This was tribal land, borderland, outside government control. As they passed a goat foraging amid the rocks, a shot rang out. Nick stiffened. There was a burst of machine-gun fire. Then he laughed. "At two rupees a bullet, that guy could have bought lunch."

"One must first sample the merchandise. I mean, these people must." Wearing a gray blazer and neatly pressed jeans, Viktor shrugged. "Besides, some things are more important than food. Yes, Nicholas?"

"I guess so." Nick's smile was fading.

"Russians know so. Perhaps on this point the Russians and local peoples agree."

"On this point."

"Of course, you have great experience with 'local peoples.'" Viktor eyed him.

"Maybe this reminds you of the good old days, my friend?"

"What good old days? Nam? No..." Nick glanced around. "What this place really reminds me of is the Old West. Only with turbans instead of cowboy hats."

Except for the occasional teashop or food stall, the road was lined with cheery storefronts, all selling armaments and ammunition. The colors were bright and gay, the designs whimsical, belying what should have been a sinister atmosphere. Instead, it was like a carnival town. You expected to see popcorn and cotton candy for sale instead of a vast array of deadly weapons. Although almost noon, there were no signs of slowdown. Everywhere men were inspecting and testing the goods, bargaining for the right price. Darra was an arms bazaar where, for the right price, any weapon in the world could be obtained. At any hour. As Mr. Yu had known when he came to replace his Beretta the night before.

The North-West Frontier Province did have much in common with the Old West: the countryside had the same red and rocky look; the law was what you made it; and everyone carried guns. Because of the Pashtun enthusiasm for blood feuds and warfare, weapons had always been a necessity of life. During the British nineteenth-century invasions, the tribesmen made daring raids to steal their enemy's Lee-Enfield .303 rifles. In a "lesser of two evils" decision, the British decided to tolerate Darra's illegal gun factories. And in a typical NWFP quid pro quo, the tribesmen guaranteed the Brits safe passage along the main Frontier roads—an agreement honored to this day, graciously extended to the Pakistani government itself.

Now there was yet another war in that martial, untamable land to the west. To meet the need, Darra's businessmen had expanded their product line from reproductions to the smuggled, stolen or captured originals; from traditional Lee-Enfields to AK-47s; from grenades to grenade launchers.

Viktor glanced at the rough wooden skeletons of new construction rising around them. "Business is booming here." He nudged Nick. "American joke. You get it?"

"Got it."

"Good." Viktor's joviality clicked right off. "So my friend, we must talk. About Afghanistan." Pronouncing it "Ahf-ahn-ee-stahn" in the local style.

"Embarrassing, isn't it? Aren't you guys ready to call it quits yet?"

"But that would be a bad precedent for our comrades in Eastern Europe. Besides, our military—like yours—is very stubborn."

"Speaking of comrades, you know what they say about the Afghan Marxists—that their Marxism is inspired more by Groucho than Karl?"

"Groucho?" But Viktor understood—too well. The Afghans were the worst allies they'd ever had. Stumbling, fumbling... until it came time to knife you in the back. Even their soldiers were incompetent and could not be trusted. "No, I have not heard such things about our loyal comrades."

Nick shook his head. "In the end, all you'll have is a bunch of Afghani restaurants in Moscow, like our Vietnamese ones. Broadens the local cuisine, though."

Viktor shrugged, turning onto a side street. "This may be, but for now it is our war. We will handle it our way, in our time. And we cannot leave without a stable government."

"Don't you mean 'puppet?'" Nick smirked.

Viktor smiled blandly. "Perhaps 'friendly' is a better word." He knew all about flies and honey. He did not want to lose Nick before even catching him. "What I wish to make you see is that this bandit—Jamal—he is a nuisance to the legal Kabul regime. He is preventing stability, he is a bad irritant—"

"—You mean like salt in your 'bleeding wound?'"

"I mean like plucking thorn from side!" He looked sharply at Nick.

"I see," came Nick's quiet reply.

Suddenly Viktor was affable again, all smiles and good fellowship. "Then your people and my people—your Afghan proxies and our Afghan proxies—we continue our friendly little war until it runs its course."

Nick just nodded.

"Ooof," Viktor groaned as he stepped in a puddle."

"A little mud never hurt anyone."

"Mud?" Viktor looked down at his Ferragamo loafers, shaking his head in disgust.

"That's what we call a euphemism." Nick grinned.

"No 'euphemism' can make it better," he snapped. "Any of it."

Nick blinked. The Russian Goliath was in deep-shit, in every sense, and Viktor had just admitted it. As his colleague paused to scrape his shoes on a piece of lumber, Nick gazed thoughtfully around the sunny back street, the town's manufacturing hub. Each concrete and brick shell housed a mini-factory. Some were forges; others handled assembly, cast cartridges, drilled muzzles or constructed stocks from *chalghoza* wood. Here, in these workshops, children learned the art of gun-making at their fathers' feet.

Viktor took in the scene, as well, and was impressed, despite himself, at the industrious enemy activity. Small boys waved, displaying their craftsmanship. No one worked so cheerfully in the Soviet Union. Then he darted an impatient look at Nick. "You can help make everyone happy."

Nick appeared puzzled. "Surely, you don't need my help to get rid of this little David?" As in 'plucking thorn from side.'

Viktor masked his anger, not wishing to reveal any more than he already had. This war went beyond a military embarrassment. It was a disaster, hurting them with the Third World, not to mention their own Muslim nationalities. He thought of the meeting in Moscow, the failure of the Spetsnaz. General Secretary Gorbachev's ultimatum. Although few would admit it, at least publicly, a military solution seemed impossible—especially given Jamal's tactical strength and growing support. "Executive action" was the only answer. Viktor could not afford to fail: his future was on the line. And that of his mentor, KGB Chairman Petrov—and Secretary Gorbachev himself.

"Nicholas." He gave his CIA colleague a friendly slap on the back. "You surprise me. You are not a capitalist? You do not appreciate the freedom to make profit? People die everyday. Jamal will die, too. Why not benefit from the inevitable situation?"

It was a fascinating proposition. Everyone wanting to get to Jamal. Talk about killing all the birds with the same Stinger! Fate was tapping him on the shoulder with impeccable timing. Nick merely had to move with caution and put all the pieces together cleanly, leaving no tracks. He knew Viktor prided himself on his cleverness. Nick didn't want to disappoint him and make it too easy. If the Russian wanted to buy him, he'd be for sale, but he would not come cheap. "Yes, people die everyday and I don't want to be one of them. I'm a civilian, you know. A government employee."

"How is your pension?" Viktor smiled.

Nick shrugged. "About as good as yours."

"But our cost of living is less."

"Good point." He nodded slowly, then sighed. "Jamal is a great hero, so his death must be worth a great deal."

Viktor met his eyes. "A very great deal."

"To compensate very great danger." As Nick turned away, pondering the possibilities, he saw a familiar shop, Gul Akbar and Sons, Arms Dealers. The overhead sign, hand-painted in English, Urdu and Pashtu, showed a shiny black automatic next to a blue globe with a green Pakistani flag rising from it. Nick had done business with the shop owner's brother, Sher Akbar, a man whose missing thumb attested to the dangerous world they inhabited. We inhabit. Shaking his head, Nick peered in at the display, as comprehensive as ever. "While we consider the immorality of war, shall we check out the captured Kalashnikovs?"

"You consider the immorality of war, while I buy a souvenir. You have seen this .22 caliber 'fountain pen?' Only eight dollars."

Nick burst into laughter. "For signing your proxy?"

Viktor stared at him. "We are all proxy for someone." Then he walked off, busy with souvenirs to take home to Moscow. In triumph, he hoped.

As the front door swung shut, Nick and Robin left a meeting with another of the resistance factions, their second of the day. Their faces were grim as they walked through the courtyard. The first group could not have been more polite and sympathetic to Robin's goals. However, despite a sincere desire to be of assistance, they were forced to decline, citing limited manpower and resources. Escorting a woman into Afghanistan would be very difficult, and their honor would not permit the risk of danger befalling an American journalist under their care. Perhaps another time, when conditions improved.

The meeting they had just concluded was even less successful. While eyeing Robin with great curiosity, the leader, an older man with a massive belly and beard, said the Qu'ran forbade the mixing of sexes. It would be wrong for his men to travel with her. Nick was tempted to lean on him a little and ask what the Qu'ran would say about his men acting as drug couriers. But he decided it was not worth making an enemy just for the sake of Robin's rather dubious mission.

At the end of the courtyard, two armed guards opened the green iron gate and slammed it after them. The street seemed more oppressive than ever. It was mid-afternoon and the heat lay over them like a heavy gray blanket. Nick was used to it after all these years, but he noticed Robin wilting a bit. If she couldn't take it... might as well get out of the kitchen.

There were more guards on the street. Nick saw that Robin was withdrawn and oblivious to their searching stares. He did not believe she had a prayer of making this trip. However, he still had hopes for the relationship and was interested in keeping in her good graces. "You know that hypocritical old fart has property in California and a fourteen-year-old wife. So it's just as well. You don't want to have anything to do with him."

"Don't humor me. What the hell do I care about his sex life?"

"Besides..." Nick hid an amused smile. "We have four more resistance groups left to try. There's another, more Western-oriented one that escorted a lady journalist last year."

"Why didn't we go there first? I don't have all the time in the world to mess around here, you know."

"But you haven't even tried. You might like it."

Robin shook her head in disgust. "Couldn't you even attempt to take me seriously?"

"I do take you seriously. You're the best-looking woman in town." He tossed an arm across her shoulders as the guards' eyes bugged out. She sidestepped and his arm dropped to his side. They didn't miss that, either.

"You know something, you're a patronizing bastard!"

"Come on, Robin, we'll give it another shot tomorrow. In the meantime, how 'bout a beer at my place?"

She stared at him. "We tried that. You were more interested in your dope deals!"

He didn't say a word: no defense.

Robin had been angry all day—still was—but that had nothing to do with business. And nothing to do with him! "In any case, I don't need your help. My driver Jhan knows his way around this town. And I can hardly do worse." She walked to a waiting brown car and opened the door, then glanced back at Nick with a sweet smile. "You'll be able to get a taxi, won't you? I'd give you a lift, but as they say, business before pleasure."

"Oh, no problem at all, hon. I got nothing much to do but 'babysit' you anyway. I'll just give Yellow Cab a buzz."

She got in the front seat, then turned and blew him a phony kiss out the window.

The Toyota pulled away, leaving Nick standing in its dusty wake. All he saw was her face framed by that windowThe guards may not have understood English, but that scene played like a silent movie. They looked at each other, shaking their heads in pity.

A horse-drawn tonga pulled up in front of the U.S.I.S. compound. Nick stepped down, brushing himself off. The sky had turned a hazy, end-of-the-day pink, but it was still hot and Nick was looking forward to some air-conditioned relief. As he moved toward the gatehouse, the door of a white Honda Accord sedan opened and Ahmed emerged, crisp as ever.

He gazed at Nick over his gold Cartier rims. "A quaint way of getting about town. Although I must say, you look rather the worse for wear."

Nick frowned. "It's a long story, but the good news is the story has a skirt in it."

"I'd wager I know whose skirt, or shall I say, trousers?" Ahmed smiled slyly. "Ahh, liberation." He paused. "Which reminds me of our last conversation. You have not forgotten, have you?"

Nick shook his head. "No, I haven't forgotten."

"Well?"

"Well, what?"

"Ahh, Nick, you can be terribly difficult. Well… have you thought of anyone?"

"In fact, a thought did happen to cross my mind." He grinned. "How long since your last tonga ride?"

"Not long enough, my dear chap." Ahmed stared at the rundown old horse and cart.

Nick reached in his pocket and pulled out a large wad of rupees, asking the driver if he might borrow his tonga for an hour or so.

"Not to hurry, sir." With a dazzled grin, the tonga-wallah placed the money carefully in his pocket and scurried off.

"Maybe then he can fix this rig up." Nick eyeballed its torn canvas top.

"I doubt he'd know where to start," sneered Ahmed, removing his handkerchief and dusting the worn wooden seat. He studied the dirt on the white cloth, grimaced, then tossed it in the road. The two men climbed into the tonga and rode off, Nick at the reins.

Scooters, even bicycles, swooped around them as the horse plodded down the suburban road. Everyone but the horse on their way home. The hint of a breeze fluttered through the heavy air, but it was more tantalizing than refreshing.

"Not exactly a F-16," Nick apologized.

"But quieter. Never mind, this ride will keep us humble, remind us how the other half lives."

A strange expression crossed Nick's face. "I live pretty humbly already. The other half I'm thinking of lives very well."

Ahmed stared at him. "Is that envy I hear?"

"Perhaps." Nick reached in his pocket and took out a thick, buff-colored business card.

Ahmed took the card, noting the address, telephone and telex numbers of the Banque Internationale de Crédit, Genève. He turned it over and saw another number handwritten on the back.

"I found someone who should be able to help you out. He'll expect bank confirmation of a one-hundred-twenty-five-thousand-dollar deposit before he leaves on his trip—and an equal amount on his return."

Ahmed nodded. His smile was merely internal. To own a CIA officer… that would be worth a fortune. If the scheme worked, the dollars would keep pouring in. And even if he didn't deliver, Nick would owe him. Ahmed knew how to make bloody sure of that. "So many are journeying over the mountains these days. Have you ever made such an expedition? It is exceptionally beautiful this time of year."

Nick gazed westward. "Yes. I've heard this is the best time to travel."

Chapter 14

Kandahar, Afghanistan

May 1986

The RPG rocket cut through the clear desert air... racing toward the tank at the head of the Soviet supply column. The thirty-seven-ton T-62 exploded, its turret and gun ripped off and hurled across the dusty highway. Flames leaped to the fuel tanker behind it. A red-orange-yellow ball of fire ripped into the sky with a devastating burst of heat.

The rear tank met the same fate.

The blocked convoy was the target of further rocket, mortar and rifle attack from the surrounding hillsides. Soviet and Afghan troops responded with superior firepower.

Their hidden enemy had the advantage, however.

Caches of ammunition exploded, sending off tracer-like blue and white eruptions that mixed with the diesel smoke and dust. The air was filled with the smell of burnt gunpowder, rubber and flesh, the screams of soldiers trapped in the deadly ambush.

High atop a craggy ridge, Jamal lowered his rifle, his crossed bandoliers half-empty. From here, he had watched the line of tanks, trucks and armored personnel carriers power toward the end of the three-hundred-mile advance from Kabul, capital of the Democratic Republic of Afghanistan. The convoy's urgent mission had been to liberate the DRA's Kandahar base, under siege for the past sixty days. Jamal knew its fall would be a major setback to the Soviets, who—unable to control the countryside—had created mined "rings of steel" around the main cities, connected by a "ring road."

Nonetheless, Commander Jamal had broken through the Kandahar "ring" and leveled the garrison's grain warehouse by a daring rocket attack. A follow-up airport strike had led to the fiery destruction of two ammunition-laden helicopters, six fighter jets, and then the barracks—also destroying the career of the local Afghan zone commander and his Soviet advisers.

Jamal saw that explosion and fire as he stared at the leaping red flames on the road below. But he was not a warrior at heart and did not rejoice at the deaths of men trapped inside their APC infernos. The armored personnel carriers had been struck by two captured 122 mm Russian rockets launched from a tripod of sticks, while the shoulder-fired RPG-7 "tank-killer" had also been captured. Jamal was fighting a traditional hit-and-run Afghan war, with guerrilla tactics overwhelming enemy superiority.

It was like fighting with one hand tied behind his back, though. Jamal knew he could be more effective with better equipment. But the leaders of the seven Peshawar-based resistance groups had insisted that all field commanders affiliate with one of them in order to obtain supplies: it was a complex game of politics, religion and money.

Jamal Durrani was too proud to play the game.

How could he agree to follow any of the "leaders"? Some were corrupt, others merely weak. He believed none of the players merited his respect. And he knew them all, having spent most of his life here. Except those four undergraduate years at Berkeley.

It seemed another lifetime now. The sixties. Those days of freedom and ease. And love. How tempting it had been. One carefree day blended into the next and there was goodness in that life.

But it was not his life. Nor his land. At the time, he had almost considered staying there—with her. Then, unbidden came the words of his ancestor, the poet-warrior, Emperor Ahmad Shah Durrani:

If I must choose between the world and you,
I shall not hesitate to claim your barren deserts as my own.

His destiny would be shaped by this land—a harsh, even pitiless place, yet emanating God's grandeur. Only amid the stark majesty of its mountains, deserts and plains did Jamal feel his truest self. He was part of it, and it was part of him. And these were his people, simple, proud, unyielding. Each man had his tribe, yet the varied cultures—Persian, Turkish, Pashtun—intermingled to create one that was uniquely Afghan. Even their Islam grew from the noble Afghan landscape.

He had left a piece of his heart in America, yet did not doubt that this was where he belonged, where he was needed. Jamal had been teaching political science at Kabul University when the various factions—leftist, royalist and fundamentalist—began to clash. He tried to moderate the differences. But the Afghan character was by nature militant. Battle lines and permanent enmities were soon formed.

Jamal had supported the King's program of gradual modernization. For others, however, it was too slow. Soon, Zahir Mohammad Shah was overthrown by his leftist cousin and brother-in-law, Mohammad Daoud Khan. Five years later Daoud was assassinated during a Marxist coup. Jamal knew that attempts at radical change would fail, for the Afghans were a conservative people. Scattered insurgency broke out. But chaos in a border state was something the Russians could not tolerate.

Jamal would never forget that Christmas Eve, 1979. One of his students, whose father worked at the airport, rushed to tell him the Soviets were landing. Jamal went to the window and saw the planes. The airlift continued around the clock for the next two days. Panic gripped the capital. Except for the rumbling overhead, the city was deathly silent. However, the silence would end.

Soon armored units of the 40th Army began pouring in. Fighter jets and gunships filled the skies. Jamal and his family huddled around the radio. At midnight they heard a gunshot as the Soviets took over Radio Kabul. Then more gunfire from the Taj Beg Palace. One president shot— by the Spetsnaz, he later learned—to be replaced by a more dependable one.

Jamal's response to the invasion was immediate. He said goodbye to his students and family, went underground and joined several other prominent figures in forming the resistance in Pakistan. But then began the inevitable jockeying for power. Jamal had no patience for such things. He did not wish power: he wished to make a difference.

And so those who stayed in Pakistan became rich, their followers well supplied. Jamal Durrani, returning to take up battle in Afghanistan, remained poor but independent.

He started small, building a secret network of bases around Kandahar, his ancestral homeland, enabling him to mount surprise raids and gradually increase his control. He and his men were able to capture weapons, or obtain them by barter from Soviet and Afghan soldiers. Supply caravans passed through his territory. Sometimes the supplies never left.

Jamal was fearless in his attacks. The government became desperate to capture and eliminate him. Yet he was elusive. His ability to appear—then disappear—at will was a mockery to them. Members of his family were interrogated and tortured in Kabul's notorious Pul-i-Charki prison. In an effort to protect them, Jamal had cut all contact with his loved ones, but the attempt proved useless.

His brave mother, among the first to bare her face in Kabul's streets, had spit on the KHAD interrogator who called her son a traitor. She became one of the thousands who never left the prison. His father, a man large in spirit as well as size, was nothing but a shrunken, silent memory when finally released. He had been forced to witness the rape of his only daughter by several drunken soldiers. The smart, lovely girl to whom Jamal was betrothed had fled with her family to their Paghman summer home north of Kabul; they were machined-gunned to death and left unburied in an open grave.

Only by implacable defiance could he avenge these losses. For Jamal, it would be victory or death. Yet whatever his fate, his people would prevail. Still, he did not underestimate his foe's tenacity. Long before the Soviet era, the Russian Bear had begun its southward push, annexing the Central Asian homelands of Afghanistan's northern tribesmen—Uzbek, Turkoman, Tajik. But the Afghans could push back. And always had.

Whoever has trodden this land, whether Alexander or Aurangzeb, Genghiz or Farangi, each met his fate with blood and tears at the hand of the Pashtuns.

A century ago, the "Farangi" had been British; now he was Soviet.

Sadly, the blood and tears were shed by all, even the innocent. There had been a million casualties, maybe more, mostly civilian. The economy had been ruined; millions of refugees had fled to Pakistan or Iran. With fundamentalists running the refugee camps, progress had ended, especially for women.

For all these reasons, he was impelled to continue his struggle. Inspired by his campaign against Kandahar, the country's second most strategic city, mujahideen were flocking to Jamal, including other commanders who saw the advantages of a united front. It was rumored his next move might be to challenge the Soviet stronghold that was Kabul. Despite his lack of supplies, Jamal had the will and patience for victory. He would continue the battle until someday, *Insh'Allah*, peace and moderate leadership would bring his country back on track. So he stayed and fought.

Over the past five years, Jamal had come to excel in guerrilla tactics, using the forbidding terrain to his benefit. Even a few hidden soldiers could overpower a mighty Soviet convoy. Jamal watched the survivors wasting their ammunition on the barren hillsides. Their surrender appeared imminent. He was looking forward to more captured weapons, fewer enemies and much embarrassment to the new zone commander.

As Jamal waited, one of his young fighters rushed to him with only the hint of a limp. Sher Ali's lower left leg was made of wood, fashioned at the Red Cross hospital in Peshawar while he was recovering from a mine he hadn't seen one moonless night. But his name meant lion, and he'd rejoined Jamal even before the doctors granted permission.

His face a mix of dirt and despair, Sher Ali reported they had no more boosters or rockets for the RPG tank-killers. "And only four Kalashnikov magazines—"

Suddenly a belching roar filled their ears. The men knew—but looked anyway—as the inevitable gunships appeared in defense of the convoy. Five MI-24 Hinds, swooping low, skimming the ridgeline in search of rebel forces. Their rotors churned the black, oily sky, charging it with their vibrations and the colored lights of anti-missile decoy flares.

The mujahideen, crouching among the rocks, were camouflaged by their long, drab shawls, but the Hinds could fly very close to the ground. Soon they would be discovered.

The helicopters were equipped with staggering firepower—rockets, missiles, cannon and rapid-fire machine guns that could pierce armor and spit fire. They could bomb and strafe the land into total annihilation, knowing that eventually they'd hit their target. Just as elsewhere, they slaughtered supply convoys and destroyed villages and farmland that supported the mujahideen. Almost invincible because of their bulletproof glass and titanium plating, the Hinds gripped the nation in a relentless reign—and rain—of terror. They were feared by brave men who feared nothing else on earth.

Flattened against a rock, Jamal stared up at the huge, ugly machines. As they buzzed closer, just above RPG range, he could see the brown and khaki camouflage paint, the dark underbelly. With a nod at Sher Ali, Jamal picked his target: a gunship that was only sporadically dropping anti-missile flares. "It is in God's hands. We will go now. After a final salute."

Sher Ali darted behind a boulder, reappearing with a Soviet SAM-7 Grail missile contributed by an Afghan deserter. Jamal took it and stepped coolly into the open, then planted his legs and lifted the weapon to his shoulder. He needed to lock onto the helicopter's exhaust heat and for that, he needed it to drop into range. The Hind banked and turned, presenting its tail rotor to him. He steadied the launcher, aimed and pressed the trigger halfway. The red light came on—SEEKER LOCKED ONTO TARGET—then turned green. He fired.

The warhead shot from its tube with a powerful burst, a flash of scarlet streaking through the dark, smoky sky at one and a half times the velocity of sound. It smashed with thunderous impact into the ship's rocket pod, but the powerful beast was merely wounded and limped off through the sky, trailing smoke from its right stub wing.

However, the SAM left its own trail. Its backblast of white smoke was a dead giveaway of Jamal's position. As more anti-missile flares—balls of glowing magnesium—began filling the sky in the attempt to lure the missiles, one of the helicopters wheeled in Jamal's direction and began homing in on him.

The mujahideen waved their fists in the air, firing their rifles and cursing the hated Shuravi and their evil machines. They had done their damage; they had challenged the enemy and would not flee before expressing their contempt.

Still, Sher Ali hoped for the day when they would do more damage. In Peshawar, his ears had been filled with talk of the American Stingers. He asked his commander when they would get them.

Jamal stared into the sky. Everyone wanted the Stingers—electronically guided, with a range of two kilometers! Such missiles would allow them to take on the evil beasts with some measure of safety. "*Insh'Allah*, soon."

Flying low, the gunship was now dangerously close. Dipping nose down, it spit its angry red fire. Rocks shattered, dust danced high, but Jamal and his men had suddenly disappeared. Only empty shells remained in the dirt.

He'd done it again! The bandit had slipped away again. How did he do it? Where did he go? He was laughing in their faces, making them look like idiots.

Sheltered under the Hind's blue-tinted dome, Major Grishkin gripped the controls as he hovered over the spot, quartering the area with keen, well-trained eyes. Shaking his head in frustration, he continued his prowl, but discovered only burnt reminders of the bandit's victory. Swooping up and down, he hugged the hilly terrain, flying at what would be treetop height—if any trees had managed to take root in this wretched land. But all he saw was cracked earth, gray-stone nothingness. His heart ached for the clean green birches and pines of his homeland.

Grishkin's anger was also directed at his comrade, Vladimir, who had put the ship in jeopardy. Why had his fellow pilot ignored anti-missile procedures? Why had he sent off so few decoy flares? Had he been low? Or merely careless? Second in their class at the Training College, Vladdy had recently taken up hashish. Unhappy, he said. Well, who in this hellhole wasn't? Grishkin had seen him smoking last night. Never mind the bandits, Afghanistan would defeat you if you're weak. His comrade was lucky to have escaped with his life, although he'd pay when he returned to the base. A negative rating would quash his hopes for higher military education at one of the Academies.

Grishkin would take no chances. He kept up the flares, red, yellow, green. His forward machine gunner sprayed and spattered the rocks into pebbles, into gravel.

A diligent officer, he had been recruited by GRU military intelligence to act as liaison with the local Spetsnaz company. They were under enormous pressure to get the bandit. The kind of high-level pressure that did not accept failure. Stomach-churning pressure from Khodinka, GRU headquarters outside Moscow. Duties that had once seemed an opportunity to rise now terrified him with their downside.

Grishkin chewed the cuticle around his index finger. He'd been certain he had the raghead today. He had watched him through the blue plexiglass canopy, low enough to see his expression of laughing contempt. Maybe, as they locked eyes, the Afghan had recognized how badly the pilot wanted him.

The major was nearing the end of his "opportunity for service to the Motherland." He had been warned. Either he would be relieved of the opportunity and reassigned to a mine-clearing battalion—or he would be accepted at Moscow's prestigious Frunze Academy and continue his career with honors.

Grishkin looked forward to their next meeting, for then the Afghan bandit would be his.

Chapter 15

Peshawar, Pakistan
May 1986

A tap at the door announced Nick's 6 a.m. bed tea, a linen-covered tray with tea, toast and fresh mango juice. Still sipping the juice, he stepped out into the pink-sky dawn. The air was already warm but still gentle, as sweet as a caress.

These were the cleansing hours, before the heat turned it all heavy and slow and somehow dark. Back in Southeast Asia, he had hit the ground running, but nowadays he took his time, savoring the fresh smells and soft light, the purity of a newborn world.

Nick enjoyed these early morning strolls. His thoughts depended on how he'd slept, what his dreams had been, how busy he was. At the moment, he was thinking about Afghanistan, wondering if they had mangoes there, if any trees were left standing. Then, he thought of the first one he'd ever tasted. Of course there had been a woman involved. A Thai woman, of course.

It had been in Bangkok. Nick was meeting with some Air America people about air support for Laos. Things were tightening up in Washington, and the "secret war" was in trouble. It was about this time that the CIA and AID gave General Vang Pao his own airline. "Humanitarian" supplies coming in, "agricultural" produce going out. But the heavy lifting was done by Air America, an Agency proprietary charged with being self-sustaining and thus given a certain latitude in pursuing business opportunities. Whatever they might be.

Friday night came along, and Nick checked into the riverfront Oriental Hotel. He had plenty of cash. Where the hell could you spend it in Long Tieng? The place blew him away: the clean sheets, the luxury and refinement of it all. He refused to feel intimidated by the elegance; he just felt happy and horny.

He had a beer on the terrace of the new wing and watched the rice barges drift along the Chao Praya. The swift water taxis raced past, sending up sheets of white foam. Even if only for a day, it couldn't have been better.

He saw her at a table on the terrace's lower level. She looked like a flower in her Thai silk dress—a tall, slim, flawless rose.

First he pretended to continue watching the river traffic, but it was a sorry pretense, finally a joke. She smiled, amused, and then nodded serenely in response to the question in his eyes. He joined her.

There was a calmness about her, a fluidity. Her curves were as graceful as the smile that lit her face. It was only later as they lay in bed, watching the twinkling lights float down the river, that he found out she was the mistress of Santo Trafficante, the distributor of Vang Pao's dope outside Asia.

Santo Trafficante! Bad guy. *Very* bad.

Talk about a small world—Air America, Vang Pao, Trafficante. It was all too close. Too dangerous.

But her eyes drew him in. He would escape—later.

It was a night of mind expansion and bliss. Then dawn arrived, washing the sky and river rosy-orange. She called room service, ordered tea and mangoes. She prepared a platter of the juicy golden fruit, cutting one in thirds, peeling another, opening the end of a third and showing him how to suck out the juice.

The juices soon covered his mouth; the fragrance filled the room. Then he leaned back and watched her, her delicate mouth devouring every morsel surrounding the oval pit. She told him not to stop; she wanted to watch him, too. That made him crazy. They ended up in the tub almost drowning in steam and hot water and almond oil.

She shook his hand as she was leaving the next morning. Her eyes danced, although her face was grave. This was but a memory.

Nick watched as she moved away, barely skimming the ground. He resolved he would not try to find her again. It almost didn't matter, though. She had put him through enough changes to last a lifetime.

He sure as hell envied her old man, but a fantasy like that could find him floating in the Mekong with the crocodiles, or lying in the forest as fodder for the wild pigs. Two days later, he learned she had a full-time minder who rarely let her out of sight—and all night the man had been looking for a tall American in cowboy boots. No female was worth that kind of trouble, although this one came damn close.

Nick gazed into his mango juice. It was golden orange, like the sun at its birth—or death. He hadn't thought about her in a long time, hence the bad poetry, he supposed. His brain clicked into gear, settling on the preparations that remained. Suddenly he felt a hard metal object pressing into the small of his back. His hand tightened around his only weapon, the juice glass.

"A morning stroll, so good for digestion," a Russian-accented voice spoke behind him. "But you may not want to bring your drink along."

Nick shrugged and set the glass down.

Prodding Nick with his weapon, a small muscular man in a tight, shiny suit directed him across the lawn and down the driveway. They stopped next to an old yellow Cadillac about the color of the guy's crewcut. The car was parked under a jacaranda tree and covered with their fallen blossoms. Its motor was running.

"What a bitch." Nick shook his head in dismay. "Those flowers are pretty but hell to clean off."

Blond Crewcut regarded the car seriously. "No problem, plenty cheap labor around. A pity, so many starving refugees."

A wiry Pakistani driver leaned over and opened the passenger door.

"Right." Nick felt himself being nudged inside. The man followed, only a gun barrel away, and sat down next to him.

The driver accelerated with a lurch down the driveway, turning left onto Sir Syed Road between St. John's Catholic Church and the Iranian Consulate. Taking a circuitous route, he turned off Khyber Road into a back alley behind Peshawar Royal Woodworks, where Nick and his friendly escort transferred into a dusty red Suzuki pickup.

Nick was now wedged between his escort—"just call me Leo"—and a large, orally compulsive driver who constantly smoked, sucked *naswar* and spit. As soon as they set off, the man opened his brass snuffbox, took a pinch of the greenish tobacco-spice stimulant and placed it under his tongue. He offered some to his companions, but they declined. Leo was more interested in his own Marlboros, which the driver eyed greedily. A sociable fellow, the Russian held out his pack. Nick shook his head, but the driver accepted with delight, first sending a long green jet out his window. Cigarette between his lips, he cracked the snuffbox, again offering it. Nick again declined, as did Leo.

The thickset driver shrugged. After a taste of *naswar*, he took another drag and then turned on the radio, smiling contently at the anguished wails of Khial Mohammad. He rolled up the window for better acoustics.

After a few minutes, he rolled it down again. Nick knew what was coming. He leaned flat against the seat. Just in time, for the wind picked up some of the green spit and sent it back into the car, bypassing him, but not Leo.

Grimacing, Leo wiped his cheek with the heel of his hand. He looked at his digital watch and started tapping his fingers on the dashboard.

Aware of his boss' sudden displeasure, the driver floored it. He began honking and weaving in and out of traffic. To avoid the noise and dust, he closed the window again.

Nick was focused on the gun in his guts, as well as the pungent BO surrounding him. The cab became progressively hotter, ranker and smokier until he felt like he was in a bar without the booze. He thought of lighting up, but reconsidered.

Making short work of what remained of the town, they followed Charsadda Road across the Khyber River Canal. Nick knew they were heading northeast, but where? And why? Did someone know what he was up to? Were they trying to head him off at the pass?

The resistance group was headquartered in a refugee camp on Peshawar's western plains. Robin had laughed, realizing she'd finally made it to a refugee camp. To Jhan's quizzical look, she replied it was a private joke. But the camp wasn't really funny. Not at all.

And now it was the same old story. Four strapping young men accompanied Robin and Jhan back to the car, followed by a one-legged, seven-year-old boy cheerfully determined to keep pace with his homemade crutch. The four mujahideen worked as gardeners at Peshawar's Islamia University to earn money for weapons. They seemed upbeat about their prospects.

"Yes, soon we go home, *Insh'Allah*, to kill more *Shuravi*. But this trip only for men. Too dangerous for a woman—even one from America!" They grinned, as if planning an excursion to the country.

Robin and Jhan exchanged glances and got in the car. As they drove away, Robin gazed at the willow-lined roadside where a woman was carrying a basket of rice and balancing a water pitcher on her head, while securing her red and purple veil between her teeth. Two young children and a goat scampered behind her.

The camps were on land leased by the government from local landowners, whose rich fields cruelly surrounded the refugees. Robin stared at the neat plots of rice, wheat and corn—green and gold rising, luminous, under the clear, wispy sky. She thought of the woman in the red and purple veil—invisible to society, yet carrying its weight. Being invisible could be an asset, but not in Peshawar. Here it just made you powerless.

And angry. Robin knew that she had to channel her fury and contain it. Still, she was reminded of the magnitude of her endeavor, the weight she was carrying on her own shoulders. She had learned much in this short period of time. She wondered if she had been arrogant in thinking she could brazen her way into this closed world and outmaneuver everyone. On the other hand, why couldn't she?

Jhan finally spoke. "You remember I am your eyes and ears in Peshawar?"

Preoccupied. "Of course, I remember."

"Well, my ears have heard something that may help you."

"What?" Robin snapped.

"My sister's husband's cousin makes very good business from mujahideen convoys. He is a rich man now with two houses, not one."

Robin couldn't care less about the good fortune of his sister's husband's cousin.

Jhan continued despite her indifference. "Someone has just purchased supplies and several pack animals." He glanced at her. "Too much for a holiday."

"Who?" she wondered cautiously.

"Since you are interested, my eyes will be looking further."

"Do that, Jhan, because I'm running out of time."

The red Suzuki pickup passed through the fertile Vale of Peshawar, northeast of town. Alexander the Great had besieged and captured the valley in 324 BC when it was the cradle of Buddhism. He was not the first, though, nor the last.

Nestled in rich countryside straddling a famous trading route, Peshawar had always been coveted by invaders. Aryans, Persians, Greeks, Hindus, Huns, Turks, Mongols, Moguls, Sikhs and British. Many civilizations had come and gone, each leaving ruins to be built upon by its successor and each relocating its capital.

It was a valley of ruins, haunted with memories of grandeur past, power past. The passage of time. An eternity of history made present by the headless Buddhas, burial mounds, monasteries and temples. By the timeless rivers that still irrigated the lush, green plains.

The Suzuki traveled a road carved through tall, densely packed fields of sugar cane. Nick could see no way out. Literally. They crossed some railway tracks and continued to the gate of a sugar mill, where the driver turned left and then right down a poplar-lined road. The bumpy track rolled past an old Hindu fort and came to a dead end at the base of a steep hill.

Nick stared up at the stony outcropping with its vast stretch of ruins. The remains of the great Buddhist monastery, Takht-i-Bahi. He sighed. "First century AD."

"You mean old." Leo stubbed out his cigarette, uninterested.

"Very old." Very dead. Nick wondered if they were trying to tell him something. "Interesting site for a picnic."

Leo gave him an insistent poke in the side with his pistol. "No picnic. Now we take hike."

"You take a hike, you bastard," Nick replied, but Leo just opened the door.

As the men got out, the driver reached down for the AK-47 wedged beside his seat. He cradled it in his beefy arms, lit a fresh cigarette and chewed *naswar*.

It was a sharp climb, and at times the men stumbled over loose rocks. Nick thought of jamming Leo with his elbow and making a run for it, but as he turned to look for an escape route, he noticed the driver covering him through his telescopic sight. One more dead stiff among all these burial mounds. Who'd ever know?

They passed some crumbling, two-story outbuildings. A voice floated to them through the clear hot air. "A bit melancholy, is it not?"

Viktor Ivanov emerged from a crumbling monk's cell. "Or perhaps it is just that I am Russian." His expression was pensive. "Five hundred years of glory. Then…" He shrugged. "I have been wondering if there is a lesson here, for all great civilizations."

"This is not amusing, Viktor."

"The fall of civilizations—or my cloak-and-dagger? Or your carelessness? Viktor's smile contained a threat. "You must have much on your mind that we were able to pick you up so easily."

"No. Just a tribute to Leo's persuasive talents," Nick said sourly. He had a headache from the smoky cab, the driver's loud music and insane driving.

Leo puffed up a bit, then deflated as Viktor regarded him narrowly. "Leonid, you are to return to the car." Leo turned and started back downhill.

Viktor pointed toward a rise behind them lined with many small individual ruins. "We'll have a better view from there."

"I'm not interested in views."

"So then I will show you the underground chambers. Some say for meditation. Others say for storage," he added pointedly.

"No tours. Okay, Vic, you've had your fun, but I have no time for games. What do you want?"

Viktor frowned at the nickname and gave him a hard stare. He needed to know if Nick would commit. The pieces were on the board, soon to be in play. "Just so… you are very busy. So much going on, but nothing yet happening. I must know. Will it happen?"

Nick gazed at the KGB man and then smiled for the first time. "Viktor, this is your lucky day." He reached in his pocket and handed him a business card imprinted with the bank's name and an account number handwritten on back.

Viktor studied both sides of the card. He nodded. "And the price?"

"A deposit of one hundred twenty-five thousand—dollars not rubles—to be paid immediately and the same when the work is terminated. No pun intended." Nick winked.

Viktor raised an eyebrow. The money was nothing. They would be repaid a hundredfold when the operation succeeded. "I only hope the enterprise will be private, that the funds do not end up in a Contra account."

"This is definitely a private undertaking."

"Another very good pun." He clapped Nick across the back. "You know, this could be the start of a beautiful friendship. Working together to bring peace."

"Yeah, your piece and mine."

"Ahh, capitalism. Everyone gets his cut."

"Even a communist?"

Viktor grinned. "Maybe next time." He filled his chest with clean country air and took in the panoramic view. Green spreading fields of sugar cane below, snow-capped mountains to the north, Peshawar to the south. Ruins everywhere. "So many temples."

Nick stared down at the ancient valley. An inaccessible expression crossed his face. "So many graves."

Robin didn't talk much on the drive back from the refugee camp. Sunk in her thoughts, she stared out the window as the cultivated land gave way to arid plains. Then out of the emptiness, there arose a large stone and beamed compound. Jhan stopped at a wooden shed extending from its far corner. A boy scurried out with a watering can, which he pointed into the Toyota's gas tank. A gas station! Robin had to smile and a part of her wished she had the luxury of being an ordinary traveler. Thinking of all those travel articles she could write, she watched the boy clean the windscreen. Jhan paid him and then backed up to the compound's entrance.

"Do not worry, I am making arrangements inside." With a reassuring nod, he walked to the red iron gate, gave it a little kick open and entered.

The gate didn't quite close and Robin peered inside. The courtyard was stacked high with crates and boxes of all sizes and shapes. She could see Japanese fans and VCRs, Russian refrigerators, TVs and bicycles, and case upon case of Stolichnaya vodka.

Jhan reappeared after about fifteen minutes to find Robin fanning herself with her notebook. Despite her evident irritation, he seemed pleased. "I am sorry if making you wait, but I must take some tea when making inquiries. It is custom, you know."

"So you've told me." She glanced again inside. "What is that place, some kind of warehouse?"

Jhan grinned. "Yes, warehouse. Vodka smuggled in from Afghanistan—"

"I've heard all about that." She shrugged.

"Many other kinds of smuggling. You can get everything in Peshawar." Jhan sent her a look. "Before, caravans paid tribute for right of passage. Now it is trucks and traders who must pay tax. If not, tribesmen are holding them for ransom."

"Why doesn't the government do something?"

"It is democracy here, Miss Robin. People liking system. Sometimes tax is paid with goods. Warehouse such as this selling them at bargain rates. Example, smuggled Soviet TV for fifteen hundred rupees. In Peshawar market, Japanese TV costing four thousand. Everyone now buying Soviet."

Robin stared at him. Every time she thought she had a handle on this place, she got thrown for a loop. Again there was the feeling of being lost in a time warp. Smuggling, trade, free enterprise. They all seemed to be synonymous around here. Even Jhan found the system perfectly normal.

Then he told her what he had learned in the warehouse and Robin was pleased to find her options expanding again. But even as she glimpsed the future, she experienced a pang about San Francisco. Her safe little world that now seemed very far away.

Chapter 16

It was late and Nick was lying on the sofa, trying to kick back over a beer and some sitar music that normally put him in a good place, only tonight nothing worked. The electricity had gone out earlier and the beer was warm. The evening raga now felt driven by a kind of intensity he wanted to escape, and its throbbing tempo would not let his mind slow down. Besides, he still had a headache from today's excursion to the burial grounds. The knock on his door was the last straw.

"Je-sus, gimme a break!" He got up, opened the door and saw Robin standing there with a bottle of vodka and a disarming grin on her face.

"'Cuse me, Mister. This the Bamboo Bar?"

Nick could feel his tension slipping away and he grinned back. "It could be. It certainly could be."

He smiled some more and she smiled some more.

"You forgot your manners or something?"

Amazingly, it all came back to him and he made an exaggerated gesture for her to enter. "*Mademoiselle...*"

"Well, if you insist..."

Nick nodded slowly. "I insist."

It didn't take long. They sat on the sofa. He opened the bottle of vodka. He started to go for some glasses. She asked him where he was going. He told her. She said, on second thought, she wasn't that thirsty. He said, y'know, he felt the same way himself. He stared at her mouth, thinking that what he really wanted was a sip of her lower lip. She let him look at her for just the right amount of time for them both to feel just a little bit uncomfortable. But it was the kind of discomfort that could be easily made right.

She took his hand. He squeezed tight and the preliminaries were over. He pulled her to him and kissed her. The kiss was thorough and decisive. She moved inside his embrace, liking the heat of his body, its unyielding strength. She would be the yielding one. He held her closer, then looked in her eyes and told her this had gone far enough.

"Not nearly far enough."

He touched the soft hollow of her throat. "No, not nearly far enough."

Nick and Robin were in bed, the music still pulsing. The sweet, heady scent of jasmine drifted through the open window on a warm breeze. The night sky glowed faintly, framed by the curtains. The candle flickered.

Robin lay in the crook of his arm and realized how well they fit. She hadn't run into one like him in a long while. She sighed. This was dangerous, but she'd worry about it later.

Nick stared into space, his fingers twirling strands of her hair. He was leaning against a pillow. His only pillow, he realized. Which said a lot about his life. It had been many moons since he'd lain quietly with a woman in his arms. There was something soothing about the feel of her body pressing against his, the rise and fall of her breath, the beat of her heart. He wondered what was inside her heart.

They knew they didn't really know each other. They were too careful for that. But as for the chemistry, they had both felt it from their first meeting. They'd been two elements waiting to combine. It had been inevitable... but now what?

He looked at her face. Her features were relaxed, the wariness gone, or at least under wraps. With her intellectual hard-edge softened, she revealed a flowing sensuality that melted all over him. But beneath the open womanliness there was more that she hadn't revealed, hidden regions that he needed to explore.

She turned to him and traced his lips with her fingers. "I think you had your way with me."

He grinned. "I'd call it the reverse, but I sure wouldn't quibble. Maybe a mutual having of ways."

"A mutual having of ways. Yes, I think I'd agree with that."

He saw a wicked glimmer in her eyes that drew him deeper. Her mystery enveloped him, creating an erotic space. He wanted to stay there.

The Indian tape was still playing. She closed her eyes and felt the rhythm roll through her. "That music is wild. Just keeps on flowing."

"An acquired taste—one that can be addicting."

"I know something else that could be addicting."

Nick propped himself on an elbow. "Oh, yeah? Wanna tell me about it?"

"I'd rather show you." She put her arms around his neck and pulled his mouth to hers.

Frank in its wanting, the kiss was heightened by a combination of the known and unknown. They'd tasted enough to want to taste more. It was delicious. Finally they came up for air.

"Pushy broad, aren't you?" He gazed at her.

Robin smiled. "I want what I want." Then she tightened her grip and folded herself around him.

It was as if she were his second skin. Yet not his own skin... unfamiliar territory, uncharted. She had invited him, but only so far. He was intrigued by the challenge.

Robin sensed he was seeking after a part of her that was untouchable. She needed to protect herself and was certain that she could.

Two strong wills entwined, entangled. Secret selves wanting to connect. Afraid where it might lead. Yet already linked in the struggle.

Nick pulled her closer, enjoying her with his lips and teeth and tongue... enjoying the pleasure he was giving her.

"Nick, please..."

"Please?"

"Please... stop."

He stared at her and released his breath slowly, then was still.

His breath seared her skin, yet she shivered.

"That better?"

"No." Her eyes blazed into his.

"Don't you mean yes?"

"Yes. No. Yes." Then she grabbed him and there was no stopping.

He could feel it, feel her rhythms change as he changed his. He let it flow over them. Like a wave that would drown them both.

The early morning breeze was fresh and sweet smelling. The candle was burnt out. And so were they. Wasted. Like never before. Nick dragged himself up, sat on the edge of the bed and then placed a hand on her warm chest. "It's been a long time, Robin."

"Me, too."

He studied her face, as if for memory. "Unexpected."

She answered with a quiet smile. "Me, too."

He sighed and closed his eyes, then opened them. He hated what would come next. "Robin... I've got to split for a while."

"What's up? I thought your duties were here—'babysitting' your journalists? At least, one of them." Her tone was light, but the softness was fading from her face.

He stroked her gently. "See you in a few weeks?"

"A few weeks? Where are you going?"

Nick felt lousy and didn't like the feeling. He wanted nothing more than to escape back into his comfortable old skin where he could control everything with a glib remark. With attitude. He tried. "That's on a need-to-know basis, hon."

She stared, open-mouthed. "Don't be that way, Nick. Not now, not after last night."

She waited. He was silent. She was silent.

She took a deep breath. "Besides, I know where you're going—and I want to come, too."

Nick gave her a sharp look. "How the hell do you know that?"

Teasing. "I have my sources."

He was furious. Hurt, too, if he were to examine it. Was that why she'd showed up here? "No way, Robin. No bloody way! This is grownup time. Go play in some other sandbox."

She regarded him in silence, her heat gone now, her gray eyes cool and opaque once again. She waited for him to get through his anger.

"Find another tour guide to seduce. Maybe he'll take you."

Robin understood how he felt—male ego, possibly more—but there was little she could do to make it better. "One thing has nothing to do with the other." She took his hand and placed it to her lips. Her look was quiet, serious. "Jamal and I were lovers."

"Am I supposed to be jealous?"

"I've got to see him, Nick. This is personal as well as professional."

"And our roll in the hay was professional rather than personal, I guess?"

"It's not like that, Nick. It's just very important for me and my career. I need to see him—and I know he'll see me."

"You know what? I don't give a flying fig about your career—or your 'relationships.' And don't worry, I'm not hurt. Just too damn busy!" Nick picked up his jeans and pulled them on—pulling on his old self as well. He felt back on familiar ground. He flashed her a big smile, self-satisfied, all teeth. "I know this old town won't be the same without me. Maybe I'll see you when I get back?"

"You won't."

He got up and walked to the bathroom. Robin watched his retreating back, then put on her shirt, reflectively rubbing her good luck pin as she stared out the window.

Chapter 17

Hudson entered with a slam. "You're a sad case, Daley. Pathetic, actually. An over-the-hill cowboy still dreaming of one-man operations in the jungle." He shook his head. "Well, say bye-bye to bygone. Your glory days are over."

Nick listened with one ear, his eyes fixed on the computer screen. "That so?"

"Yes indeed, that's so. This is a brave new world. No more improvising. You go through channels, play by the rules. Or you don't play. Period."

Nick seemed oblivious to the silence in the room, his mind on the message he was crafting to send over the scrambled phone lines.

A strange expression dawned on Hudson's face. "I've just received a rather interesting communication from the Director. He seems to know nothing of your extracurricular activities."

Nick shrugged. "Maybe he doesn't think you 'need to know.'"

"But don't worry." Hudson smiled. "You'll have plenty of leisure to contemplate the changing times: you're on 'vacation' now and for the foreseeable future."

Nick smiled back. "That's an oxymoron, isn't it? The 'foreseeable future,' I mean?"

"Not according to the Director, it isn't. He can see very clearly." Hudson cut him a look. "As for my crystal ball, you're not even in it." He paused, waiting for the reaction from Nick that—infuriatingly—never came. "So if they don't can you, your next outpost must be way off my map. And that's all I care about, since I can't afford to have you stirring up my Pakistani pot anymore. Have fun, wherever you land." He turned and walked out.

Nick stared after him, wondering how much he knew. In any case, it didn't matter. He was on his own now. With a shrug, he returned to the computer and typed a number.

A red light blinked on the modem; the words, CARRIER ESTABLISHED, appeared on screen. He began to type.

Jhan turned right at Chowk Yadgar and squeezed the Toyota into a sliver of space along the central square, near a beak-nosed hawker of dates, raisins and walnuts. After they got out, he locked the door. "Before war, we are never having to lock our cars."

She regarded him sadly. "War is a tragic thing, in every way."

The two entered the dusky holstery bazaar with its smells of leather, uncured animal skins and oil simmering in the midday heat. Fierce-looking, craggy-faced men were intent on pistol holsters, rifle slings, ammunition belts and bandoliers—too intent to heed even an unveiled woman in trousers.

Near the end of the lane, Robin and Jhan reached a narrow stall with a corrugated metal roof and a faded awning that brushed his head as they entered. The hot, dark space enveloped them and Robin squinted, trying to get her bearings.

From the shop's dim recesses, a tall, turbaned figure in white approached, a curved, turquoise-studded dagger thrust into his belt. "*Salaam Aleikum.*"

"*Aleikum Salaam.*" Jhan then inquired about his health. "*Khub hasti?*"

The man, Masud, spread open his arms in an expression of abundance. Things were evidently going well in the holstery business. "*Zendeh bashi.*" He hoped Jhan would live forever.

After they completed their expressions of goodwill, Jhan introduced Robin as the person they had spoken about. Masud gave her a hard stare.

Robin extended her hand. Masud took it, but his grip was weak and awkward. She let go quickly, remembering her first—and last—handshake with Jhan. It occurred to her that one could write an interesting piece on cultural relativity, for what might be good manners in one locale was an utter faux pas elsewhere. Faux pas translated to false step and she couldn't afford to make any more.

"What you need, it is my duty to help you succeed. Any information, any advice. From now on."

"Thank you." She nodded gravely. "From now on."

She and Jhan exchanged glances. Jhan thanked him and they left the stall.

The man watched them go, shaking his head.

As they continued through the densely packed lane, Robin could feel trickles of sweat moving down her legs. Her hair stuck to the back of her neck. Her khaki T-shirt was clammy. One thing she'd learned: T-shirt fabric was not cool and it never dried.

The weather was oppressive, but it was not just the heat. It was also the smoke rising from the coals of the kabob sellers, mixing with all the other scents of foods and spices and body and animal odors into some kind of pungent Eastern stew. One that she might still consider exotic even though she knew better.

Robin pulled her damp shirt away from her body, trying to let in some air, but it didn't really help. Her wardrobe, which had seemed so appropriate in San Francisco, was not adequate. She needed some new clothes. She looked at Jhan, apparently unfazed by the heat in his loose tunic and pants. "There's something to be said for the traditional ways, at least in the clothing department."

Jhan nodded. "Yes, sometimes traditional ways are better."

"Maybe so." Robin wiped her forehead with the back of her hand and lifted the sweaty hair off her neck, instinctively pausing to rub her good luck pin. "Isn't the ladies' bazaar around here somewhere?"

Jhan pointed. "Turn left at this corner and you will reach Meena Bazaar. Very nice quality ladies' clothing there."

"Okay, perfect. I think I'll do a little shopping. I'll meet you back at the car." With a nod, she turned and walked away.

He saw her figure disappear into the stream of turbaned men and shrouded women flowing through narrow passageways under dark canvas awnings. Then Jhan headed back through the bazaar the way they had come. As he passed Masud's stall, the man gestured to him. He re-entered, a quizzical smile on his face.

"There is one who must speak with you," Masud said by way of explanation.

Jhan followed him to the rear of the dim shop. Afghan operative Syed Hussein emerged from the shadows and placed a calm hand on Jhan's upper arm. "Very well you have performed your duty. We commend you. And now a final burden we must be placing on your shoulders—" Masud's curved blade plunged into Jhan's upper back, at the base of his neck, while his strong left hand reached around Jhan's throat and forced him further into the knife.

His eyes already glazing over, Jhan stared at Syed Hussein, terminally puzzled.

With a twist of the knife, Masud severed his victim's spinal cord. As the "Ox" stepped aside, Jhan fell forward onto the floor; the turquoise-studded hilt shuddered and then was still.

Hussein gazed at the body and shook his head, his eyes cold but not unfeeling. "We are all called on to make some sacrifice." The communist enforcer glanced at Masud. "They say human skin makes finest leather."

Masud's face reflected his horror at this kind of mutilation that would make the victim's soul unacceptable to Allah. Jhan was not that kind of enemy. "But defiling his body? He will not go to paradise."

Syed Hussein gave him a look of scorn. He was not motivated by tradition or tribal loyalty or religious fervor. He believed in a new system, to be realized in the Democratic Republic of Afghanistan. "Peasant, we no longer follow old ways. We are modern; we are rising above these kinds of superstitions." He paused and then smiled with gentle irony. "So I would like a fine quality holster for my pistol."

Masud swallowed. The sound hung in the silence.

Syed Hussein pulled out a 9 mm Makarov and pressed its cold barrel against the flesh of Masud's nose. "As a murderer, you will be knowing about the need for such things."

Without a further glance, Hussein opened the rear door. The tiny door that forced him to duck and turn sideways in order to exit. Cursing this country of small people, he finally emerged in the alley. Then he rounded a corner and saw the white BMW with blackened windows. He got in the backseat, where Viktor Ivanov was waiting.

Viktor shifted over to make room and regarded him with a raised eyebrow.

Syed Hussein glared at his patron. What did he know of the pitiless reality that was Afghanistan? The ruthlessness necessary to survive? His former KHAD chief—now President Najibullah—had ascended to the peak from atop a pile of bodies. But all Viktor Ivanov knew was his own ambition. What Hussein was called upon to do in the name of progress, he would do with pride, for himself and his honor. He would do it for his poor backward people who understood only cruelty and power. But as for the Russian, he would just as soon spit on his arrogant corpse. Make of him a pistol holder.

Then he remembered that they were using the Russians to advance their own cause. It was a mutual need. He looked at Viktor and nodded. One less obstacle. Syed Hussein spoke softly. "When we achieve victory, we will end war."

Chapter 18

The crescent moon was outshone by stars that dazzled the velvet sky. Yet all this radiance seemed lost amid the endless desert sands. So it was in almost utter darkness that the road curved westward toward the inky mountain horizon. It was a rough, lonely road, crossed only by a wild cat, its eyes bright and hungry. Then two more rays of light cut through the night—the high beams of a speeding vehicle, a brightly painted truck.

CLANG. The driver did not see the red metal gates that suddenly slammed shut. He heard the sound, though, and screeched to a halt. The gates were connected to cement posts on either side of the road. Off to the left, a small wooden structure with an extended roof rose from the hardscrabble ground, its window sending off a faint blue glow. The truck had arrived at one of the customs checkpoints scattered along the government road running through tribal territory.

The guard controlling the gates turned and called inside the post. Two tribesmen emerged, shouldering their rifles as they passed a man sleeping on a wood-framed *charpoy*. He opened an eye and watched them join the sentry, then wrapped his blanket tighter and turned over. The two off-duty guards wore long, shirt-tailed tunics and red badges on their dark caps. The sentry had epaulets on his shoulders, a cartridge belt slung over his chest and protruding belly. They were Afridis, tribal militia hired by the government to police the checkpoint.

"Papers," demanded the sentry.

Nick leaned across his driver Hash, short for Hashmatullah, and handed over the three stapled onionskin sheets that constituted his "visa" to traverse tribal land. The guard studied the signatures, stamps and dates.

Then he showed the papers to the other men. After serious consideration, they exchanged a look, tilting their heads sideways in assent.

While his fellow tribesmen pointedly checked their rifles, the sentry walked back to the post. Returning with a long gray ledger, he made some notes and then handed Nick his papers. "You may pass."

One of the guards kicked open the red gates, while another fired his Lee-Enfield into the air. Whooping with laughter, the three Afridi tribesmen returned to the guard shack, back to their well-worn *Irma La Douce* video, the largesse of a cousin in Kuwait.

Nick's truck lurched forward, his youthful driver rushing through the gears, trying to pick up speed, and they were off again, deep into North-West Frontier Province territory. The plains eventually sloped upward to meet the foothills. The road became rockier, but the truck kept up its pace.

Behind a clump of tall plane trees, a darkened vehicle waited until the truck curved out of sight, then rolled out and began following at a distance.

The night was still, but Nick felt the presence before he heard or saw it: the road was no longer deserted. Sure of his instincts, he turned and spotted the jeep.

"Let's hit it!"

Hash didn't need to be asked twice. Grinning, he floored it. A kid from the Chitrali mountains, Hashmatullah had gone looking for work in Peshawar, where—thanks be to God!—he'd met Nick. He had enjoyed the rewards and excitement of big city life, but this was more than he'd ever dreamed. Just like the cinema!

The jeep accelerated, zipping around corners in hot pursuit. The chase was on. Over the next few miles, it never managed to catch up, yet they were unable to lose it. Nick would not be allowed to disappear into the night.

Rounding the next bend, they were assaulted by a powerful flash of lights. A helicopter was touching down in the middle of the road. Hash slammed on the brakes and shimmied to a stop.

The jeep came to a smooth, gliding halt and pulled off into the shadows.

General Farouk emerged from the halo of lights with a smile and a cigarette. He was followed by a half-dozen armed soldiers.

Nick threw open his door and jumped out. "What the hell?"

"Such a delightful warm evening. I simply could not resist a little spin amongst the stars. But then looking down, I was shocked to observe a speeding vehicle, reckless in its disregard for law or safety. I thought to myself, such dangerous behavior cannot be permitted." He clucked his tongue.

"You're a paragon of virtue, you sonuvabitch."

"But Nick, my dear friend, how was I to know it was your truck?" Farouk's face was long, momentarily disturbed by the quandary of friendship versus duty. He soon resolved the dilemma. "Of course, there is no question. I must face my obligations. I'll have to confiscate it—and its contents."

Shadowed by his soldiers, Farouk walked to the rear of the truck and lifted the tarp. He peered inside and saw two men guarding several crates marked DRILLING EQUIPMENT. Six crates, in fact. His Stingers! The very ones he'd sold to the "Iranian businessman." He didn't have to check the serial numbers—somehow he just knew. Just as he'd known Nick was up to some mischief. What surprised him, though, was the Iran connection. Not exactly America's best friend. He was also puzzled about the Chinese middleman in the deal. Time for a little chat with Mr. Yu.

Farouk walked back to Nick, shaking his head with dismay. "Nick, now I am truly appalled. Of course, we are all supporters of the noble mujahideen… But black market arms dealing? And with such a dubious cast of characters? What would Ronald Hudson say?"

It didn't seem prudent to Nick to throw the black market dealing back at the general. There was nothing to be gained from it, at least not now. So he remained silent.

Farouk stared at the American for a long moment. "Perhaps you will be able to hitchhike back to town?"

Nick looked up and down the deserted road. "No problem. Lots of traffic here."

The jeep revved its engine, spun around and sped off.

General Farouk snapped his fingers. Two of his soldiers ordered Nick's men out of the truck and disarmed them. Then one of them jumped in beside the Stingers, while the other got behind the wheel and drove away. The Sikorsky's rotors began to spin.

Farouk smiled at Nick benevolently. "You are lucky we are friends, so do not worry, I leave you your trusty weapon."

"I'm much obliged, General."

Farouk clapped a hand on Nick's shoulder and then turned his face upward. "When was the last time you looked at the evening sky, Nick?

Really looked at it?" He gestured toward the heavens. "Awe-inspiring, is it not? And so clear."

"Why don't you stick around? Enjoy it."

He smiled again. "I have been enjoying it. Unfortunately, I must push off now. Pity." He strode back to the helicopter, which roared up and away.

Brushing off the dust, Nick watched the Sikorsky disappear into the black night. Then he removed the beeper from his waistband and pressed the button. After the return beep, he slipped the device back on and joined Hash, Amin and Kamal squatting by the roadside. Staring at the forbidding mountain barriers to Afghanistan.

It was not long until an old, tarp-covered Bedford truck—a plain one this time—arrived. Taj leaned out and saluted, his face one big grin.

"Going my way?" Nick inquired.

"You bet, boss!"

Nick hopped into the cab with Taj. Hash and the two Afghans got in back, making space among the supplies, which included several long, burlap-wrapped bundles: the six Stingers.

Taj swerved off the road onto a bumpy track rolling southwest. Except for a few blank-walled villages, the landscape was silent. Empty.

Nick was too wired to sleep. He gazed ahead at the dark, seemingly impenetrable ridges. Somewhere among them, the Kohat Pass connected the Peshawar valley with Afghanistan—like the Khyber to the north. South of Kohat, in this lawless borderland, was the Darra gun bazaar. Nick recalled meeting there with Viktor, when the KGB officer had first "popped the question." The real question was: Who was using whom—or was it somehow mutual?

In Pashtu, "darra" means both valley and pass. Nick watched the valley rising, gradually closing in on itself and narrowing into a pass etched through sheer granite. The road climbed and snaked, ultimately reaching the summit of the Kohat Pass.

An imposing stone fortress controlled the pass from the crest above the road. Fort Mackeson rose as if part of the mountain itself, its granite walls punctuated only by tiny openings, just big enough for British rifles. Now a Pakistani garrison, the fort was named for a colonial commissioner who had met an enemy's bullet in Peshawar and died far from home.

The green Pakistani flag was whipping in the wind from the checkpoint's pitched roof. A drowsy government soldier stepped out, one hand raised for them to halt, the other on his sidearm. He stared at the broken-down truck, typical of the kind used by local tribesmen. The road, running through Afridi territory, was notorious for smuggling and the sentry was under strict orders to search all suspicious vehicles. He peered at the driver and a sleeping passenger.

The passenger was wearing khaki pajamas and a ragged turban that fell over his face. He barely breathed. They were breaking every Pakistani law on the books. Besides the posted regulation—*Foreigners Not Permitted In This Territory*—there was the matter of Nick's official position with the Agency, not to mention his unofficial business. And last, but certainly not least, his lethal forbidden cargo.

"*Salaam Aleikum*," Taj greeted the soldier.

The soldier nodded but did not reply, debating whether to search the lorry or return to his dream. He glanced toward the rear of the vehicle, knowing his duty...

As the man took his first step, Taj reached under his seat and pulled out a carton of Marlboros. "Sorry to be disturbing you at this hour of the night, sir."

The guard paused. "What cargo are you transporting?"

Taj shook his head and shrugged. "Some rice for my family, onions. Fodder for animals. We are poor people." He sighed. "Also my very sick brother, who is having high fever, wrapped in blankets in back. He wishes, if it is God's will that he die, to die at his home." Taj then indicated Nick. "This other brother is working so hard—also tired and sick, but not so high fever. I myself am trying very hard to stay well."

The Pakistani soldier took a step backward. "Put away your cigarettes and good luck." He waved Taj on, then turned back toward his warm post.

Taj drove off, not so quickly as to signal his relief, but quick enough to escape a changing of the guard's mind, or the mind of any other interested party. He glanced at Nick, who circled his thumb and forefinger in approval.

Nick was fond of his agent. Taj's loyalty, cleverness and good humor were a rare combination. His fate would not be that of the loyal Vietnamese and Laotians he'd seen abandoned when America moved on. Nick's life had led him to make certain deals with his conscience, compromises with his Sunday School grandma's values, but not with his belief in taking care of his people.

Taj was unaware of Nick's thoughts and the complex dangers he faced in the company of the tall American. He raced happily down the twisting road. The color of the night was changing, the blackness now washed with gray. Nick looked at the plunging ravine below, all loose tumbling stones and gravel and coarse red clay soil with no moisture to hold it together. He saw the sign on the roadside—*Speed Thrills but Also Kills*—in English and Urdu.

Nick wondered what it was about driving in Asia, at least getting behind the wheel. It was a constant game of chicken, testing the limits, near misses with eternity. He didn't know whether such fatalism was a blessing or not, but maybe it was a state of mind to cultivate. At least, where he was going.

Chapter 19

Mr. Yu's black Mercedes slipped into the shadows behind Lala's Grill and parked at the rear of the Nanking Chinese Restaurant. It was dawn. The trash containers in the dingy alleyway reeked from last night's business, but were not yet overflowing. He stared at the bin on the far right: his property was inside. His wealth.

Yu had been relieved to get the message from Nick. He was advised that the drop would take place during the night, but to avoid suspicion he should not collect it until the following morning. This morning. Anxious, unable to sleep, Yu was ready at the first light of day. He had an eager customer for the dope, a long-time Bulgarian colleague who'd caught the bug of free enterprise.

Yu studied the terrain before getting out and saw no unusual activity. He glanced at his Rolex. It was six in the morning and Peshawar was just waking up. The watch was a Hong Kong imitation, which he kept as a souvenir of his beginnings. Soon he would have a genuine gold one with a diamond face.

In Singapore. It had been three years since his first visit to the small city-state, as part of a company delegation. He'd been struck by how clean and organized it was, how prosperous. At once he could envision a different kind of future. However in Singapore, drug-dealing had a penalty of death. But an arms merchant… that was a respected profession. He was now amassing his venture capital.

He left his car and walked toward the row of trash bins.

Mr. Yu was no longer alone, though. A jeep pulled up and parked behind him. The driver had barely turned off the engine when Lieutenant Rashid jumped out.

"Yu," he called.

Startled, Mr. Yu turned.

"General Farouk is wanting to see you."

"Of course. I am honored." He nodded and hastened his pace.

"Where do you think you are going?"

Mr. Yu recognized the arrogant tone in the lieutenant's voice, the tone that came from position, family, access to power. Everything to which he aspired. He paused. "Oh... I... something I left at dinner last night. It's just over—" He cast his eyes down the alley, then continued on. How could he stop now?

"I am ordering you..." Rashid put a warning hand on his weapon.

His mind racing, Mr. Yu tried to determine how to play this moment. Suddenly a burly man exited the Nanking Chinese Restaurant carrying several large sacks of garbage—terribly smelly, like Shanghai back streets and Guangzhou fish markets. Yu wondered what he was doing at work so early, when he realized that the man was also heading toward the line of trash bins. Possibly to his!

"A moment. Please." Mr. Yu shot an anxious glance at Rashid before elbowing in front of the worker.

"No moment. No please." Rashid was livid at the disrespect.

The worker cursed the foreigner and pushed his way past him to the container on the far right. Angrily, he tossed in one trash bag. Then the rest. The sacks broke open, their contents splattering around.

Stunned, Mr. Yu watched as his package, the key to his future, was buried in refuse.

"NOW." The lieutenant drew his machine pistol.

"Yes, yes." He tried to collect his wits.

Rashid moved deliberately toward Yu. Just then a large garbage truck approached from the opposite end of the alley.

Mr. Yu stared, frozen, eyes sweeping from truck to bin to Lieutenant Rashid's MAC-10 machine pistol.

Waving his weapon, Rashid reminded the restaurant worker that the West Cantonment police station was located down the street. That he should be gone quickly, or he'd find himself locked inside. The man hustled away.

Two bullets spattered in the mud on Yu's best shoes, butter soft black leather lace-ups from Singapore. He smiled nervously, knowing he must stall and somehow extricate himself from this nightmare.

The garbage truck moved inexorably closer.

"I will make you very rich man," he promised, hands outspread.

"I will be rich in paradise when I die an honest man. Now come!"

All of Rashid's hostility at being manipulated by Taj was focused on this fool of a Chinaman. Farouk would pick his bones almost dry—then leave the rest for the vultures—if he ever learned of his nephew's treachery. Rashid's career would be finished and his father destroyed. Rashid knew what it meant to be a powerless nobody in Pakistan. The faces of poverty and terror were everywhere, surrounding you, threatening you, reaching, taunting for you to join them. You would do anything not to be there.

He grabbed the man's arm, pulling him to the jeep. As they drove off, Mr. Yu watched in desperation as a grimy trash collector got out of the cab, lifted the bin on the far right and dumped its contents—Yu's fortune—into the back of the truck.

Nick's truck passed several more checkpoints scattered along the Frontier road after Kohat. These posts were little islands of government authority, in the midst of territory referred to on official maps as Tribal. Even brave men hesitated to go there. The road was lightly traveled, and mostly bad. Sometimes scenic, the tribal borderland became progressively more parched, dry and barren as they continued southwest.

By the time they approached Thal, they were surrounded by a stark, windblown desert. The sense of desolation was heightened rather than diminished by the forbidding sand-colored fortresses dotting the landscape. Fortresses whose walls were topped with thorns and broken bottles, the message clear: Keep Out. In this inhospitable land, outside life rarely dared to intrude.

The brief presence of life that emerged from time to time only emphasized its absence. Once they passed a camel caravan transporting wood from Afghanistan. Later they saw another *kafila* moving westward, kochis returning from winter camps to graze their fat-tailed sheep in cool Afghan mountain pastures. Many of the nomads were on foot, proud, handsome men with kohl-rimmed eyes and waxed moustaches, brightly-dressed women wearing bangles and beads, carrying shoes on their heads for the rocky trails to come. Then suddenly they were gone, seemingly swallowed by the desert, and emptiness again reigned.

As the road got worse, the local militia manning the government checkposts became progressively more interested in the beat-up truck.

Now it was no longer a matter of possible smugglers, but saboteurs they were concerned about. Every vehicle was a potential time bomb of terror.

Just after noon, the sun blazing overhead, they were stopped by a scholarly-looking soldier, wearing a beret and blue sweater with chevrons on the sleeve. A pistol was at his side. He asked Taj a few questions, then glanced at Nick. Taj explained about his ill "brother," while Nick coughed and moaned a few times. The man continued to stare, rubbing his moustache pensively. "This man is needing care."

"I am taking him to family in Miranshah." Taj's expression was grave.

"Yes, yes. So many strangers with family in Miranshah. Amazing how so few families have so many relations visiting, especially in such a remote border town." The soldier raised an eyebrow at Taj. "We Pakistanis are not really that stupid. Lucky for you I am not too inquisitive. But my advice is to hide your 'sick brother' from sight before the next checkpost. Out of sight, out of mind, you know."

With a tilt of the head, he walked back to his post along a path lined with white-painted stones. Once inside, he took his seat in front of the fan and returned to his British spy novel.

As they drove away, Nick and Taj exchanged a glance. Taj pulled off the road as soon as possible, then they got out and moved to the rear. Their three comrades were delighted to be able to stretch their legs and relieve themselves. Taj wrapped Nick in a blanket and placed him between the sacks of food and the weapons. Then Hash climbed back in and settled against a burlap bag of rice.

Kamal and Amin joined Taj up front while Hash drifted off to sleep. So during the remainder of the trip, Nick was alone with his thoughts.

He found himself free-associating about his life. His strongest, most powerful memories, of course, were of Southeast Asia. War never left you. You were indelibly marked with its wounds, but you wore the scars with pride, and someday, when you got old, you'd reflect on what it had all meant.

Nick remembered the people he'd loved and the people he'd killed. Sometimes they were one and the same.

He remembered the woman from Bangkok, the woman from the Oriental Hotel, Trafficante's mistress. She'd contacted Nick several months later, wanting to meet him again, this time in Saigon. He battled with himself, and in the end he went. They met at Givral's cafe under the tamarind trees on Tu Do Street. Their espressos had barely arrived when she commented on the heat... too hot to wear underwear, n'est-ce pas? He stared at her, asking where was her "keeper." She said she'd given him a woman he could not resist. Then smiled, mentioning her nice, cool room at the Continental Hotel. He threw a huge amount of piasters down on the table and they left.

He kicked the door shut behind them and grabbed her. She pushed him away, unbuttoned her dress and let it fall, revealing golden skin and a white silk g-string. With a small nod, she moved to the bed, carrying a small beaded bag. He felt he'd follow her anywhere, but for now, traveled only as far as the white sheets where she awaited him.

She spoke soft musical words he didn't understand, and he was transported to another world.

Later after relocating his mind, he held her, thinking they would marry and live on a white sand beach somewhere forever and ever. She turned to him, saying she had something she needed to ask. Anything, he grinned. Well, it was like this: They wanted Nick to be Trafficante's Laotian liaison, she smiled innocently. After all, he was a logistics expert and certainly not being paid what he was worth. Then another smile, not so innocent. He thanked her but declined; he still had the remnants of a Midwestern morality then. Also, he was pissed off, hurt, his perfect fantasy destroyed. Obviously their romantic interlude in Bangkok was but the preliminary to the setup.

She tried to bribe him with various means at her disposal. Finally, with Trafficante's retribution. He was a good friend—but a very bad enemy. Still no go. At last, she pulled a dagger from the beaded bag and pointed it into Nick's groin. Why not be a rich man instead?

He called her a whore, worse than the hookers at the Dragon Bar. Her eyes flashed, and he watched her draw blood, realizing she wasn't joking. He wrestled her for the knife, and she fought back with blazing intensity. Then suddenly, she was dead.

Anthony Poe, top CIA adviser to General Vang Pao, had fixed it for Nick. Of course as Vang Pao's case officer, he knew Trafficante. The three men formed a triangle of mutual interest: they all owed each other. Now Nick owed Poe.

Tony Poe was a man who offered Lao fighters five hundred kip (one dollar) for a Pathet Lao ear and five thousand kip for a head if accompanied by an enemy army cap. One day he'd ordered Nick to shoot a rebellious seventeen-year-old Hmong soldier. The kid didn't want to be part of their war; he wanted to go home. Nick stared from Poe to the terrified boy. Nick had trained that boy, known him for the past year. He'd brought rice to his family; the old grandmother had mended his pants. Nick said, let him go. Poe reminded Nick about following orders—and the consequences of not following them. Consequences that could be fatal. Nick obeyed Poe's order. The example set, there was no more talk of going home, at least that day.

Poe arranged for Nick to be hired by the Company after he finished his third tour with the Special Forces. Nick was their kind of guy.

There were things you didn't like to recall. You could escape their memory most of the time—until you found yourself riding in the back of some truck, wrapped up like a mummy in a sauna. Thinking about it all. All the wounds you bore from service to your country.

Toward late afternoon, the dirt track came to an end. They had passed their eighteenth checkpoint a few miles back and covered two hundred odd miles. The truck lurched to a halt beside a brushwood hut with a corrugated iron roof, the only evidence of human habitation in sight. Taj hurried around to unpack Nick, who was thankful to get out. There was only so much contemplation a body could handle.

Nick stretched and took a deep breath. The air was dry and hot, the sky brilliant blue. He looked around. The world was the color of dust, perhaps the dust from which the first man sprang. To which we all return. This was God's world, not man's. Other than the shack, the landscape was barren and empty… except for the faint path rising into the mountains of Afghanistan.

Five Afghans emerged from the hut to welcome them, each wearing a hat—embroidered skullcaps, turbans or karakuls of lamb's wool. Two of the men were from Taj's village outside Kabul and the others were southerners from Kalat, near Kandahar. After Nick and Hash were introduced, they all embraced, exchanging the string of traditional greetings. Nick grinned, knowing Taj had seen them just two days earlier in Peshawar when he'd packaged their little tour.

The men had been gardening, driving trucks, doing a little black market trading—anything to earn funds to go back and fight *jihad* against the *Shuravis*. Now they would be paid for fulfilling their hearts' desire! With

Taj's money, they could take care of their families in the camps and return to *jihad* sooner than expected—with brand-new weapons from Darra. The three from Kalat planned to stay and join up with Jamal, who was operating in the Kandahar area, near their homes.

Behind the shelter were a dozen Tennessee-born mules and small but tough Afghan horses. Taj had rented the pack animals from a market that supplied the mujahideen convoys. Big business back in Peshawar.

They helped off-load the truck. Stingers, guns and ammunition, food, fodder for the animals and other supplies. Each man set aside a new automatic rifle for himself, then everything else was placed in wicker nets, balanced and lashed to the animals.

It was sundown. Hash took a compass from his pocket and the men lined up their *patous*, facing west toward Mecca. They kneeled and bowed, palms upturned, foreheads touching the ground. Nick watched, almost envious of the certainty of their belief. After their prayers, they settled down to wait until dark.

General Farouk's office in the Bala Hissar fort was simply furnished, with a fine teak desk, high-backed armchair and antique Bukharan rug. The windows were located high on the walls, allowing plenty of light but no prying eyes. The freshly whitewashed walls displayed framed pages of the Qu'ran, some dating from the eleventh century. The artists were among the greatest Islamic calligraphers, men who married spirit and art. It was a valuable collection. Whatever the state of General Farouk's piety, there was no questioning his taste.

It was commerce that paid for art, though, and if one's business were in disorder, then his collection was in jeopardy. Today there was chaos. On the silk carpet in the middle of the floor were two open crates marked DRILLING EQUIPMENT—their contents straw and rice. Next to the crates, Mr. Yu sat, disheveled and bound to his chair.

Leaning casually against the wall, Rashid smoked a cigarette, watching the proceedings with intense, but veiled interest.

General Farouk was livid, and not only because of the rice he'd impounded instead of Stingers. Nick had played him for a fool, yet it was Yu who would suffer. The "Iranian's" briefcase was open on his desk, its contents as fake as the Bottega label. As he ranted and raved around the room, Farouk periodically lit yet another bill on fire, waving each under his prisoner's nose.

"—Some very big mistakes. Your greed has led you to dangerous areas where only Pakistani hospitality protected you." He lit a hundred dollar bill. "But this, your latest adventure, has gone beyond the limit good manners will bear."

Farouk grabbed the glasses off Mr. Yu and smashed them underfoot. The businessman cringed. "But I didn't know."

"Didn't know? Then you must answer for stupidity, as well as greed."

"Yes, yes, General, of course, but our friendship—"

"Friendship? *Friendship?* Passing counterfeit CIA money is friendship? Conspiring to swindle me is friendship? No: it is treachery. For this, you must pay!" General Farouk turned abruptly to his nephew, unaware of his part in the betrayal. "Rashid. I'd like you to show our Chinese guest the sights... from five thousand meters."

Mr. Yu was also unaware, and Rashid had hopes he'd remain that way. The man was entirely too close to the "Iranian" plot for Rashid's comfort.

"But I cannot see... My glasses—"

"No need to see where you're going."

Hatred and fear combined in Mr. Yu's eyes as he tried for one last deal. "How much? Whatever you ask. I have thousands of dollars, hundreds of thousands."

"Stolen or counterfeit? No matter, I will never know." The general waved his hand in dismissal. "Get him out of here."

Lieutenant Rashid bit back a smile. He would be delighted to take the man up and show him the "sights." He stubbed out his cigarette and then moved to the center of the room to untie the prisoner's ropes.

Mr. Yu rose calmly, having decided he'd find a way to bribe the lieutenant once they left General Farouk's office.

Farouk's anger began to subside. He stared after them as they left. It was not as if he were in this for the money. He was a patriot. His country had special problems and they needed American support. Their situation, however, was precarious. The Soviets had been quite explicit: *Let the Stingers through and we will invade.* So General Farouk knew that disposing of them on the black market was only good politics. It was a pity politics made such untrustworthy bedfellows.

Chapter 20

Taj turned to Nick and grinned as he pointed toward the mist-shrouded valley below. "Afghanistan."

"Afghanistan," Nick echoed with a sigh, wrapping his shawl tighter against the nighttime chill. While Taj saw his homeland, he saw only darkness, the view as murky as their future.

They had left at deep dusk. The sickle-shaped moon rose soon after the caravan set off up the sandy track, their silence broken only by the wind murmuring through the pines, the thumping footfall of the animals, the rustle of their harnesses. One of the locals from Kalat moved ahead, checking for mines. The track led upward through the rocky Waziristan Hills, one of the thousands of secret trails used by tribesmen who either did not recognize the "border" or were oblivious to its very existence.

And now they had reached the crest of the Tochi Pass—in sight of their goal. It was midnight, clean and clear and quiet. To the north, they could see the snow-capped peaks of the Hindu Kush.

The Afghans fired into the air. Home! Taj joined them as they laid down their *patous*. It was the time and place to pray.

When they finished, Taj found Nick still staring in the distance. "I envy you, Taj."

"Why?"

"Your faith."

"Faith is necessary, boss. Without it, how can you live?"

Nick peered in Taj's eyes and saw only peace. He nodded slowly. "What next?"

"We continue till dawn, then rest. From now on we are traveling only by night, so Antonovs do not spot us."

"Mistake us for real mujahideen, huh?"

Taj glanced at the other men. "Some of us are real mujahideen."

"Yeah, they have business here. However, last I heard there is no U.S. presence in Afghanistan. Official or otherwise." He glanced skyward. "So we'd be quite a prize for some lucky spotter pilot. Shot—or captured and paraded on TV. Probably cause some kind of international incident."

Taj smiled. "*Insh'Allah*, no incidents.'"

"*Insh'Allah*, no Antonovs."

Yet they both knew that even darkness was no protection against the AN-26's infrared, night-sighting equipment. The technology was all on the side of the Soviets. So far.

Taj reached under his shawl for a pack of cigarettes and offered one to Nick.

Nick shook his head. "Don't you know smoking is hazardous to your health?"

Taj put a cigarette in his mouth, struck a match under the shelter of his palms and lit up. He took a long inhale. "Where we are going is even more hazardous to your health."

It had been a magnificent sunrise over the desert, the colors rich and deep as jewels. The sky shimmered pink and gold. The Black Hawk helicopter glided and wheeled like a real bird of prey. But this hawk already had its quarry inside its belly. It was ready to spit out the remains.

Lieutenant Rashid turned to Mr. Yu and offered him a cigarette. The man's feet were still bound, but his hands were free. He had used them to straighten his tie, slick down his hair and brush off his suit. His white silk handkerchief was poking neatly from his breast pocket. His head was high, his nearsighted eyes fixed on some inner vision.

"I said, would you care for a cigarette?"

"Cigarette? No... no," he murmured absently, then looked in Rashid's direction. "I thank you for your gift—this beautiful sunrise."

Rashid laughed. "Your last."

"So it is beyond price." Mr. Yu sighed, shaking his head in puzzlement. "You lie to me and mock me. You steal my money. Why have you chosen me for your enemy?" He did not whine. Having come to terms to his imminent death, he projected a sense of dignity he had not achieved before in life.

Rashid glanced up at the pilot, who had on his headphones. The man was loyal—knew when not to listen, not to look. Not to speak. Still, even a loose word could be dangerous... and a loose rotor screw could bring down even the most skilled helicopter pilot. An expensive "accident," but perhaps necessary. He flicked open his gold lighter and lit another cigarette, then grabbed Yu's white handkerchief to wipe the sweat from his forehead. Strange, it was cool up here. Why was he sweating like a pig? "You make dangerous friends, Chinaman. You betray the wrong people: You have chosen poorly." He stuffed the soiled handkerchief back in his prisoner's pocket.

Yu's dark eyes flashed. "You privileged young fool! What do you know of choice, what do you know of necessity? I have fought all my life to escape from the 'iron rice bowl' of socialism. I have struggled to rise and achieve something beyond my stomach, something to remain after me. A memorial to my life."

Rashid stared at him. He could admire Yu's refusal to beg. He was a changed man from the groveling coward in the general's office last night.

After they'd left, Yu had tried to bribe him. Rashid locked him up and said he'd think about it. He arrived before dawn, pretending to agree. They went to Mr. Yu's office and extracted several thousand dollars from the safe. Real, not counterfeit dollars. Yu asked only for enough to buy a ticket to Singapore. Rashid played with him, saying the plane wouldn't be safe, too many soldiers hanging around. A train would be better. Train? To Singapore? Well, to Delhi, then fly. Okay, fine, Yu agreed. Back in the jeep, Rashid said he changed his mind. The airport would be safe enough.

But when they arrived—and Yu saw the green helicopter—he knew. That was when his transformation began.

Yu had clawed his way up, and he now realized this was as high as he was meant to go. Literally. This helicopter represented the pinnacle of his life, its final meaning. He would face it as a wise man.

Rashid experienced a sense of respect that led to a moment of pity. He questioned his task. But there was no question, not really. He could never cross his uncle. He must always behave with care and obey his will perfectly. And perhaps, *Insh'Allah*, his treachery would remain a deep secret. He gazed at Mr. Yu. "Sadly, I know too much about choice and necessity. I know that none of us is having any choice and we are all ruled by necessity. I am wishing only that you are a believer and I could be sending you on to paradise."

"What is your paradise?" Mr. Yu asked seriously.

"Beautiful cool green gardens. Beautiful young perfect virgins. Perfumed, flowing fountains. No desert and no fear." And no loose bowels.

Mr. Yu nodded. "My paradise would have been Singapore. Success. Respect. Sons. But none of them pathetic, dishonorable, cowardly fools like you."

Rashid's head buzzed and his stomach churned as a wave of anger engulfed him. He felt the warmth of his insides begin to flow out. He grabbed Yu by his clean white collar, twisting it as he pulled him to his bound feet, their faces inches from each other. With his other hand, Rashid slid open the cabin door and grabbed on tight. The wind rushed over them. "One thing I must tell you now, Chinaman. It is not true that you die before you hit the ground!"

Then Rashid pushed. He tried to push out all the anger and fear, but all that disappeared was Mr. Yu.

The formidable mountains had blocked the sunrise. But the pale glow of dawn was creeping across the night. They could finally see their feet again, then the stones under their feet, then the patches of snow on the pine-covered hillside to their right and the sharp drop to the shadowy valley below. They continued their march down into Afghanistan.

Soon they reached a wooded ravine. The mist was lifting; the sky turned a cool, muted blue just the other side of gray. A crystalline light washed over the world and everything shone with freshness and promise. The Sulaiman Mountains rose above them, covered by pine, willow and mahogany trees every shade of green. The trail ran along a rushing stream lined with creamy dwarf irises and purple campanulas. The water skipped and sparkled over smooth black rocks. Birds sang and three small quail bobbed their heads with disapproval as they sped from the intruders.

Nick felt the fatigue from the long night creep dully through his body. He didn't want to think he'd become soft, but he sure wasn't twenty anymore. The fast-flowing stream seemed clear and inviting. He knelt on a patch of tall grass and splashed some icy water on his face. He curved his palms into a bowl and could almost see his reflection, then dipped his lips to taste—

"Nick! No." Taj cried out.

Nick looked around and saw the bloated carcass of a dead horse lying upstream. A large brown and white vulture wheeled in the sky overhead.

Nick opened his hands and watched the polluted water fall away. "Thanks, Taj. Now that we're on your home ground, I guess you're the boss."

Taj grinned. "Right, boss."

After prayers they continued back up the trail. Soon they would have to stop for the day and hide, but until then the mood was joyous: the men were home. Or at least on familiar terrain in the case of Hash, the Pakistani mountain man. As for Nick, he had crossed to the other side of fatigue; he was into an action high.

Traveling in Afghanistan was a matter not of time but destination. No one even risked wearing a watch, whose metallic glint might attract an Antonov. What mattered was to forge onward to the next ridge, a place to rest. Before long, they reached it—a narrow plateau overlooking a fertile valley of Paktia Province.

Then gunfire erupted and colorful tracers lit the pale morning sky. From the northern ridge across the valley, mujahideen guerrillas were firing down at a DRA convoy returning to its base in Khost. Retaliation soon followed. Soviet/Afghan artillery hit back, but they were firing blind. They bombarded the mountainside, yet there was no return fire, no sign of life at all. The enemy had melted away. Soon the gunships appeared, big and black and buzzing with anger.

Nick and Taj looked at each other. They could not afford to get caught in the crosshairs. Taj ordered the men to take cover off the bare ridge. They scurried down the slope and into the trees, where they tethered the animals, camouflaging them with brushwood and large khaki tarps the color of the shawls draped over their own heads. Then without a word, Taj set off across the hillside.

By the time the men had settled down to wait, Taj was nowhere in sight. At first concerned, Nick began to wonder if he had misjudged his agent. Had Taj deserted?

Then out of nowhere, he reappeared. Without pausing to explain, he indicated they must follow. Now! As they leaped to their feet, he was already on his way, leading them downhill and toward their left.

They reached a narrow clearing amid the trees and brush. Taj moved to a small mound of stones and leaves, pushing them aside to reveal an opening. He sat at its edge, turned and began to descend. The other Afghans grinned, as Nick watched in puzzlement. Taj gestured for him to follow. Then he disappeared.

Nick looked inside. All he could see was a rough wooden ladder propped against a dirt wall, but leading where, he couldn't tell. He climbed down the shaft into a subterranean passage, dank and moldy. As his feet touched the ground, he felt a tap on his shoulder. Taj took his arm and led him further into the darkness while the others made their descent. Soon Nick could no longer stand upright. Bits of clay crumbled on his head as the ceiling closed around him, and he was forced to stoop. He didn't have a clue what was going on. "What?"

"It is ancient irrigation channel. We are calling such tunnels *karez.*" Taj pronounced it to rhyme with "breeze."

"Manmade?"

Taj lit a match, nodding proudly. "This *karez* was dug through mountain from one 'well'..." He indicated the entrance above and then pointed downhill. "To next, following natural flow of water. We have many, all over Afghanistan. Some still are bringing water. Others are dry, like this."

"Very clever, you Afghans."

"Russians think so, too." His eyes sparkled in the dying flame. "We wait here till dark."

"It already is," Nick replied as the match sputtered out, and they were again enveloped in cold blackness.

Taj cleared a space on the pebbly tunnel floor and they settled in against a wall. They could hear the crunch of footsteps on the ancient streambed, an occasional cough or nervous laugh as another clod of earth fell on someone's head. Nick wasn't enamored of the loose rooftop, but at least he didn't suffer from claustrophobia. He remembered the VC who had run their operations from an underground headquarters. A fairly safe space, considering the alternatives.

When the men joined them, they spread their shawls on the damp ground and lay down to rest. But Nick was too tense and tired to relax. Too many pebbles under his ass. As he listened to their untroubled snores, he became more and more obsessed with everything that could go wrong. His worries turned into troubled dreams, and he slept a fitful sleep.

Suddenly brilliant flashes shattered the darkness. The walls were crumbling around them. The blaze rushed closer. Nick gasped for air, but all his lungs could grab onto was smoke. Then he was shaken by another eruption. White phosphorescence melting into his eyeballs. Red flames searing him.

His brain exploding, Nick was jolted awake. He saw Taj lighting Kamal's cigarette, then his own. "Let's get this show on the road," Nick snapped.

"Right, boss." Taj shook out the match. He seemed rested and good-humored as usual.

The men made their way back toward the pinpoint of light above the ladder. One by one, they climbed up into the dusk, the last man pausing to re-cover the well with stones and leaves. It was the end of their first day in Afghanistan.

The horses were waiting peacefully, but the mules were irritable, impatient at being tied up so long. And hungry, having emptied their feedbags. The men stretched and breathed deeply. They, too, were ready to move on. On to the next valley.

As the light was fading, Nick restlessly scanned the terrain from the track underfoot to the distant landscape. Then something caught his eye. Maybe the shadows on the bluff below were smooth round rocks, but maybe not. Maybe they were huddled figures overlooking the trail.

He nudged Taj and pointed. Taj froze, taking in the scene, then slowly nodded. Nick reached for the small of his back and grabbed his Colt as Taj unshouldered his rifle. After checking their ammunition, they cut off the track, determined to surprise the strangers from behind.

Creeping through the brush, they approached the group. It must have been some dry leaves or a twig, but the noise seemed to resound through the air. Tightening their grips on their weapons, Nick and Taj rapidly covered the last few feet. But they had been overheard. Two shrouded figures, two sets of eyes turned and stared. Taj thrust his rifle in their faces. He ordered them to identify themselves.

Wrapped in a faded blanket, a man spoke. "Our village is destroyed. We were fleeing to take refuge near Kandahar, but were hit by a gunship attack. I, Mustapha, am wounded in my shoulder. I need help to bury *shaheed*, our martyrs. Thanks be to Allah you have arrived." He gestured to the two blanket-draped bodies lying next to him. The other figure sat silently, covered in a brown *burqa*, its only opening a narrow grille at eye-level.

Taj looked at her. "And your wife is unhurt?"

Mustapha bristled. He glared at Taj from under dark bushy eyebrows. "Do not dishonor me, young man."

Nick sensed an unpleasant undercurrent. "What's up, Taj?"

Taj shook his head. "I asked about health of wife. I have been in Peshawar too long. Such things are not proper."

Nick smiled slightly. "Shocking disrespect."

"That is what husband is saying. So what are you thinking we should do? He wants our help."

Nick shrugged. "Can't leave 'em like this."

Taj nodded, knowing that without proper care of the remains, the soul would have no body on Judgment Day. He turned to Mustapha. "We will help bury your martyrs, then you may travel with us as you like. Our group, too, is going to the Kandahar region."

"We are most grateful," Mustapha said, with a sideways tilt of his head.

While Nick sat perched on a rock keeping an eye on the Afghan couple, Taj scurried back up to the trail and told the others to join them. They tied down the animals, who went ravenously to work on a patch of meager grass. The men then pitched in to dig the hole. The earth was dry and they had no shovels, but their knives were gradually able to hack away a depression large enough for two men to await eternity.

By the time the grave was completed, twilight had given way to night. The stars shone fiercely overhead. They looked uncomfortably at one another. Taj fidgeted, staring at Nick.

"Now what's the problem?"

"I am sorry, Nick, but it is too late. Burial is forbidden at night. This is our custom."

Nick shook his head with a sigh. "When in Rome."

They decided to complete their duty at sunrise and try to make up some time under the cover of early morning mist.

Everyone was awake well before the coming of the sun. The corpses were placed in the grave, feet facing Mecca, so the bodies could sit up and face the Holy City on Judgment Day. At the first ray of light, each man tossed in a few handfuls of dirt. Then the hole was refilled and rocks piled on top. A small green martyr's flag was wedged into the mound, and the caravan continued.

Chapter 21

A shot cracked the gauzy stillness. The men froze... and listened... as the echo died away, leaving only silence in its wake. They were safe, at least for now. Although they were pushing their luck, traveling past dawn.

The stony, snaky terrain was treacherous on a downhill. This was the killer Sulaiman Range, second only to the Hindu Kush in its awesome stopping power. The path was marginal at best, imaginary at worst. Nick thought of Kipling's description, "Never a road wider than the back of your hand." Traveling in Afghanistan was literally a matter of peaks and valleys. Up to ten thousand feet, down to six thousand, back up to eleven. Freezing morning and night, sweltering at midday. The going was grueling and relentless, but when you finally crossed the mountains, you would reach the rust-red desert sands—and they were endless.

In the dim light, both men and beasts struggled to keep a foothold, moving from rock to gravel to fine white dust, soft and deep enough to engulf their feet. Suddenly one of the horses stumbled and fell, twisting its ankle. It stared at them, helpless. The men exchanged glances. There was silence... then Taj stepped forward with his rifle. He nodded at the horse and fired, knowing the sound would place them in jeopardy, yet also knowing they could not leave the animal to its lonely fate. More silence, then they moved on.

Soon the mist began to part. They were exposed now and in dire need of refuge. Their pace quickened as they headed down the trail, passing beneath a shady green knoll. There, tucked against the steep mountain wall, was a straw-covered mud and rock hut, the local *chai khana*. Sheltered by spreading walnut and mulberry trees, the teahouse brought whoops of delight from the men. While Mustapha and his wife waited off by themselves, the others tromped inside.

The dirt-floored room was covered with an ancient carpet and cushions. The men sank down with relief, oblivious to the bees' nest in one of the rafters and the glassless window covered by floral curtains. They nodded approvingly at the painting of a Russian jet being shot down by an AK-armed mujahid.

The blackened samovar was steaming over the fire, and a young boy handed each traveler a chipped china cup. He apologized that he could not offer the traditional black *chai-sia* with milk, but milk was hard to come by these days. No one seemed to mind. The boy moved around the circle, spooning out brown sugar and serving green *chai-sabz*. He laid out a platter of biscuits and *kishmish*—dried fruit—then busied himself refilling their cups as soon as they were empty. The tea was always hot and always sweet.

The men swapped jokes and stories; it was like a party. Nick faded in and out and told Taj not to bother translating. The war seemed far away. He felt almost narcotized by the comfort.

They passed the day talking and dozing. Nick went outside once to relieve himself and saw Mustapha and his wife seated against a tree, staring in the distance. He thought they must be mourning their losses. Suddenly the war returned. It was everywhere; there was no escape anywhere in Afghanistan.

They set off again at dusk. The boy watched them go. He was only passing time until he, too, was old enough to join *jihad*. That day would come soon. And soon, he would avenge his parents' death.

The trail led to a boulder-strewn valley that became a raging river in those years when heavy snows were followed by a hot spring. Now spring had long passed. The hills were semi-barren, sandy, covered only by sparse scrub. And yet ahead under the pale night light, they could see still another fearsome range of snow-capped mountains.

They crossed the mountains. Their movements became instinctive; each step led only to the next step and the next. The meaning of life became the placing of one foot in front of the other. Reality was to endure.

They had left the safe mountain hideouts of Paktia and Paktika Provinces and were now halfway down to the Kandahar plains. Shortly before dawn, they reached a flat open plateau. No teahouse, no safe place to halt. The ground was crisscrossed with fresh tank tracks. It was a wasteland of charred bushes, littered with empty Bulgarian ration cans, cartridges and clips from a recent battle.

Taj conferred with the men, who pointed west toward Kalat. "Big Soviet base," he explained to Nick. "This is not a good place to be."

Through his exhaustion, Nick smiled briefly. "That's what we call an understatement, my friend."

The party had to find a place to halt for the day, so they pressed on across the plateau and soon saw the Lora River. Their spirits rose and they marched more swiftly, even the animals. From a silver strip winding through the tawny countryside, the river grew larger... and then the caravan reached its barren eastern banks. Fed by the massive Sulaimans, the rushing water sparkled in the early morning light. Curving along a rocky hill, the western banks were overhung with low bushy trees and appeared to provide good shelter. They would just have time to attempt the crossing.

Nick raised an eyebrow and looked at Taj. "Do we swim, 'boss'?"

Already digging in the supplies, Taj grinned. "I have brought boat."

"This I gotta see."

"You will be seeing soon."

Taj began calling out commands. The men knew exactly what to do and soon had inflated four cowskins, which they lashed to a wooden pole frame—a traditional design used in these regions for centuries. They attached two rough oars to the *jaala* and were ready to go. Hash had crossed many a mountain river in such boats, so he and Taj carried it to the rushing waters for a trial run.

They pushed off and Taj rowed the thirty meters to the other side, arriving slightly downstream of the embarkation point due to the strong current. Hash stayed to begin a fire for tea, while Taj returned for the next load of men and supplies.

As Taj landed, they heard a faint drone. In the distance they saw what appeared to be a tiny dragonfly, but the drone grew louder and the "dragonfly" larger. The gunship drew ominously close. Nick and Taj looked at each other. They were exposed. There was no choice but to continue the crossings, trying to reach shelter on the other side.

The gunship was interested in Nick's group, but not in the way they feared. It had other business. Business at the highest level.

Colonel Viktor Ivanov did not care for war. He preferred wearing nice suits with clean shirts, but today he was in uniform. Three stars on his red and gold shoulder boards, shiny black jackboots. The previous day he had flown from Peshawar to Kabul to instruct some local agents and then shuttled down to Kandahar this morning. As he flew over the barren region, he found it desolate and ugly, utterly lacking in poetry. Were he not an atheist, he would have thought God had forsaken this place. The bandits deserved their wasteland.

He looked down at his convoy. The payoff was coming. Trained by the Executive Action Department of KGB's First Chief Directorate, Ivanov was a specialist in *mokrie dela*, the "wet affairs" of assassination and sabotage. Sometimes "executive action" was the only means to achieve political results, but it required subtlety and patience to develop such an operation. His success in directing it would enable the Soviet Union to leave Afghanistan with honor. There would be no limit to his advancement. Chairman General Petrov would make room for him at the top, perhaps even recommending Viktor as his eventual replacement. No more dusty Peshawars, only the good life in Moscow and sophisticated European capitals, the finest of suits and cleanest of shirts. That was the life he merited. A life in the center of the Center, as predicted for him by the renowned Georgian psychic.

With a smile, he ordered the pilot back to the base, where he would catch a return flight to Kabul. He was looking forward to a drink in his hotel suite. And there was the pretty desk clerk—no one like her in Peshawar. With two hundred rooms and eight guests, the Kabul Inter-Continental took great pains to insure the comfort of its guests.

Nick and the others crouched on the eastern bank as the gunship circled overhead, but it must have taken them for peasants because they were not attacked. While Taj continued to ferry back and forth, the fearful pack animals were coaxed into the swirling waters.

At last Taj returned for the final trip with Nick, Mustapha and his wife. As they were midway across, one of the mules stumbled and knocked Taj into the river. The *jaala* capsized and they all fell in.

Taj was struck in the head by a corner of the frame. He reached for the boat, but the current was already carrying it away. Dazed, he could only tread water. Mustapha grasped an oar with his good arm and turned to help his wife. But encumbered by her *burqa*, she was being pulled under and down river. Mustapha was unable to save her. He stared at Nick in desperation.

A strong swimmer, Nick struggled against the forceful currents but found himself losing. He fought harder, slashing the tumbling waters with his arms, twisting and kicking, filling his lungs when he could. Finally he resurfaced near the woman, who was choking and gasping for air. He grabbed her shoulder and upper arm. The current tugged her away. He yanked her back, but she was like dead weight with all that fabric. Then it ripped, exposing her face... Robin's face!

"What the hell?" he finally sputtered through a mouthful of water.

Robin spit some of her own water back at him. "Peshawar just wasn't the same without you!"

He was still holding her, their bodies entangled. They could go down together and he wouldn't care. He stared in stunned disbelief. What the hell was she up to?

Robin was too exhausted to deal with him now. Mustapha was thrusting the oar her way and she reached for it, gulping down air as he pulled her toward shore. Turning, she panted her thanks to Nick. "My hero."

Nick was staggered, his mind blown by her deceptions. Her treachery. Her betrayal. It seemed like he'd been there before. Then he let the thought go; now was not the time. He dogpaddled in place, trying to sort it all out. He ran through the entire scenario in his head while watching them struggle toward the riverbank. Only when he had made some sense of it did he swim to safety himself.

He reached land about the same time as Taj, who had been jolted by the scene in the river and was trying to figure out why the woman seemed familiar. But Nick ignored his quizzical glance and strode directly to the clump of pomegranate shrubs where Robin was trying to dry off in privacy. He stood there drenched, his eyes blazing.

Defiantly, she returned the look. "Well, don't drip all over me."

"If I want to invite you, I invite you. But I didn't—and I don't. No one makes plans for me—I make my own. Now, what are yours?" Nick knew the force of his rage and part of him wanted to let loose. Make her pay. He'd been there before, too, and that was not a place he wanted to be. Not now. He held himself together through sheer force of will, knowing that violence was a tool. *Use it or let it use you.* He had more important things to do.

"No change. I'm continuing on." Robin spoke casually, almost flippantly, not wanting to engage with his anger. What did he expect? That he was the only one with an agenda? She could match him in determination, and he couldn't handle it. Couldn't handle an independent woman. Sure, there was something between them—they both knew it—but it was also an "all's fair" kind of a thing. Was it love? Or were they just in different wars?

"Not with me, you're not. No way. You're going back."

"I never go back, only forward." Her lips curved in a half-smile.

"Not with me, you're not," Nick repeated.

Her smile faded. They stared at each other implacably. Heatedly.

"You're one sneaky bitch."

"Well, you're a cold bastard. I was convenient you used me—"

"'Used'? You're talking to me about used? You got a good offensive, hon. Ever considered the NFL?"

Robin's shoulders loosened. Her eyes softened as she met his. "Come on, Nick. It'd be too quiet without me."

Chapter 22

At dusk the convoy set off again, despite the shocking turn of events. Her *burqa* roughly mended, Robin disappeared back inside even though it was not quite dry. The stunned Afghans kept their distance, for in their culture a man did not travel with a woman who was not his wife or close relation. Although Hash's upbringing was equally traditional, he'd seen a bit of the world since working for Nick in Peshawar and yet he, too, found the situation troubling.

The same could be said for Taj. By then he had recalled seeing her in the car with Nick after tailing Mr. Yu to the mosque. It was evident, though, that Nick had been as surprised by her appearance as all of them. Except Mustapha, who was viewed with distrust. Taj kept his own counsel, but the others could tell that he knew more than he was saying. In any case, they were quite sure she was a foreigner. Possibly an *American?* Nick, now wearing a turban and shawl, kept his words to a minimum. Naturally, Mustapha was not talking. And his "wife" spoke not at all.

By dawn they were descending the final range of foothills, each deep in his own thoughts. Then in the distance, they could make out the ancient minarets of Kandahar, named for Alexander, or Iskandar, as he was known in the region. The hills sloped into a desert plain that surrounded the town. As they entered the desert, the heat rose to envelop them. The walled compounds, the unpaved roads, the soil, the dust—everything was the color of sand, except the neat green fields and scattered flashes of brightness from women who abruptly covered their faces at the sight of strangers. The mules tried to stop to graze, but were prodded onward.

Led by Taj and one of the locals, they climbed a stony rise overlooking the fields outside a low-roofed mud village. To the north, south and west, they could see more village oases scattered through the arid plain. "Jamal's territory," Taj told Nick.

Nick looked down on a nearby wheat field. A young boy was driving a pair of yoked-together bullocks round and round in circles, their hoofs throwing up a haze of chaff. Beyond were rows of grapevines, melon fields and leafy groves of apricot, peach, fig and walnut trees. The world seemed timeless, life continuing as it had for thousands of years, despite invasion, despite hardship—despite even despair. The Afghan people had no choice but to endure.

Next to the field, a small bomb crater had been turned into a fishpond bordered with pink-flowered shrubs. "Idyllic," Nick muttered.

"We are using everything." Taj smiled quietly, then pointed toward the gully below.

Nick stared. The rocks on which they stood curved around the gully to form natural northern and eastern boundaries; smaller rocks and some trees and shrubs protected its southern exposure. An irrigation channel running through its center carried water from the foothills to the village fields. The stream, lined with young saplings and tall blue daisies, was fast flowing and fresh. Nick and Taj looked at each other, then nodded. Camp. The area, about twenty meters long and fifteen wide, offered good security, requiring only a guard where they now stood.

"Taj, you organize the men and start setting things up. I'll go scout out a hiding place for the Stingers and other weapons."

Taj appeared disturbed. "We must make separate sleeping area for Robin. The men will be not be relaxed with her near."

"I don't care where she sleeps."

"And what about her 'husband'—Mustapha?"

"We'd better keep him around in case I decide to send her packing." Nick scowled.

Taj stared at his face. He had never seen it so cold and dark. The woman had caused Nick trouble and pain; maybe he loved her, maybe he hated her. Taj was not sure. He knew from the cinema how different were the ways of Western men and women.

Later that day after they were settled and rested, Nick and Taj prepared to make an initial foray to the village.

Robin approached, wrapped in a long black shawl. "I'm coming, too."

Nick was still furious at her manipulations, but would not give her the satisfaction of a battle. She was there; he didn't care what she did now. He regarded her coolly. "Where's the *burqa*?"

"Still wet. Those damn things never dry! You try marching all night in a wet shroud."

"Next time maybe you'll make different vacation plans. Until then, keep the veil on and your mouth shut."

Robin shrugged her assent. Besides, Nick was equally camouflaged. Yet he didn't seem in costume. He appeared so at ease in this environment, his suntan and dusty face only adding to the effect. The man was a chameleon. What was he really up to?

The sun was low in the sky as they drew closer to the village and entered its shadowy maze of blank earthen walls and crooked little alleys. From inside gates and around corners, suspicious eyes followed them. Even in normal times, each village was a world unto itself; trust was a scarce commodity. Now during wartime, fear was at a heightened level. Informers were everywhere. No one arrived unknown and unannounced. And no mujahideen traveled with women. So these two strangers must not be mujahideen—and therefore, not friends.

Nick, Taj and Robin found the local *chai khana*, always the social hub and center of gossip, and so a good place to inquire about Jamal. The hut was dark and smoky with an ancient copper kettle bubbling on a fire, the dried poppy stalks used for fuel stacked beside it. A chicken scratched the dirt floor. A cage held a trained fighting partridge. Three elderly male patrons stared.

The proprietor, a toothless old man in an embroidered skullcap, approached the newcomers. He wore a flowing, striped robe over his shoulders, its sleeves dangling to his knees. "*Chai?*"

"We thank you kindly, but next time," Taj replied. "We are looking to find Commander Jamal."

The man's face shut down. "I know no Jamal."

The three patrons turned their backs and continued sipping their tea.

Nick looked at Taj, who shook his head imperceptibly. You couldn't force these people. They walked back outside. Taj decided to search out the bazaar and try there. He set off down a dusty lane, followed by Nick, with Robin trailing a few paces behind.

Some of the houses were still standing, their flat roofs covered with corn and fruit drying in the sun. Some had suffered partial damage—black scorchmarks, window frames blown in, stone walls fractured. But others were destroyed—charred timbers reaching to the sky, bombed-out rubble returning to the earth.

Two small girls in bright yellow with only two legs between them looked up from the mudcakes they were baking and smiled in shy curiosity. Women peeked through clutched veils as they carried water or fruit from the fields. Old men gossiping in the late day sun stared without losing a beat. The bazaar was a poor one, offering bare necessities, no consumer goods. A baker piled stacks of warmly-scented naan; a butcher laid out a neat array of animal parts. Flies swarmed everywhere, droning insistently.

Then another insistent low drone gradually separated and became louder.

The Antonov emerged from cloudless blue. Nick and Taj looked at each other, only too aware what the appearance of the reconnaissance plane meant. Taj took off toward the edge of town. Nick grabbed Robin's hand and followed. Desperate for a place to hide.

The four-engined spotter plane was flying low and slow through the clear desert air. Raid commander Major Grishkin and his two photographers would have a perfect view of the upcoming battle. While his last encounter with Jamal had been from the distance of a gunship, today Grishkin hoped to see the whites of the man's eyes—and the red of his blood. It would be a major offensive, the most important of his career, as well as a supreme demonstration of Soviet power.

His commands were two-pronged, military and political. Under orders from his general, he would punish the villagers for their part in Jamal's deadly raid on the Kandahar jail. His orders from GRU military intelligence were more specific: Nail Jamal. Grishkin felt this would be his day of triumph. He bit his cuticle as he stared at the village below. Those fools had helped the bandits. Now they would suffer.

He switched on the radio. "Commence attack."

Major Grishkin turned his gaze toward a village to the southwest. Four Hind helicopters swooped down like hawks, laying smoke trails to guide the air strike, warming up the area with some preliminary bombing. Red flares slashed the chalky blue skies. Grishkin felt a surge of excitement.

Then they came, the two Sukhoi SU-25s shrieking through space, diving to send their cluster bombs hurtling to earth, then climbing again, soaring weightless and free. Grishkin smiled as he watched the fragmented bomb explosions casting up flames, smoke and dust. He'd enjoy making it last, the pleasure of sticking it to those peasants and their bandit friends.

Hearts pounding, Nick, Robin and Taj raced away from the crumbling, mud-brick walls, searching for cover. The ground was shaking beneath their feet, wave after wave of explosion. Then a barefoot young boy rushed up to them. He stared at Robin, grabbed her veil and pulled her along with him. Nick and Taj ran after them until the boy stopped at a four-foot deep trench planted with grapevines.

They pushed aside the branches and climbed inside, huddling together as the reverberations became more powerful. The thunder overhead was growing louder, the blasts nearer. The boy curled against Robin in terror, eyes fixed upward. She gazed into his little face and then back at the darkening sky.

There was nowhere else to look. Nick waited for the inevitable. The jets howled closer, releasing more bombs from beneath their wings. Clouds of white and gray smoke rose. Only then, slightly out of sync, came the crack of the explosion. He felt Robin grip his hand... her nails digging deeper as, suddenly, a goat crashed through the branches into the trench. It was moving in circles, bleating in fear. The boy whispered to the goat, calming words they did not understand, but soon it settled at their feet. Robin released her grip, smiling ruefully at Nick. He did not smile back.

Their double rotors a faint blur, two gunships appeared, hovering overhead—one higher, one lower—secure in their invulnerability, firing rockets and cannon with deadly efficiency. Nick had been up there. Now he knew what it was to be down here.

Another, larger helicopter appeared. Dropping orange flares throughout its approach, a MI-8 troop carrier landed in a corn field, unloading two dozen blue and white T-shirted Spetsnaz commandos and Afghan conscripts. Carrying portable radio units, they fanned out through the area, machine gunning, bayoneting, burning.

Nick pulled his automatic, not knowing if they were the focus of the raid or merely "innocent bystanders."

Then a cry rang out. "*Allahu Akbar!*" God is great!

Hidden mujahideen assaulted the invaders with grenades and rifles. The invading troops dove for cover, strafing the landscape with their

AK-47s and 74s. The smoky air was filled with the flat pop of shells, the hissing, the crack.

A stocky, suntanned commando hit the rocky ground with a curse. Spotting a glint of metal in a nearby trench, he nudged his comrade. They crawled toward it, aiming their assault rifles inside. But as they fired, they themselves jerked into spasms, spattering bullets everywhere.

One of their bullets hit the boy. Hearing his cry, Nick looked at him and then at Robin's stricken face. Nick leaped up to fire on the attackers... but they were already lying dead alongside the trench. He turned to see a tall mujahid lowering his rifle over their bodies. Their eyes met. Before moving for cover, the man stepped closer and stared at Robin, now unveiled. A burst of gunfire forced Nick to duck back down. When he arose, the phantom Afghan was gone. Again.

Robin gazed after him. "Jamal," she murmured.

She turned to the boy, cradling him in her arms. He touched her cheek and smiled sweetly, then cried out once. She watched him die. Where did the light go? The life? Robin had never looked at death before, and didn't know how to feel. Better not to feel. Until it was over.

Taj whispered, "*Shaheed*. He is now martyr."

Robin glanced up at Taj... Nick. She shook her head mutely.

"This is what you wanted. Right?" he demanded.

She saw the criticism in his eyes. He was telling her this was real, not an idea. Real blood. Real danger. She understood now: How could you prepare yourself except by being here? In the middle of war.

She nodded. "Be careful what you wish for."

Mouth tight, Nick handed her his automatic. The goat ran back and forth in panic, then climbed out, apparently deciding to take its chances elsewhere. Nick and Taj grabbed the two dead men's AK-47s and their extra banana-shaped clips. They set the rifles on AV—automatic—then hunkered down in the trench, waiting for the onslaught.

Another gunship flew toward the battle. Inside, Colonel Viktor Ivanov yelled into his radio. "You must halt this attack! Immediately!"

From the Antonov, the surly words of Major Grishkin crackled back to him. "We have sighted the bandit. We are too close to stop now. When I get him, I halt. Not one moment before!"

Because of Jamal's elusiveness, the operation to roll over his southern strongholds had been developed in top secrecy. Viktor had only learned of it last night on his return to Kabul. He set aside his own plans—the relaxing vodka, the Inter-Continental desk clerk—and began calling in favors. He was determined to protect his own operation from another heavy-handed military attempt on Jamal.

Now in the air over Kandahar, he had no doubt who would prevail. He was higher ranking than Grishkin. And KGB. "Then you face very early retirement. I have an operative down there on a mission of highest priority!"

Major Grishkin broke into a sweat. His teeth cut through a sliver of remaining nail on his index finger. He reached the skin and drew blood. He had no recourse; his general was back at the air base in a drunken stupor, trusting Grishkin to handle it, or not caring.

He swallowed hard. "I wish you much success, Colonel," he said belligerently, trying to save some face with his crew. Although now, what did it matter?

"And you, Major." Viktor smiled slightly.

After flipping off the transmission switch, Grishkin slammed his fist into the metal wall. "*Yeb tvoyu matz*, Ivanov!" he cried out in anguish. Fuck your mother!

He was oblivious to the pain. Oblivious to the stares of the men. It was all over. He could not disobey a superior's order, but GRU had warned him that this would be his last chance. Either succeed or fail. That KGB bastard had just destroyed his career.

Nick and Taj knew their hiding place had been revealed, that more soldiers would be soon following. They waited for the next onslaught. Nick glanced at Robin, who was staring dully at the boy's body. He wondered what was going through her head. And what the hell was she doing here? Independent or not—a woman had no place in the war zone. Russian soldiers were animals. If they found her... He shuddered inside. Should he kill her before letting them take and brutalize her? He contemplated the horror of this choice, and prepared himself to act.

The moments seemed endless... but at some point they noticed the sounds of battle fading—the rolling thunder, the thumps, the pounding. There were no more flashes or crashes. The earth stopping shaking and rolling. Now the only sound was one of mute terror, the absence of sound caused by shock and despair. It was an eerie stillness that had settled over the land, finally broken by the anguished braying of a donkey.

Nick stuck his head out and saw the smoky wake of departing Soviet air power, taking with it the blue of the sky, the green of the earth, leaving but charred remains.

Taj rose grimly. He had wrapped the boy's body in his *patou* and was holding him in his arms. "I must try to find family. He must have proper burial." This could have been his own son, he knew.

They stood and watched Taj go in silence. Silence was the only response to what they had experienced. Robin let her breath out slowly.

Nick turned to her. "Put the goddamned veil back on. *Now.*"

Robin gripped the dark fabric, trying to stay in control. "I hate this thing!" she lashed out. "I can't run, can't see—can hardly breathe."

"Get used to it!" Nick barked. "If a spy reports a Western woman, it'll bring down another attack. I don't suppose you'd want that on your conscience, too."

Robin glared at him through the haze and dust and grudgingly draped the *chadar* back over her head and body. At least it let some air through—unlike the *burqa*. That was like a tomb. "I'll live with my own conscience, thank you. Besides, who are you to talk—Mr. Vietnam?"

Nick shrugged. He didn't want to get into it with her, didn't have the will or desire or energy. As he regarded her shrouded form, the anger and fear started seeping away, and a sly smile began. "Anyway, your face is dirty and your hair's a mess!" She didn't respond. He patted her ass. "I know it's under here somewhere."

She shook her head in disgust. How could he be so damn callous? "Very funny. Keep your rotten hands off me."

"In these parts, hon, you'd be considered my property," Nick gloated, finding relief in the banter.

"Over my dead body!"

"It would've been dead if it weren't for me."

"*You?* It was Jamal who saved us!"

"Jamal, huh? Too bad he didn't stop to say hi. I could've used the intro."

"Oh, that's why you're trying to butter me up. Typical." She paused. "I think he already knew we were here."

Nick stared at her. Could she be right? Had Jamal just happened to be in the right place at the right time? Or had he gone out of his way to save them? If so, why? In any case, they owed him now. And Nick didn't like the obligation.

The dusk began to close upon them. Robin lapsed into a preoccupied silence as they headed back to camp, picking their way amid the debris of war—stones, glass, metal bomb fragments, smashed fruit and shattered tree stumps. She felt him reach for her arm and shrugged him away.

Fine, let her stumble, he thought. Let her go through her changes alone. You never got used to it, though.

It was awesome and terrible and surreal. They passed a neat row of fresh craters. An uprooted, reeking outhouse. A padlocked door connected to nothing. A headless chicken covered with flies, frantically running—nowhere. A dying goat leaking intestines. Robin stared, wondering if it was their goat.

Overhead, vultures were cruising.

Frightened villagers carried their wounded, returning home from caves, trees, ditches, whatever shelter they'd been able to find. But whatever it was, wasn't enough. Nothing was safe and the familiar had become strange. Terror was in the air—along with the foul invasive odors of gunpowder, rocket and aviation fuel, burnt fields and flesh.

Nick scowled. "Maybe it's a good thing you can't breathe."

"Yeah." She nodded briefly.

He paused to survey the scene. The valley was ripped apart, as if by simultaneous hurricane, earthquake and fire. "War," he said softly, then turned to her.

Robin read his dark eyes and realized he wasn't as insensitive as he seemed. Tough, maybe—callous, no. She looked down and whispered, "I was scared."

Nick shrugged. "Who wasn't?"

They studied each other. Time for a cease-fire?

"Thanks, Nick. I know I've made it rough on you."

He shrugged again. "Well, you're here now. I only hope you get what you want."

Her smile was quiet, her eyes thoughtful. "I hope we both do. If that's possible."

It was dusk as they approached camp. Almost safe. Then angry voices hit them. They froze, casting their eyes about wildly. Through the dim light they could make out a group of Nick's men gesturing and shaking their fists. Mustapha was shouting back at them. As Nick and Robin rushed closer, they saw the guns—and then a wounded Soviet soldier with close cropped hair and dirt-streaked face. Blood soaked through the left side of his blue and white striped T-shirt.

The prisoner's frightened eyes locked on to Nick's. "*Gospodin, zhalosty!*"

"Sorry, don't speak Russian."

Robin stared at him. "He looks scared to death."

The men's hatred for the Soviet enemy was palpable. Nick didn't need to know the language to comprehend the curses.

The prisoner acted out how he had played dead until the Russians left. He pointed at himself. "Alexei." Then he pointed at the hammer and sickle on his belt buckle and shook his head no. He fell to Nick's feet, pleading for mercy.

Taj came trudging back, sick at heart from his bitter errand. He had experienced the parents' anguish, and his mood was black and unforgiving. When he saw the prisoner, he stared in revulsion. This man stood for all who had destroyed their land, killed their children. "We do not want *Shuravi* here! We give him to villagers—or get rid of him ourselves."

Nick looked down at Alexei and then back at Taj, normally sunny, now angrier than he'd ever seen him. Nick spoke firmly. "We'll care for him until we make contact with Jamal. He may want him for a prisoner exchange. As local commander, he'll decide."

The men exchanged dark glances.

Nick turned to Robin. "Take a look at him, will you? No one else will."

She gazed at the terrified soldier. "I'll see what I can do."

They all went quickly to sleep, to escape the day, but not their nightmares. Robin had never smelled death. Its stench was invading her dreams, acrid fumes of cordite, foul odors of burning and rotting flesh.

A hand clamped down over her mouth. Startled, she bit hard and kicked wildly. She saw a bushy moustache and then only darkness as a larger hand covered her eyes, only to be replaced by a cloth. Another cloth was tied over her mouth, then two pair of hands grabbed and bound her. Sandals were slipped on her feet.

She had an instant's absurd relief that she had fallen asleep in her clothes, but realized it didn't matter. Dressed, undressed, she was helpless. There was no one to turn to. She had been convinced that somehow she'd make it... get out of here alive, live to be an old lady with great exploits under her belt. Memoirs to write. Now she realized what an innocent fantasy that had been. How completely isolated she was. And alone. Inside a primitive country where a woman was no more than a piece of meat.

Chapter 23

Overpowered, bound and blindfolded, Robin was carried from her tent by the two husky captors. She went limp. The fight had left her. Maybe she'd have another chance later. But for now she was helpless.

One of them slung her over his shoulder and they moved swiftly through the dark fields. She tried to remain alert but was disoriented and time seemed endless. Maybe it was minutes, maybe longer, but at some point they stopped… and were suddenly carrying her down a ladder. The air became musty and heavy. Then one ahead and one behind, they dragged her along.

She fought to keep her wits about her. All she knew, she was in some kind of tunnel. She had to crouch to avoid banging her head. She felt the walls closing in on her. It was awful. Robin had once been locked in the trunk of a car, and this had that same sense of psychological confinement. All she had thought then—all she had allowed herself to think—was: *Where's the air?* It was a feeling beyond terror. She feared being entrapped, in any way. With black humor she wondered if that were her problem with "relationships." Suddenly she stubbed her toe and swore, loudly. The sound echoed away to nothingness. Then her focus returned to drawing her next breath. And worrying there would be no more.

Finally they stopped. They removed Robin's blindfold and untied her. She felt a hint of fresh air and a flood of relief followed by anger. Adrenalin surged through her body, but it was dark and there was nowhere to escape. The man with the flowing mustache turned to smile before ascending a rickety ladder. The guy behind pushed her up, but not before she jammed her elbow into his groin. He merely laughed.

The first one grabbed her and lifted her into the fresh night air and—
Jamal.

Robin blinked and felt her heart stop. There was a stillness in her body, in the universe. Then reality kicked in. She took a deep breath and brushed the dirt off her shirt and jeans, but not really caring. He just smiled, that dazzling smile.

She saw Jamal as if for the first time. Strength radiated from him— along with an incandescence that burned even brighter than before. He was wearing clean white pajamas and a tan shawl. His eyes and skin were golden, his dark hair shiny, his teeth very white. He had a simplicity about him, yet he was larger than life.

They stared at each other. This was not how she had planned the encounter and she felt off-balance, filled with emotion. Way too much. She would not cry, not with these bastards watching her. She couldn't, however, control the shiver of apprehension that ran through her. Jamal removed his shawl and placed it over her shoulders. He wore a black vest threaded with gold and an automatic in a shoulder holster.

"Hello, Robin."

"Hello, Jamal." She kept a steel grip on herself.

They continued to stare at each other. The feelings that poured through them were too powerful for words; their silence was deeply expressive. Sensing the power of this encounter, Jamal's guards backed off, while keeping their weapons trained on her.

Jamal placed a hand on her arm, jolting her with his heat. But she ignored the hand and the heat and hoped he would, too, unless he hadn't felt it, but she was sure he had.

He led her through his camp, located in a canyon so narrow the opposite clifftops seemed almost to touch. At its base were reinforced stone walls with caves for supplies and shelter against bombing raids. There were many armed men, no women. Stars glimmered through the slash of black sky. A baker plunged a stick into a smoky pit and removed several rounds of *naan*. The warm smell filled the night with memory of home.

They reached a secluded spot under a walnut tree where the rocky canyon floor widened. An upended Soviet bomb was filled with purple petunias. A fire was burning behind an antique carpet and cushions. Jamal gestured for Robin to sit. He sat beside her, not quite touching. He didn't have to—the sparks that leaped between them were not from the fire.

An old man with a long white beard brought a tray of tea, sugar and red grapes, deep red the color of the flames and carpet. Jamal served her, as dictated by Afghan hospitality, filling her glass half-full with brown sugar.

To fill the moment, she took a sip and winced. "Too sweet." She smiled. He smiled.

They studied each other, each admiring the warm fire glow on the other's face.

"That was a dirty trick—"

"What are you doing here?"

As the years compressed into instants, they burst into the comfortable laughter of old friends. Then again spoke simultaneously:

"I came to interview you."

"I am sorry but..." A stern expression passed over his face. Jamal held up a hand.

She had forgotten how long his fingers were, how delicate.

"I must ask you about your friends. Who are they? What do they want?"

"They're not really my friends. I just needed help getting here. The American is CIA. He's brought you Stingers."

Jamal frowned as he pondered this information. Could it truly be so simple? "Trust is a luxury I can no longer afford—that includes you, my little bird, I am sorry to say. That is why you were brought here this way... blindfolded. Our camp must remain secret." His smile was gentle. "I hope you are not offended, Robin. Now you are my guest." He looked at her fondly but from a distance.

She had been observing her former lover carefully and was aware of his many changes. Always noble, always kind, Jamal had grown into greatness. He projected an air of authority combined with grace and wisdom. But also there was the reserve. His choices had molded him and taken him elsewhere. She knew his strength and needed to match it. "Who'd have ever thought my old friend Jim...?"

He nodded at the memory of another life, so far away. "Who would have ever thought? Who can ever know what path life will offer?"

Robin gazed for a long moment into the fire, feeling its warmth—and menace. "Who can ever know?" Then she turned to him. "I want to tell your story to the American people. They haven't a clue what's going on in Afghanistan."

"Probably they do not even know where my country is."

She nodded soberly. "Geography is not an American strong point. Half of them never heard of this war. The other half doesn't know where it is."

Across from them a man was playing a banjo-like stringed instrument, singing with two others. Their sounds were haunting. Robin recalled a similar instrument she'd seen at the "Bamboo Bar" in Peshawar. With Nick.

"A very old *dhamboura*, made by this man's grandfather," Jamal explained.

"What are their songs?"

"All about love. He goes away. She goes away." He smiled into her eyes.

For an instant, a bare instant, Robin forgot why she was there. The man was like a god come to life, his skin the color of honey. She remembered its sweetness. And she remembered the passion… but passion had originally meant suffering and martyrdom. She could not forget that, either. If she had stayed with him, she would have been a martyr to that love. That passion would have brought her here, to this land that scorned women and wrapped them in living tombs. And yet looking at the man, Robin could still imagine that choice. She shivered again and picked up the tea, but it had gotten cold.

The old man approached tentatively. At Jamal's nod he refilled their cups, then padded away on felt slippers with upturned toes"The first cup, as you must remember, is for thirst. The second pledges friendship."

She raised her glass, but did not smile. "Friendship."

The warmth flowed through them. He regarded her intently, noticing the pin she still wore. Her auburn hair was burnished by the firelight. He wanted to touch it. Touch her. "Still so beautiful. My little bird, still wearing my little pin."

Robin's cheeks flushed. She had not heard that nickname in so many years. It frightened her, that name with all the meaning it held. Instinctively, she touched her pin. This pin connecting them through the years, connecting them still, to an unknown future. Then she shook her head. She was holding back. She had to. "This is a professional visit, Jamal."

"Of course." He nodded in dignified assent. Of course. Too much had changed. And yet...

And yet... Had he spoken those words? Or had she just felt them?

Jamal fixed her with his gaze. "Any time you wish your interview, you are welcome to return."

"Thank you." Mission accomplished.

He didn't reply, still looking at the woman who had been such a part of his life. His eyes reached out to her, asking her to enter his memories. "Only tonight, let us forget our professions and remember our past. Like the day I gave you a little gold robin."

She remembered, and could not escape those eyes—hot and liquid, molten gold. She nodded as the fire flickered across their faces and drew them in.

The same two men accompanied Robin back to camp the next morning. Only now the mood was friendly. Still wearing Jamal's shawl, she smiled and raised a hand, indicating for them to wait. Then she saw Nick, back against a rock, squinting down the barrel of his automatic.

Nick was preparing to defend her, take out her kidnappers if need be... until she smiled. That damn smile. He could see she was in no jeopardy, none whatsoever. He went from concern to relief to anger in no time flat, more of those twisted emotions she seemed to put him through. That's where he stayed—pissed.

Around dawn, he had gone to offer Robin some breakfast. Unable to find her, he'd torn the camp apart and sent men out to search the area. She was nowhere to be found, and he felt responsible—even though he knew he wasn't. With nothing else he could do constructive, he settled in near her tent, watching for her, cleaning and oiling his pistol while reviewing yet again his options.

As she approached, Nick spoke, masking his concern by gruffness. "And where the hell did you go last night?"

Robin continued inside the "tent," a tarp draped over a center post with sticks supporting each of the four corners. Her flippant words floated out. "I was kidnapped."

"By who?"

She reappeared in a clean T-shirt, holding the shawl. "That's my business," she replied blithely.

"Wrong. Since you landed in my lap, everything you do is my business." He pointed at her. "Got that?"

"'Cuse me a sec, will you, Nick?" She brushed past his outstretched index finger.

Mouth tight, he watched her move away.

She returned to the two mujahideen, folded the shawl and handed it to them. "Please thank Commander Jamal for his hospitality."

Nick stared at Robin… then at the men who were departing amid cordial nods. Then back at her.

Robin felt the heat of his glance. Aware of the anxiety mixed with his anger, she walked over to him. "I'm glad you missed me, Nick, but I've never liked possessive men."

She was teasing, playing with him, but he was in no mood for any headtrips. He grabbed her chin, tilting her face toward his. "Understand one thing: This is not a game with me. It's not career advancement—and it's sure as shit not fun! I want to do what I came for—and get out alive."

Robin shook him away. "What did you come for?"

His look was hard. "Don't turn it around on me. I need to know. Where were you?"

"Why should I tell you? I don't know anything about you. CIA. Stingers. Drugs. I don't know what all you've got going." She wanted to, though.

He stared at her in a test of wills. Refusing to give her anything.

Finally she shrugged. "If you must know, I spent the evening with my old friend Jamal."

"You get your big interview?"

"No. We'll do that next time."

Nick didn't react. He may have been jealous, but he sure as hell wouldn't admit it. "Next time, huh? Great. Maybe you'll get a Pulitzer. Or maybe, just laid."

Robin's eyes blazed, then cooled into tiny dark embers. "Maybe."

He backed off a little. Probably he'd gone too far. "Look, I came all this way to see Jamal. I need to know where his base is."

"I wish I could help you, Nick, but I promised not to reveal his whereabouts."

Nick watched her face close in upon itself. It was as if she didn't know him any more, had never known him. Her lips clamped shut, setting in a stubborn line of defense. He wouldn't even try to cross over.

"You got a lousy sense of priorities, lady." He turned abruptly and strode away before smacking her back to where she came from. Wherever that was.

Robin was too wired to rest. She went to see Mustapha, who was sitting by the stream cleaning his rifle. He said he didn't feel secure in the camp. The men did not like his defense of the prisoner. Not to mention his association with her. They were all aware of Nick's anger toward the American woman.

She shrugged. "Don't worry, you'll be out of here soon. How is the prisoner?"

He glanced up at her, then ran his index finger across his throat. "They killed him during the night."

"Who?"

Mustapha sighed. "Who can say? He was hated by all."

Robin nodded, but before she could respond, they heard Taj's voice crying out.

"Nick! Watch yourself!"

Robin whirled around and saw Nick draw his pistol.

Nick was standing in the center of camp, staring at the rocks overhead, the trees and bushes behind. They were completely surrounded by armed Afghans. *But on whose team?*

Robin looked from one man to another, trying to sort out this latest development. Then she recognized two faces among those closing in on them, weapons drawn.

As Nick moved in to back him up, Taj pointed his rifle at the invaders. "Friends or enemies? What do you want?" he demanded in Pashtu.

Nick had to size things up—quickly. He gazed around at the fighters and then recognized the two men who had escorted Robin back. Now it made sense.

At that moment, a tall, bearded Afghan in an oversized black turban stepped forward. "Steen-gahrs."

Shaking his head emphatically, Nick pointed at himself. "I bring them to Jamal."

"Our leader will not see you." Black Turban drew himself up fiercely. "We will bring Steen-gahrs to him."

Taj realized that Nick knew these people. Or thought he did. "He says 'our leader' will not see you. They'll take the Stingers—"

"No way! I've seen many mujahideen weapons delivered—but never to the right man. This time I'll make sure they are."

The rebels stood there. Silent. Defiant. Armed.

Nick pondered his next move. Then unexpectedly, he smiled. "Okay, no problem. I'll give you one Stinger as a sign of good faith. And you will deliver my message to Jamal: I'm a U.S. official, and must speak with him on a matter of life and death." Now he wasn't smiling. He was negotiating from authority.

The mujahideen scrutinized Nick and deliberated among themselves. Black Turban locked eyes with Nick and then inclined his head in approval. Nick nodded at Taj.

Taj left, returning a moment or so later with a burlap-wrapped Stinger. He handed it to the spokesman who hoisted it on his shoulder. The men hurried away.

Nick noticed Robin watching from under a nearby tree. His smile contained malice rather than humor. "With your pull, I should've had you set up the meeting."

"You don't need my help."

"Normally no, but then I'm not sleeping with the chief."

"Fuck you!"

"You already did that." Ignoring her blistering stare, he took a toothpick from his pocket. It snapped at the first contact with his teeth.

"That was the worst mistake of my life."

"You didn't seem to think so at the time."

"Bastard!"

He nodded. "Whatever you need, whoever you can use."

"You should talk."

"It's okay, we all got our priorities. And right now, I need to cut me a new toothpick."

Nick turned and split. He grabbed a few extra clips from the stock of ammunition, wrapped himself in turban and shawl and then slipped across the fields outside camp. He quickly picked up the trail of the mujahideen, determined to track them to their destination. Keeping his head down, he followed their path along the irrigation canal.

As the group moved east, Nick saw the clue he'd been looking for. Black Turban kicked aside a mound of stones and earth, passed the Stinger to the man behind him and dropped from sight. That man handed the weapon down the opening, then he and the other mujahideen followed. The last one reached up from inside the shaft and carefully covered the hole behind him. There was no trace they'd ever been there.

It was as if the earth had swallowed them up. And it had. Literally.

Nick whistled softly, realizing they'd entered a *karez* just like the one Taj had discovered. The countryside must be full of them. He waited a few moments to make sure he was alone, then hurried to the well. Once inside he closed off the entrance, and he, too, disappeared.

Nick crept through the dusty darkness. It was quiet, like a grave. Yet the men were there, somewhere, so he didn't want to risk lighting a match. He moved slowly, cautiously, finally seeing a ray of light and then a ladder. Was this where they had exited? Nick straightened up briefly, rubbed a shoulder, then decided it was too soon. He crouched back down and continued on.

On to another entrance shaft, then more darkness. A bat brushed his face, but otherwise he was alone, moving uphill through one of the underground tunnels crisscrossing Afghanistan. The perfect means for a guerrilla leader to appear and disappear with ease.

Chapter 24

Nick lost track of time. Maybe it was an hour, maybe longer. Then he reached a dead end where the earth had caved in, or it could have been just the unyielding granite. He backtracked to the previous shaft and climbed the ladder, stopping below the surface. He peered out at the mouth of a secluded canyon, its narrow entrance partially blocked by large boulders. Several dozen mujahideen were scattered around—some on patrol, others cleaning their weapons, eating, drinking tea. Robin's two "kidnappers" and Black Turban were showing the Stinger to Jamal.

Grabbing the Colt from the small of his back, Nick shimmied out, taking shelter behind some brush. Watching Jamal study the Stinger, he reflected that if he were to do what the Russians and Pakistanis had hired him for... *now would be the time to act.*

Suddenly five rifles were staring him in the face. Two more guards yanked him to his feet and disarmed him.

Raising his arms, he grinned. "Take me to your leader."

No one moved; they glared at him.

"Just a joke, fellas. I'm here to see Jamal."

Jamal strode forward, covering the ground in long strides. He smiled without surprise at Nick and told the guards the man was a guest. They lowered their weapons slightly, their suspicions not at all allayed.

Jamal extended his hand. "Welcome, Nick Daley."

Nick stared at him, then reached out to accept the handshake. He sensed a calm strength, a mysterious self-confidence in the man. "The famous Commander Jamal."

Jamal smiled again. "You are a most resourceful man, the first outsider to discover our camp. You must wish very badly to speak to me, so of course we will talk. But first you must take some tea."

As Jamal led him through the canyon, Nick was impressed by the camp's size and security. If he were truly the first outsider to penetrate it, he had gained valuable intelligence. But could the Afghan leader afford to let him walk away with it?

When they reached the quiet spot under the walnut tree, Jamal gestured to the antique carpet. They sat and the old man brought tea. Jamal spooned a large amount of sugar into Nick's cup, a smaller amount for himself and then poured the tea. Nick thanked him and took a sip. It was too sweet, but he knew about such things and didn't react.

They drank it slowly, both outwardly relaxed, but inwardly wary and guarded.

"You are enjoying your tea?"

Nick nodded. "Very sweet."

"The more sugar, the more honor to the guest."

"I'm flattered."

"Yet the tea is bitter. It is like Afghanistan, both bitter and sweet."

"I've heard about your way with words, Jamal."

"Our culture values these things." Jamal inclined his head in acknowledgment, never taking his eyes off Nick. "You are enjoying your stay in Afghanistan?"

Nick grinned at his courtly manner. "It couldn't be more delightful."

And yet he felt the danger. The dark suspicious eyes. The glinting gunmetal. Surrounded. That's why they pay you the big bucks, he thought mirthlessly. He put his cup down.

"More tea?"

"Enough, thanks. Let's get to it."

Jamal regarded him with mock disappointment. "Oh, you Americans. No subtlety, no patience."

"That may be, but what we do have makes up for it."

Jamal knew where his visitor was headed, just as he had known Nick would follow his men back here. At least one of them understood the use of subtlety and patience. "And what do you have?"

"Stingers. And an offer."

Jamal gave him an even look. "As to the Stingers, we have requested them for a long time. They are the only way to defeat the gunships that terrorize our people. But all we receive are out-of-date weapons, limited supplies of ammunition." He stared closely at Nick. "I know others benefit from American aid, others get rich."

"Others?" Nick met his eyes.

"My enemies in Peshawar—including the fundamentalists—block my supply convoys. The ISI's Afghan cell repacks your crates with modern weapons on top, old surplus ones underneath."

"That doesn't surprise me. Pakistani intelligence is in bed with some nasty folks. Dangerous—and not just to the Russians. It seems your holy war is a magnet to *jihadists* everywhere."

"Especially the Saudis. Using us for their own cause." Jamal shrugged.

Nick glanced around the armed camp. "You're not fighting empty-handed, though."

"We get weapons wherever we can. By capturing or buying them from the Soviets. Or from Afghan conscripts secretly loyal to the mujahideen."

Nick wondered where he obtained the money to buy his weapons. Some commanders traded in drugs.

Jamal put a hand on Nick's shoulder. His expression was grave. "You must understand one thing: The resistance will prevail. We have no deadline and few requirements. We need only our hearts, our bodies, our faith in God."

"That may be—but the Stingers will help even the odds a little."

"This is true." Jamal gave him a gracious nod. "So, you have Stingers. And what is this offer of which you speak?"

"My people would like to back you."

Jamal stared at him, considering the American's proposal, with all its ramifications. After a thoughtful pause, he answered. "We accept your offer, even as I understand your backing of our struggle is in your own interest."

"Common interests, you might say." Nick grinned.

Jamal smiled back. "You use us, we use you."

The hook was in. Now Nick wanted to wrap up this business and get the hell out of Dodge. "You'll consider this the first delivery of many. And as to future shipments, we'll work out some form of payment. Drugs, whatever's easy." He took a sip of lukewarm tea.

Jamal studied him, but remained noncommittal. "And you bring how many Stingers in this first delivery?"

"Besides the weapon your men took this morning, I have five more, each with two missiles. Since the valley is swarming with Russians, it'd be safer if I bring them to you."

Jamal laughed, showing his fine white teeth. "I fight the *Shuravi* invaders everyday. I am not afraid. We have an old saying: Presence of danger tests presence of mind."

"Does keep you on your toes." Nick agreed.

"I will come tomorrow night."

The two men rose, still sizing each other up.

"Watch your rear. Some people don't like you very much." Nick wondered if Jamal had any idea of the power of his enemies.

"Thank you for the advice. And now, we will protect your rear and escort you back the way you came—so you don't get lost."

"And my gun?"

"Until your safe return, you will not need it. You are under our protection." He smiled. "*Pashtunwali.*"

Nick shrugged, accepting the inevitable. "I know all about a host's obligation to his guest."

Jamal nodded his approval. "Especially such an educated guest."

When Nick wandered back to camp that afternoon, he checked in with Taj and briefed him on what had happened. He said that when Jamal came for the Stingers the following night, the men from Kalat could join up with him, as was their plan. Taj grinned; the Afghans were anxious to kill Russians.

Aware of Nick's return, Robin hurried to him, wearing the veil draped over her head and shoulders and a warm smile.

Taj looked at the two of them. "I am going to tell the men they will soon be fighting *jihad.*" He walked away.

Robin gazed in Nick's eyes, her anger seemingly gone. "Did you chop down a whole forest?"

"Huh?"

"You went looking for toothpicks? Remember?"

"Oh, yeah, right."

"Cut you a few, did you?"

"No, I didn't."

She smiled again. "So, what did you do?"

"That's my business," he repeated pointedly.

Robin got the dig and nodded. "Cute."

He remained silent. Stone cold and silent.

"No... really?"

"Really what?"

"Really, where were you?"

"None of your damn business."

Robin looked down, then touched him lightly on the chest as she met his eyes. She brushed a strand of hair off his forehead. "I was worried about you."

"Worry about yourself, lady."

"Look, Nick, I feel uncomfortable about how I tricked you. And I'm sorry for being such a witch," she apologized sheepishly.

"There's another word."

Robin winced, nodding. "Maybe. But now I'd like to make amends." She fixed him with a certain look. "A little dinner by the fire, maybe? Nothing fancy, just the usual bread and rice and tea." Her eyes danced with promise. "And some good company."

Nick knew it was a peace offering in more ways than one. He saw the invitation in her look. "I'll check my datebook."

Robin had cleared a small area behind her tent, sheltering it with brushwood, decorating it with daisies and sprigs of pink oleander. Mustapha had dug a pit and helped build the fire. The tarp on which Nick sat was anchored with melons and bowls of apricots. The only sounds were the crackle of flames and the warm desert breeze through the trees.

"Sorry, no wine," Robin apologized as she served the food. She smiled. "From a 'dry' country to a dryer one."

They stared at each other, suddenly feeling like old friends who've been through the wars together. Literally.

He nodded. "The Bamboo Bar."

"Yeah, the Bamboo Bar."

Robin sank down beside him. She took a deep breath. "I know you think I'm manipulative. But then, who isn't?" She drew the veil around her face, gazing at him innocently, but not really.

He laughed. "When you want something, you go for it. Right?"

"Right."

"Well, I wanted this trip." She grabbed onto his eyes. "I also wanted you."

"Might've done the same myself."

"I guess we're both pretty unscrupulous characters." Her lips curved.

"Shameless."

"Double-dealing."

"Conscienceless."

"False-hearted."

Nick grinned. "At least we understand each other."

Then a cloud passed over her face. "Nick. If something happens here—and uh... Or if one of us gets hurt or something—I uh..."

He watched her. The firelight turned her gray eyes silver and made them sparkle. "Nothing'll happen. You got your good luck pin," he teased.

"I lost it."

He waited, knowing she wasn't finished.

"Nick, I—I didn't think I was going to feel this way."

Nick slipped a hand under the veil and cupped the side of her face. "You're not so bad yourself."

"So I wonder if we can call a truce, make up?" The look in her eyes was seductive but serious. "As in kiss and make up?"

His fingers stroked her warm cheek, flushed from the fire, and he realized how much he cared for her. He hadn't expected anything like this and was stunned. But the timing was all wrong; he had to keep it light. "Is that a proposition?"

"It's anything you want, Nick. "Which way to that tent of yours?"

"I was hoping you'd ask."

Robin took his hand and pulled him to his feet, matching her stride to his.

He glanced at her. "You know, that veil's quite provocative."

"Maybe they do know something we don't know. You said that to me once, about them all wearing pajamas. Back in your bungalow—remember?"

He nodded. He did remember.

She gave him an enigmatic smile. "Where did you go, anyway?"

"Sorry, hon, but I promised not to reveal his whereabouts." Teasing but stubborn. Again repeating her earlier words.

Robin nodded. "You saw Jamal, didn't you." It was a statement, not a question.

He stopped and stared. Why was she so interested? He sure as hell didn't want to know about the two of them. "Okay, Robin, he's coming for the Stingers tomorrow night. And then we'll head back. So you've got between now and then, for your—interview."

She turned to him. "I didn't sleep with him last night. Sure we thought about it, but those days are over. Now it's professional." She moved closer. "But you, Nick—I knew you were trouble from day one. It's never been 'professional' between us—it's something else."

"It's something else, all right." His eyes crinkled. "And you can't quite put your finger on it."

"But I'd sure like to. Right now, I've got a hot lead I want to follow up."

He pulled her to him. She grabbed on tight. There was refuge in that embrace and neither wanted to let go.

Then he whispered, "I want to get to the bottom of it as much as you."

They entered her tent and dropped the flap behind them. It was small and dark. But they were inside together, alone. The center post was the only place they could stand upright. They gazed at each other and then at the faint shadows of fire dancing out there in the world.

No one made the first move, but they flowed together. Nick pulled the veil down to her shoulders and looked at her. The connection was so powerful, and suddenly there could be no space between them. And yet his desire was fueled by anger, for despite the laughs and the seduction, he was still angry. Darkness clouded his vision and her features changed from beautiful to treacherous... and then his fingers were digging into her and he was shaking her.

Her head snapped back against the post. Her eyes opened wide, stunned.

Equally shocked, he dropped to his knees, pulling her gently with him, and cradled her in his arms. "I'm sorry, Robin. Forgive me." She was crying. He kissed her wet cheeks, her eyes, holding her, consoling her. She sobbed. He rocked her like a baby.

"Oh, Nick," she moaned. Over and over.

He stared at her moist, glowing face, then smothered her moans with his mouth. He pushed aside the veil and moved his lips to her neck.

"No..." she whispered. "Don't."

"Don't?" He stared at her incredulously. Was she back to her games?

Her features became twisted with pain. "I can't trust you—and you can't trust me. How can we make love?"

"Oh, Robin, I know." His eyes told her he understood. "But leave that outside. All that is outside. Here, it's just us."

She stared at him for a long, long time and then nodded. She took an end of the veil and wrapped it around him, pulling it tight until they were in a cocoon. That wild, seductive smile returned to her face. "Don't say I didn't warn you."

"You didn't have to."

With those final words, Nick pressed her to the ground and wrapped her in his arms. They remained locked together until somehow they escaped their clothes and she cried out once... and they lost themselves in a long slow dance of forgetfulness.

Chapter 25

Nick was up with the dawn. He and Robin had watched the sun rise over the eastern mountains. There were no words. None were needed. They had burned their way into each other like a brand and that pain would be there forever.

Now he was uneasy. He had a feeling... something was about to pop. He moved nervously through the quiet camp. He rechecked the Stingers, their supply of weapons and ammunition. He spoke with each of the men, making sure he knew everything they knew. Unable to find Mustapha, he asked Hash to check him out.

Hash moved to go, but then paused, as a thought occurred to him. "After..." His gesture seemed to include all of Afghanistan. "I am inviting you to my home in Chitral mountains. For trout fishing."

"It's a deal, Hash." Nick smiled, his eyes still wary. "But on those roads, I'll do the driving!"

The kid laughed easily. "Okay, Nick, but I am thinking racing in mountains is still safer than walking in Kandahar."

"You may be right—" Nick stopped.

He caught a glimpse of a man lying belly-down among the rocks. He turned and spotted another figure flattened against a tree. Whose men were they?

AK-armed, Taj rushed up to warn them. Then saw his boss already knew.

"Visitors." Nick was calculating their odds. "Only problem, you can't tell the players without a program around here. Time to get out the big guns, fellows. Spread the alert. And haul ass!"

Taj and Hash hustled off. Nick grabbed a rifle and ammo, as well as protection for Robin, then hurried to her tent… where he was surprised to see her in jeans and a T-shirt. "Hey, what happened to the veil, Robin? You stand out like a sore thumb."

"Huh?" Robin glanced up, preoccupied with folding a tarp—last night's tablecloth.

He checked her out. "Make that sore eyes. As in 'sight for sore eyes.'"

She intercepted his look and shook her head. "Male chauvinist to the end."

"I won't touch that with a ten-foot pole." He grinned but saw the tension in her face.

Her eyes flickered. "Quit while you're ahead."

His grin fading, Nick handed her a .38 revolver—not too big but big enough—and no chance of jamming. "Looks like it's starting to hit the fan. I know you're an old Berkeley peacenik, but promise me you'll use this if you have to."

"Don't worry." Her face was grave. "I will."

As last night's memories rolled over them, their eyes connected, but then today's realities struck. They disconnected and all bets were off.

"Be careful, Robin."

"You, too."

Nick turned away, his thoughts on the defense of his camp—and its valuables. He hurried to join the others.

Then the shadows converged on him, and he was looking into the rifles of Jamal and about a dozen mujahideen.

"Sorry for not ringing first, Nick, but we decided to surprise you."

"Always a pleasure, Jamal." Although irritated with his methods, Nick respected Jamal and understood it was a strategy he himself might have followed. "I suppose you're here for those Stingers. Okay, let's get 'em."

Nick led them to the large overhanging rock under which the missiles were stashed. The mujahideen carried the Stingers to their waiting donkeys.

Once the animals were loaded up, Jamal turned to Nick. "Thank you. We will make very good use of them. But as for the rest of your 'offer'…" His eyes flashed. "If the price of more Stingers is to be the connection for an American drug dealer, then you have insulted my honor. And you are lucky I do not cut your throat!" Instinctively, Jamal shot a glance at a clump of trees south of camp. His guard was gone. He scanned the rocks overhead: Empty!

Nick saw the leader's concern. The two men exchanged a quick look of understanding. Despite their mistrust, they were now allied against a common danger.

There was an instant of awful stillness, then Nick could almost hear the adrenalin rushing through the men, both his and Jamal's. Rifles were unshouldered, ammunition checked, commands shouted.

Nick understood the bad vibes he'd been feeling. *The double-cross is turning triple!* The mujahideen had walked into a trap. Betrayed—but by whom?

He tried to grasp the extent of the treachery, knowing he had but moments until the attack. Then time ran out. The now too-quiet morning was cracked open. Gunfire thundered around them. He moved for a boulder at the edge of the clearing, as Jamal took cover nearby.

Taj ran up. "Now we will kill *Shuravi.*" Grinning, he fired a volley at a figure in the surrounding trees.

Nick could see that Hash and the others were similarly excited. This was jihad, what they had come for. He knew the odds were against them, though. They were penned in and outmanned at least three to one by elite enemy troops—not only Spetsnaz, but tough Afghan Frontier Security Forces.

Then instinct took over. Nick was engulfed in the rush of battle, its colors and smells, its roars, whizzes and crashes. The hot blue sky vaporized into a haze of dust and black smoke, shot through with angry red flashes, singed with the stink of cordite.

Suddenly he thought of Robin. He hit the ground and crawled to her tent, but she wasn't there. Then he saw her crouching against a rock, the .38 in her hand. Her eyes met his without recognition. He ran to her, gripped her arm and led her to a sheltered irrigation ditch in the fields west of camp. Just a quick look—then he was gone.

As he was sprinting back, Hash leaped up to cover him, not noticing an enemy rifle aimed in his direction. Nick shouted to warn him, but the kid didn't hear and a bullet slammed into his knee. Nick whirled and shot the Soviet, then raced to Hash and dragged him behind some rocks.

Oblivious to the pain, Hash grinned. "Remember I am telling you walking in Kandahar more dangerous than driving in Chitral mountains."

Nick smiled weakly, staring at Hash's shattered right leg, seeping blood and flies. "At least, now I'll have to drive. Take care of yourself, Hash." He handed him a fistful of extra clips and turned away.

Nick dropped to his belly, scrambling back toward the center of camp—and Jamal. Definitely not an innocent bystander this time. If he did manage to get out alive, they'd probably nail his ass for violations of the U.S. Neutrality Act. A bullet skimmed his spine. He ate dust, then kept moving.

Looking up, he saw Jamal take out an enemy soldier in blue and white stripes. The victim's fallen rifle was quickly retrieved by a mujahid, who just as quickly put it to work. He, too, was slain. Jamal picked off his killer and coolly nodded at Nick.

The CIA officer and Afghan leader fought shoulder to shoulder, while still reserving judgment on the other. Their confrontation would come later. But at this moment, in this battle, Jamal was a sure, unflinching presence and Nick was grateful.

Taj showed up again, still brazen, but the grin gone. The mujahideen had suffered many casualties. The encounter was turning into a rout.

The angry buzz of helicopters joined the roar of traded ammunition, amplifying the tension, drowning out the moans. One copter hovering overhead, one landing across the clearing.

It was all happening too quickly. Attack. Defeat. Invasion.

Nick looked around. Jamal had disappeared. He was relieved to spot Robin… until he saw the rifle poking in her back. She was being led away by Soviet soldiers! Nick leaped to his feet, but Taj grabbed him and pulled him down.

"Fuck you, Taj!" Nick was furious at his friend, furious at himself for not being able to protect her. His worst fears realized. God only knew what they'd do to her, a foreign reporter. A girl.

"Saving her not possible, Nick." Taj held him in an iron grip.

Nick watched Robin being forced onto the helicopter, its rotors whirling. The door slammed behind her. Enraged, Nick shook Taj off, but it was too late. The rotors whirled faster. It was lifting off.

She was gone.

At that same moment, Jamal emerged… Near the gunship, aiming a rocket launcher. He fired. There was still a chance. The ship was not too high in the sky. But Jamal had only a thin tree as cover, and the helicopter machine guns were shooting at him.

Hash peered out from behind his rocky shelter. He could not allow Commander Jamal to be mowed down by the *Shuravi*. He pushed himself up with his rifle—then turned it on the helicopter. But the machine gun from the sky got him. Another burst hit Jamal, grazing his arm before he ducked out of sight.

There was nothing Nick could do. Only watch helplessly as Hash died. He was sickened. That brave, crazy young kid. Robin. And the others, there because of him. But Nick couldn't afford the emotion and cut it off, quick. The pain would surface. Later.

Now he had to take care of business. Nick made a dash across open ground, back to Jamal. He noted that the leader's wound was slight, then grabbed his good arm.

"Let's get out of here."

Jamal stared at him, scornful. "How can I leave my men? And how can you leave yours? Better to die bravely in battle than safely in bed."

"Look—that may be another fine old Afghan saying, but you won't die. You'll end up a war trophy for the Soviets. They're after your ass!"

Besides the truth of Nick's words, Jamal realized the battle was nearing an end; most of his men had been killed or wounded. The survivors were even now disappearing into the landscape. He nodded soberly. "We must bury the martyrs as soon as possible."

Nick took a last look at Hash and the other victims. Then he and Jamal crawled into the fields west of the gully. Seeing them begin their escape, Taj raced to cut loose the donkeys carrying the Stingers and shoo them away. He caught up with Nick and Jamal as they began circling back toward the eastern foothills.

They kept to the rocks and shrubs and brush when possible, but there was little cover. They could hear the gunships on the prowl, flying low to the ground, hugging the treetops, whipping up their leaves and churning the dirt. They smelled their stink.

Then through the dusty haze, the men spotted the entrance to the *karez* and crept toward it, Nick bringing up the rear. Suddenly two enemy commandos jumped him. In swift silence, Nick slashed one soldier's throat with his bayonet and shot the other.

Taj and Jamal whipped around. There was no time for them to do anything. No need.

Jamal nodded. No matter what else, the American had proved his courage today.

Taj cleared the opening and climbed in the tunnel, followed by Jamal and Nick, who reached out to cover it again. Once down the ladder, Nick rehinged the bayonet and reshouldered the rifle, then grabbed his .45.

The men moved quickly through the darkness, Nick and Jamal filled with thoughts of Robin. Her fate.

Nick cursed himself for not doing more at the time. He wracked his brain for any action he could take, and wondered if he might get Viktor to intercede—and how much it would cost. Whatever that price, he'd pay it; he'd do anything, other than betray his country. The blackness surrounding him mirrored his inner reality. He had found her and then lost her. He felt her loss physically, as if she had been ripped from his body. For she was there—had been there—inside him, filling that angry emptiness. He wanted her desperately.

Jamal remembered his first sight of Robin hiding in the trench with Nick. He had been shocked by the intensity of his feelings for her, still strong after all those years. Jamal knew there could be no future between them. It was not meant to be, just as before it had not been meant to be. He knew also that Nick loved her, had laid claim to her. Yet Robin was his youth, his first love. He had hoped to help her, to see her happy and safe. The *Shuravi* had destroyed that hope, too.

Nick willed his emotions back under control. Pistol in hand, he stared tensely toward Jamal's back.

Jamal stopped. He turned to face Nick, sensing the weapon. "I suppose there is a big price on my head."

"A very big price."

"We all have our time, our qismet. Our fate is in the hands of Allah."

"Yes, we all have our time." Now, Nick decided. "But it's not yours yet, Jamal—and it's my job to make sure of that!"

Jamal was still. He waited. Taj waited.

"I'm here on a special mission for the President of the United States to investigate our covert aid program… and you, Jamal Durrani."

Nick struck a match. "And I've got a tale of inefficiency, diversion and greed that will knock their socks off! After this report, Jamal, your friends will far outnumber your enemies. Because, I can almost promise, they're going to back you heavily as the future leader of a free Afghanistan!"

Taj broke into a great, triumphant grin.

Jamal took a moment to absorb it before speaking. "I believe you, Nick, but one thing I do not understand—?"

"The drug business? Sorry about that. It was one final character test. You passed."

Jamal smiled gently at the CIA man. "And you passed, too, my friend."

The match burned down to Nick's fingers. He didn't feel it. Felt only relief that the truth was finally out. *Or what passes for truth.*

The darkness settled and they pushed on in silence, following the gradual rise uphill toward Jamal's camp. Nick reflected on how he had got to this place. The past two years in Peshawar. His many identities... media specialist, case officer, double agent, arms and drug dealer, scam artist, sting expert.

The sting that killed.

Stinger.

Nick had accepted the risks when he was assigned to Peshawar. He didn't give a damn about the politics of it all. Originally, it had been just another posting, another gig. But he soon developed a solid respect for mujahideen bravery—while disdaining the politicking of their "leadership." And he became aware of the inherent corruption of the covert aid system. He saw everyone taking their piece—leaving just crumbs for the real fighters.

Like Jamal. Especially Jamal.

The mujahideen leader had sounded too good to be true. This was the final part of the operation. The endgame. Nick had to see him face to face—despite violating the U.S. Neutrality Act by going in personally with the Stingers. He was committed to gaining the best possible intelligence for the president, and he didn't care how he did it. But because this mission didn't exist—officially—he had been allocated no official funds. It was one of those self-financing operations. He'd been there before and knew how to improvise.

The Stingers had been furnished by the U.S. government, via Farouk. The drug bust in the mosque had raised cash for supplies, as had the Russian and Pakistani "advances," with the surplus remaining as a cushion. For this operation—or his retirement in Bali. You never knew. If there was one thing he'd learned in all these years with the Company, it was about the marriage of drugs, arms and politics. You couldn't be too pure. Just pure enough.

Perhaps that was why he was there. Whatever. It sounded a little corny, but it was an honor to have been chosen.

Taj smiled to himself as they continued their ascent. He had known Nick was an important *malik*, but not how important. To think Nick was working for the President of the United States! That meant Taj was working for the American President, also. It made him so proud. Soon he would be telling his wife and his sons. He would be a very big man before their eyes.

To be able to serve his people. That was why he had taken the job with Nick; the money was for his family. But to be able to serve them in such a big way, to help Commander Jamal become victorious. The next ruler of their country! Whatever else happened to him, he had done his duty. He was honored to have been chosen.

Jamal's feet knew the way through the karez, leaving his mind free to contemplate the unexpected turn of events. He was in no way overwhelmed by Nick's revelations. He had always known he had a destiny, even back in Berkeley, even as a child hearing stories of the great leaders of Afghanistan's past. But if it were true that Nick represented the President of the United States in his offer of support, then now there would be no question of their victory!

He would be able to achieve all his goals. First, defeat the Soviet invaders. Then, prevent the fundamentalists from taking power. And finally, but most important, help lead his beloved country into the modern age. He was honored to have been chosen.

Chapter 26

The three men climbed out of the *karez* into Jamal's camp. Safe.

Then—Robin stepped from the shadows.

Nick blinked. Waves of emotion washed over him, too intense to sort out.

Jamal smiled, deeply thankful. "Robin! You are safe. But how did you find us?"

Robin smiled back, then raised her right arm and pointed a pistol at him—the .38 Nick had given her. A Makarov automatic was tucked in her waistband, two extra magazines in each pocket.

"Luck, you might say." She nodded toward the Hind gunship behind the walnut tree. Four jumpsuit-clad soldiers were covering her, three mujahideen bodies lying nearby.

Nick stared. At Robin... and her gun, aiming at Jamal.

It's Jamal she's after! She's gonna take him out. Nick felt as if he had been slugged in the gut. He almost staggered from the blow. And yet deep inside, he had known. There were too many pointers along the way... including the staged meeting on the trail, complete with fake husband and prop corpses! The truth flooded over him with some kind of obscene clarity. It must have been a spotter plane that nailed them. A girl journalist on her own? How the hell did he think she'd found him, of all the trails in and out of Afghanistan? He should have averted this. But she had tap-danced her way into his heart and prevented him from seeing her awful truth. It was on his head—and would be, till the end of his days. *All these deaths.* And now, Jamal, the man he was here to support. He reached for his automatic.

"Hey, Nick, you don't want to do anything stupid. You told me to use this if I had to. Remember?" Robin's pistol—and her gaze—were still on Jamal.

Of course, she wasn't looking at him. Probably never has. Nick was filled with disgust. At her. At himself. Yet as he gazed at Robin with her wild hair and jean-clad body, he still found her beautiful. Desirable.

"Come with me, Jamal. Please. I don't want you to be a dead hero. Come with me." Robin knew her power over her former lover. And now she focused on him, holding his eyes, drawing him to her. She did not want to shoot Jamal. She just wanted to stop him. So they could end this stupid war and reopen the schools. Free the women.

Jamal didn't move. He was stunned. He stared at her, speechless at the betrayal.

Nick's face was dark. "Your material needs work, Robin. Now I guess you'll tell him everything Russia can do for his poor underdeveloped country." He spit out his words, his contempt unable to shield his insides that were twisting on her knife.

Robin knew Nick was peripheral to her main objective. She couldn't let him sidetrack her. "What do you believe in, Nick?"

"I almost believed in you, Robin."

She clamped down hard on her feelings, as she had all these years. Accepting the tradeoff: A "normal" life for one with meaning. The chance to make a difference. "It's nothing personal, my friend. This is strictly politics. It's about the fundamentalist bullies. And the little girls who have to get married instead of learning how to read. And the women in those stupid—fucking—HOT—veils! Even you couldn't like that kind of system!" Her next words were directed to the man whose world had, finally, become hers. The man at the other end of her gun barrel. "Jamal. You know what I'm talking about."

Jamal had seen what war could do to people, but never such treachery as this. He shook his head.

Nick grimaced. "Get off your soapbox, lady. They're using you."

"Maybe. Maybe I'm using them. It's a toss of the dice—for all of us. But I'm prepared to lose... on the chance I might win." Her eyes flashed, but her arm remained steady.

She radiated passion and for an instant Nick loved her as much as he hated her. But then the love died. "Selfish to the end, right? Take everyone down on your ego trip."

"No. It's more like our little problems 'don't amount to a hill of beans.' *Casablanca*—remember? And yeah… I guess we're just two people who met at the wrong place in the wrong time." She allowed herself a regretful shrug. "I am sorry."

Nick could feel his heart shrinking back into the cold, unlit place where it had waited so long. "Here I was thinking I was with the right person, at the right time, and in the right place—for once. Yeah, sorry is the word." Being cool didn't seem to matter now.

Robin's grip on the .38 did not waver. With her left hand, she gestured to the pilot. "Come with me, Jamal. You can talk to them. They'll need an Afghan leader. Who better than you? Think of your mother. She fought to get rid of the veil, too."

Jamal's voice was cold. "You shame yourself by trying to use my mother's name. She spit on those people."

The mujahid with the long white beard had been dozing up in the cave by the hidden machine gun emplacement when he'd heard the thunder-that-was-not-thunder… but a gunship! Then he'd heard the woman's voice… seen her holding a gun on Commander Jamal and two others—one, the American with the Stingers.

The old man sprang to life. *Insh'Allah*, he would defend his leader. He pivoted the Ziqriat down toward the woman—Jamal's old "friend!" He aimed and fired. She jerked backward, allowing the American to flee behind a boulder—however Jamal was still in danger. The old man ducked as a machine gun burst from the helicopter nose was directed at the cave, followed by shots from the *Shuravis* on the ground.

Fighting not to lose control, Robin managed to keep the .38 on Jamal, while aware of her own sudden vulnerability—especially with Nick gone to cover! But the backup commandos were surrounding her in a strong counterattack. "Don't move, Jamal. Please!"

Feeling like he was twenty again—a warrior!—the man in the cave turned his longer-than-one-meter double barrels on the *Shuravi* gunship. Bullets ricocheted everywhere on the narrow canyon walls.

Robin concentrated all her will on Jamal. He stared back at her, his eyes hard, implacable. As unyielding as hers. She had hoped to convince—or force—him to come with her. The unexpected resistance put her plan in jeopardy. But despite all opposition and all obstacles—including her own heart—she was committed to Operation Birdwatch. To saving Afghanistan from itself. She read something in Jamal's body language—and made a split-second decision, not allowing herself to feel.

She pulled the trigger... as Jamal raced to join Nick behind the boulder.

Taj dove in front of Jamal, taking the bullet in his stomach. Jamal scrambled back to Taj and dragged him to shelter. Something roared in Nick's brain; he became wild with fury. He whirled around and saw Robin retreating behind the walnut tree. He fired at her, but missed.

The old man on the Ziqriat continued shooting at the beast from the sky. Gleeful, he killed one of the *Shuravis* climbing aboard. He kept firing—and got another. Then another.

The pilot watched the fiasco through his blue plexiglass canopy, the single vulnerable spot on the armored gunship. Never mind his helmet— that bandit machine gun from above could get him. He revved the engine for takeoff. If he had to leave the woman, so be it. He was no fool. Returning with the valuable Hind was priority number one—KGB operation or not.

Robin saw the gunship preparing to lift off. She realized she was going to be killed or captured. The rotors were picking up speed. It was all over. The surviving soldier took her arm and they raced for the helicopter. As the ship began to rise, he grabbed the door grip and leaped inside, pulling her with him.

At that moment, a bullet from Jamal hit the Russian commando, spattering his blood all over Robin. She watched the body fall to the ground. Was he aiming at me? She slid the door shut. The double-barreled Ziqriat was still ripping into the Hind, wounding it, but unable to bring it down.

With a deafening howl, the mighty gunship maneuvered upward through the narrow canyon walls. Robin leaned against the metal door, heaving deep gasping breaths, trying to steady herself. She had survived, but she had failed. Was there a part of her that was secretly glad? That would be too awful to confront, because if she did not have her commitment, then she had nothing. Still, she looked outside, looking for them both. Jamal was safe. Then she saw Nick. She stared. She wanted to tell him something—but it was too late.

Nick watched her face at the rectangular porthole on the fuselage, beside the red star. Their eyes met. The Hind was roaring toward the rear opening of the canyon. Despite the distance, Nick felt sure he saw the regret in her eyes. He stood rooted to the spot. Then he shook his head and hurried away.

Jamal stared scornfully—defiantly—at the escaping helicopter. At Robin. The air was murky and turbulent; the winds were shrieking and churning. Pieces of the mountain were crumbling into whirlwinds of dust and grit as the gunship continued to fire down at them.

Nick returned, carrying the one Stinger in Jamal's camp. Steeling himself against the pain of what he had to do, he lifted it to his right shoulder and uncovered the launcher tube. By now, the ship had almost disappeared over the ridge. Only seconds left. He planted his feet and went inside himself to an awful place... then steadied the weapon and lined up the target in the cross hairs of the sight.

The words he spoke were so soft, only he could hear them—and maybe Robin. "*Insh'Allah*, we'll meet again—in hell."

Nick pressed the trigger. The missile was locked onto the target and knew where it had to go. With a terrible blast of red heat, the Stinger was launched, flashing upward through the blackened skies. Twisting and turning as it chased the Hind gunship.

Robin was still staring down at the retreating camp, her retreating past. She saw the ray of dazzling light. The awesome brilliance of it all. It truly was her past—but it was coming toward her, not receding. Then she knew: it was her future. Her now.

Like lightning, the fireball streaked toward the Hind—and Robin. Then came the roaring collision... the sheet of flames. The shattered machine plummeted to the jagged cliffs below.

Nick stood motionless, holding the grip-stock limply by his side. He felt drained of all life, hollow. The world was a soulless place and he didn't care anymore. He just didn't care.

His face ashen, he turned and walked to the boulder where Taj was propped up, arms crossed over his stomach, holding his insides in place. Still watching the action.

Nick kneeled and cradled him in his arms. "You're a big hero, Taj."

Taj shook his head no. "You are big hero, Nick. I am just little hero."

Nick swallowed hard. "I'll take care of your family, Taj. Send the boys to school in America, if you want."

Taj grinned his old grin. "Sure, boss." He grabbed Nick's hand. "And do not worry for me. I am happy. I am going to paradise. This is all I could ask for."

Nick nodded and watched his friend die. Then he kneeled and closed Taj's eyes, gently covering him with the shawl Taj had given him back in Peshawar. The rest of his heart seemed to go. He was used up, empty. Not even a tear left.

The old man climbed down from the cave. A trickle of mujahideen survivors from today's ambush returned through the *karez*.

Nick got up and made his way to Jamal. They looked from the rising column of dark smoke to each other. They knew that each had loved Robin; they shared the pain of her treachery.

The victory was sweet for the old man, bittersweet for Jamal—and sour for Nick, who had lost Taj as well.

Jamal remembered his duties. He gestured to two mujahideen. "Gather some men. Return to bury our *shaheed*..." He glanced at Nick. "Including our Pakistani friend."

"Hashmatullah." Nick honored his name.

Jamal nodded. "Hashmatullah." He had buried many men, many men who lived in his heart. "Then find the donkeys with the Stingers."

Nick recalled his duties as well. "Don't worry. You'll be well supplied from now on." His voice was flat.

Jamal shook his head, deeply troubled. "But how did she find the camp? She was blindfolded, brought by way of the secret *karez*."

"'Luck, you might say.'" Her words were etched as if by acid in his brain. He gazed into space, remembering everything now. "Luck. Damn good luck, if you ask me... Did she happen to be wearing her little gold robin pin when she was here?"

"Yes, she wore it."

He fixed an unpleasant stare on Jamal. "Where's your bed?"

Jamal stared back. "Why do you ask?"

Nick smiled mirthlessly. By now, he knew how she operated. She had lied to him about everything else; she'd probably lied about that, too. "We may find her 'luck.'"

Jamal turned and led him to the small cave that served as bedroom and headquarters when he slept here. Nick made straight for the low, wood-framed charpoy against the granite wall. He lifted the blanket-shawl and saw pinned to the bed's hemp webbing a little gold robin—Robin's good luck pin.

Nick picked up the pin and held it in his palm. "Here's the 'luck' that led her here. A damn homing device! She told me she lost it."

The men looked at each other. Two men who loved the same woman. Two men betrayed by the same woman.

Jamal spoke first. "I think I know how you feel—felt about her, Nick. I must tell you we did not make love that night."

Nick nodded, expressionless. Maybe he believed it, maybe he didn't. He'd have a lifetime to decide.

Jamal gazed at the mountaintops, both comforted and bereaved by their constancy. Some things you could never understand. He had trusted her. She was his first love. He loved her still.

Nick took a last look at the little robin pin and dropped it in his pocket. "I guess I didn't know her at all," Jamal said sadly.

Nick responded with a cynical shrug. He earned his living by deceit. Why should she be any different? As to the rest, he didn't want to deal with his own feelings now. "You were leftists back then, weren't you?" he asked matter-of-factly.

Jamal shook his head. "Idealists. Like so many students, we wanted to change the world." He shook his head again. "But I don't think she was a communist in those days. I don't know what changed her. I know she always envied my commitment. She wanted something to believe in. She said she wanted to make a difference." He sighed from the sorrow of all these years. All these losses.

"Yeah, she made a big difference, didn't she? But as for her belief or commitment..." His mouth twisted in scorn. "Nah. I think she was just an adventurer. Period." Bitterness weighed on Nick. Life had gutted him and he couldn't remember what they were fighting for. He wondered about Jamal, who seemed subdued but with spirit intact. Maybe he had stared into the gorge of human existence before; maybe he had fallen into it—and climbed back out.

If so, he was equipped for the rest.

Nick looked coldly in Jamal's face; the man surely deserved to know what he was up against. "I was sent to assassinate you, too. Whether as Robin's backup or vice versa, I don't know. Or care. And not only the Soviets—the Pakistanis also paid me. They both paid a hell of a lot of money—and would've paid a lot more if I had gone through with it. You're quite an unpopular guy."

Jamal nodded soberly, aware of the forces arrayed against him. "I do not doubt some of your own people oppose me as well."

Nick's gaze didn't cut him any slack. "Yeah, some of 'my' people would like to 'fight down to the last Afghan.' It's all about bleeding Russia, and so your strength is a threat to the stalemate they favor here. But my report to the President will change that—and..." He smiled faintly. "*Insh'Allah*, you will be victorious."

Jamal thanked Nick with his eyes, for everything. "*Insh'Allah.*"

Chapter 27

Peshawar, Pakistan

Nick strolled into Lala's Grill, trying to shield himself with some of that old attitude. It was his first afternoon back in town, a busy but grim afternoon, shadowed by Taj's absence. Leaving the harsh metallic sunlight, he squinted into the room, clocking the action—especially at the rear table. There they were, his "colleagues"—Russian, Pakistani, Afghani—men of societies both ancient and ageless. Societies that had borne the weight of history, with its invasions and succeeding empires. Nick realized that his was just the latest empire.

They knew it, too, deep in some genetic memory: *Empires come and empires go.* Yet for that moment in time, America was the power they had to placate—or fight. They all had their roles.

He moved toward them. It was as if nothing had happened. In a funny way that was true, but the parallel truth was that nothing again would ever be the same.

Viktor observed Nick enter. His eyes narrowed into hard shiny disks. Of course, he already knew. He had been waiting at the Kabul Inter-Continental, the iced vodka ready to toast his success. Then word came, and it was disastrous. Robin's guide, the KHAD operative Mustapha, had escaped and reported back to Kandahar headquarters, which relayed the information to Kabul. And now he looked like a fool. Both agents failed. Aware of his gamble in trying to run Nick as a double agent, he had nonetheless been fairly confident that the woman would succeed. He had misjudged Nick, whose cynicism was merely an overlay for typical American idealism.

That was Nick's problem. His problem was the failure of Operation Birdwatch. Viktor knew he had best come up with an alternate plan, quickly. For General Secretary Gorbachev's edict was still hanging over all their heads: Solve the Afghanistan problem! KGB weakness brought out the long knives, and Chairman Petrov was even now scrambling against their enemies. As Viktor must do here, in dusty Pakistan.

And so, there were professional relationships to nurture. He overcame his anger. "Ahhh, Ni-cho-las," he crooned. "It has been too long."

Without comment, Nick settled into his usual seat facing door and window.

Ahmed nodded his greeting. "Yes, far too long." Ever the good Pakistani host, he passed Nick a sweet glass of tea.

Viktor had something else in his tea. He raised the glass. "To your safe return home. And to us—your dear friends."

Nick smiled back, yet his eyes were shrouded in clouds. "I bet you guys were bored without me."

"Very bored," Viktor agreed. "But I have had time to learn a new word of American slang. The word is 'sting.'"

"An interesting addition to your vocabulary."

"Very interesting." He watched the American closely. "And very clever—your 'sting.'"

"Clever? I'm flattered, but what sting are you talking about?"

"You have not heard of Operation Birdwatch?" Viktor saw Nick blink, then compose his features.

So did the Afghan spymaster, Syed Hussein, who was privately pleased by the Russian's failure.

Nick took a deep breath. *Birdwatch*, huh? Clever? It was she who was clever. He had not outsmarted Robin; the termination of Operation Birdwatch was nothing more than dumb luck. Luck, you might say. He regarded the Soviet impassively. "Operation what? I've been on vacation, you know. Mountain climbing."

"Did you do any hunting?" Viktor inquired. "Shoot any birds?"

Nick met the KGB man's gaze. "Yeah, I did." He shrugged. "Didn't plan on it, but it was hard to avoid. Wildlife abounds, you know." Especially the "fowl" kind.

"And what about our contribution to your 'holiday'?"

"Contribution?" Nick appeared puzzled, then grinned with genuine humor. "Oh, the money you donated to the account of Commander Jamal. I hear he promises to put it to good use."

Viktor knew he'd been doubly had by his "double-agent." His smile was cold, his eyes colder. "You'll be careful, will you not, Nicholas. Next time you may be feeling sting."

"I'll be very careful." Nick was going through the motions, playing the game. Trying to care.

The others had been following the proceedings with interest. Ahmed realized that he, too, had been had. However, there were other means to achieve the same end. Means already selected. He gave Nick a knowing look. "I am glad to hear Jamal is alive and well. May he lead his people on to victory—but not just yet."

Nick winked. "I think it'll take at least a few more months."

Ahmed understood that some deal had been struck, some offer of support. His nation was determined to be on the winning side. "In that case, you will make sure he is aware of Pakistan's generous contribution."

"I'm sure he is most grateful. As are we, for your hospitality."

"Hospitality?" Ahmed looked at Nick, then Viktor. "Yes, we are hospitable to all our guests. We are neutral in this unfortunate conflict, you know."

Nick had noticed that one of the other "neutral" parties was missing. "And Mr. Yu? Where is he these days?"

Ahmed shrugged. "A most tragic accident. How, we do not know. They found his... remains in the desert. He seemed to have taken a fall, from some distance up. And the strange thing—probably a coincidence—his body was lying next to a crate of drilling equipment filled only with straw and rice."

Nick stared. Another victim of the killer sting. That one was his. It was in the line of duty, of course. More tally marks on that great Tally in the sky. He shook his head, still waiting to slip back into that old self of his, so amoral and free. And elusive, it seemed. With effort, he returned to his role. "What a shame—but there are times when upward mobility takes a downward turn. Maybe now, though, some of the Chinese weapons shipments will make it to the rebels—instead of the black market."

The Afghan Syed Hussein scowled. They were gossiping like a bunch of hens. Ignoring his contributions, as usual. Under his direction, KHAD agents Jhan and Mustapha had handled logistics for the operation, performing very well—despite their unfortunate fates. It was the others who had performed poorly. The American female had bungled it. The

KGB had shown stupidity in selecting a woman. And from what he was hearing, Nick had been merely lucky. The only one Syed Hussein truly respected was his countryman Jamal. An enemy to be sure, but a heroic figure of power and poetry. There were rumors President Najibullah's brother would go over to his side. In Afghanistan allegiances could be so fluid. It was always possible to embrace the enemy—a fellow tribesman, after all.

In the meantime, what was this ridiculous American talk about closing the black market? Syed Hussein gazed at Nick across the table, as if across a great divide. That divide was history. The Americans had no history; they had only their youth. Youth was a good thing, but once you lost it, you needed other skills in order to survive. His people knew when to put their head down and when to rear up. But those were merely tactics. They would continue to follow the old ways—and they would never submit. "You Americans are very smart, but sometimes very simple. Do you not realize smuggling is the oldest game in the world here?"

"Next to war." Ahmed sighed. "Which, sadly, is so good for business."

Nick nodded. "Seems I've heard that before."

Viktor didn't care about business, but he did care about the game. He raised his glass. "To your missiles and your women—both very dangerous."

The two men exchanged a hard look. Nick's fingers closed around the glass; he lifted it in silence. Didn't drink.

Viktor realized there was more than political gamesmanship involved here. His deep-cover agent had crawled under Nick's covers—and his skin, too—from the looks of it. A most interesting bit of information. He filed it away for use later, when someday he'd tell his CIA friend just how and when he'd recruited Robin. A glint in his eye, he downed half his glass and then raised it again. "Another toast: To the Superpowers and their 'Great Game.'"

Nick slipped away from under the shadow and joined in. "Friendly adversaries."

Syed Hussein kept his glass on the table. "May our nations endure." He glanced straight ahead, ignoring Viktor, but all knew to whom this was directed. His nation would endure. Independent. Under no one's thumb.

Then it was Ahmed's turn. "To the Great Game—and its beneficiaries."

They clinked their glasses and studied each other, wondering who really were the beneficiaries of this prolonged bloody war.

Ahmed leaned toward Nick for one final clink. He smiled broadly. And then, they all knew.

It had been a long day. Nick sat at his computer late that night, realizing just how long. He had returned the previous morning, then crashed for twenty-four solid hours. It was more than the fatigue; he dreaded the awakening. But he dreamed about what he had to do over and over and over....

Until finally, he was there—in her small, tidy tent in the refugee camp. Taj's shy wife stared at him. She slowly put down the broom and glanced at her two boys playing a game with sticks and pebbles. Nick had visited before but never without Taj. It was improper, but when she looked in Nick's tired eyes, she forgot all that. She forgot to offer him tea, because she knew. She held herself with dignity, her thin fingers grasping the pale blue *chadar*. Nick told her that her husband was a hero—a martyr—*shaheed*. He would never forget her reaction.

She bit her lip, gazing at her young sons. "Too many *shaheed*."

Nick explained about the money she'd be receiving every month. She asked, what good was the money? Nick had no answer; there was never an answer for that one. We use them up, then give money to the widows. The boys were tugging on her shawl, where was baba? Nick looked at them and told her they would go to school in America, praying all the while they wouldn't have to go to war first. She smiled sadly, her delicate young face already too wise. That would make Taj very happy. He loved America.

So nothing that took place afterward at Lala's Grill could compare with that. At Lala's, he just went through the motions, touching base, catching up. He waited until evening to return to the office, not quite yet up to facing Ronald Hudson. By the following morning, his boss would have received a communication "reinstating" him in his old job. Nick could only imagine Ronald's delight.

He sat at his desk, trying to get his head together. He needed to debrief himself and file his report to the DCI. It would be an important one. He'd have to "sell" Jamal—and he didn't want to leave anything out. Except the part about him and the girl. That would die with her.

The president had issued a finding that ordered the director to get him some hard intelligence. He feared a Soviet takeover of Afghanistan—but also a fundamentalist one. Jamal seemed the man to back, but the president wanted to check him out first.

The DCI sent Nick. When the director was COS Saigon, he had sent Nick on similar private ops, such as investigating just how deeply Vietnam's President Thieu was connected with General Vang Pao's Laotian opium. The revelations about their allies were embarrassing—and therefore buried—but Nick had come out with his career intact.

Nick knew the director thought of him as the perfect rogue operator and had told him as much. He was unorthodox and not afraid to run with the ball, but he was dispensable and could be hung out to dry if need be. Good old dispensable Nick. A case officer who was the director's own private agent.

Nick switched on the modem and typed in the number of the secure scrambled line. When the connection was established, he gave his identification code and password. Then he began his message.

Epilogue

Panama City, Panama
March 1988
The old ten-inch television was sitting behind the bar. A corner of the glass was broken; scotch tape seemed to do the trick. The bartender periodically reached in front of the screen to grab a bottle of booze, but that was infrequent, as most customers preferred the basics and just stuck with beer.

For one who cared, that was Dan Rather's voice reporting over the news footage: "What the longbow was to English yeomen and the V-2 rocket was to the Germans in World War II, the Stinger anti-aircraft missile is to the Afghan rebels today..."

Three Hind gunships appear over the mountain ridge, skimming close to the ground. Suddenly a mujahid emerges from inside a cave, aims his Stinger at the rear helicopter and fires. The missile shoots through the air until it reaches its target. The Hind explodes.

The other two ships bank and turn, but before they can let loose with their machine guns, they are blown from the sky—victims of two more Stinger missiles launched by two more guerrillas.

"Before the Stinger," the newsman continued, "the rebels were vulnerable to bombing and strafing from fighter jets and helicopter gunships..."

Tanks and stationary machine guns manned by Soviet and Afghan government troops surround the rebel stronghold, pinning them in for the final air assault. Several mujahideen crawl through the mined fields, but draw fire from patrolling Hinds.

Then from behind the rocks, Stinger-armed fighters appear. Standing boldly, they take aim and fire their missiles. The gunships fall amid walls of flame.

"But since the Stingers have been brought into operation nearly two years ago, they have downed enemy aircraft almost daily..."

On its approach to Kabul Airport, the Antonov makes a circular descent, dropping defensive flares. Just before landing, it is hit and crashes into the tarmac.

"As Soviet leaders announce the withdrawal of their forces from Afghanistan, military analysts increasingly cite the role of the Stinger anti-aircraft weapon in influencing their decision to seek an end to their eight year-old 'bleeding wound.'"

A MIG fighter flies high in the sky to avoid enemy missiles. Then it explodes.

A guerrilla fighter stands tall on a mountaintop. Holding a Stinger at his side: Jamal, a victorious smile lighting his face.

Nick looked down from the TV and picked up his glass of beer. On the bar in front of him was a two-day-old New York Times. Dated March 15, 1988, its headline read: "SOVIET SETS MAY 15 AS GOAL TO START AFGHANISTAN EXIT."

Nick finished the article as he sipped his beer. Then he just sat there, staring in the glass. He had been too burned out at the time to care much when they yanked him from Peshawar soon after filing that last report.

Back at Langley, the Director had explained that as a result of much soul-searching, he'd decided it was not yet time to seal all those pipeline leaks—or go all-out for victory. But he promised that "Nick's man" Jamal would be well cared for, at least well enough. Nick was quick to clue the Director to the fact that Jamal was nobody's man but his own. The DCI nodded and went on with his account of how they'd had to sweet-talk the President a bit to see reason, but finally he did come around. After all, we needed to keep our Pakistani allies happy. And watching the Soviets squirm was just too much fun.

So the bottom line was, Nick had done a damn good job. Maybe too good. It was best for everyone that he be reassigned. Nick understood. It was just politics. And they were all—all of them—expendable, to be consumed, used up, replaced. The only one who rejected that definition was Jamal. He'd be consumed by his own vision, never theirs.

Like Robin. For he'd come to accept that she did have a vision. He had to give her that.

His beer finished, Nick reached in his pocket to pay. His fingers curved around something and he pulled it out. The tiny gold robin. He looked at it lying in the palm of his hand. Yeah, he'd loved her, and yeah, he'd been a fool. But being a fool for a woman sort of went with the territory. She wasn't the first. Maybe she'd be the last. Maybe not.

Then he tossed down a couple of dollars, because in Panama the dollar was still the official currency. Official, too—at least nearly—was the familiar linkup of arms, drugs and money.

So they'd sent Nick. He had plenty of experience with corrupt generals. But there were degrees of corrupt—and this one had crossed over the line. Noriega was out of control, and his grandiosity was becoming a threat, even to himself. For only a madman would boast, "The United States is like a monkey on a chain. All you do is play the music and the monkey performs."

Nick was playing from a different score, and the general was not going to like the performance. You build them up and then you bring them down.

He walked outside, back into the green world of the tropics. He heard the thunder. As the first drops began to fall on his head, Nick wondered if it was a coincidence that he was on another mission to investigate another leader. He wondered if he'd have to assassinate him this time.

The End

About the Author

Diana R. Chambers has always been a bookworm. As a child she wandered the musty aisles of libraries, drawn by the promise of discovery, distant lives and distant lands. She has traveled widely, including many far corners of Asia.

An importing business in India led to a Hollywood design career, which later evolved into writing for television, film, interactive and travel media. Research for various projects put her on the road again. She loves spicy food and her bag is always packed.

Her work has been praised for its riveting plots, unusual characters and deep sense of place. A member of Writers Guild of America, Sisters in Crime and Mystery Writers of America, Diana lives in a small Northern California town with her husband, arty daughter and brilliant mutt, the best writing companion ever.

For more on the author, please visit www.facebook.com/DianaChambersAuthor, www.twitter.com/DianaRChambers and www.dianarchambers.com.

Also by Diana Chambers

Meet Nick Daley's new agent Evelyn Walker in *The Company She Keeps*

What would you be willing to do for your country?

The daughter of a military man, young Evelyn Walker ends up in Washington D.C., alone and with no money. Appealing to her sense of patriotism, CIA officer Nicholas Ross Daley—back from Afghanistan—recruits her to work undercover for The Company. As she struggles to balance her sense of duty with her personal values, "E" enters the international world of espionage with its deceit, glamour and sexual intrigue.

Her case officer, Nick watches over E. And yet, he is forced to send her into danger. A world of danger, from Europe's grand boulevards to Iran's Grand Bazaar.

"A fascinating story about making hard choices and living with the results, as Evelyn and Nick both learn that every decision bears a heavy cost.... When the storyline takes E... to the Iran of the Ayatollahs, a somberness and a realism steps in that is impossible to put down."

— Randall Masteller, www.spyguysandgals.com

"Chambers has created a world of three-dimensional reality... the intrigue-filled corridors of Washington, the romance of Paris, the danger of Tehran. And each page literally brimming with suspense. This is a book I did not want to end, whose story and characters I wanted more of."

— Harold Livingston, *Star Trek: The Motion Picture*

"A fast-paced tale of a young girl's transition into womanhood. It gives us an inside look at... the shadowy side of The Company. I recommend this book to anyone who likes romantic suspense stories.

— Jennifer Glick, www.myshelf.com

"This is a fabulous book and a fast read... an espionage thriller (that) will pique your interest from beginning to back page. Plots and twists are never-ending. You don't read far to solve the current mystery. But... you'll quickly find the heroine embroiled in yet another more intricate and sticky situation."

— Deb Killarney, *CoastViews* magazine